MY SO-CALLED LOVE LIFE

LAUREN BLAKELY

ABOUT

I've got a list of people I absolutely don't ever want to be stuck with on a boat, or a plane, or a train, and it starts and ends with the broody, grumpy, too-sexy-for-my-own good Axel Huxley.

Also known as this romance novelist's number one nemesis.

The man is legendary for his mighty pen and his even mightier scowl. I tried to work together with the cocky thriller writer once upon a time, but the two of us are like vodka and good decisions. We don't play well together.

Only now, our publishers are sending us on a joint trip across Europe to mingle with our most devoted readers on an old-fashioned luxury train. And thanks to a booking snafu, we have to share a sleeper car.

You guessed it--**there's only one bed.**

I'm not sure I can survive the next seven days and nights with my dangerously sexy enemy and all our fiery tension.

Which explodes one night in a desperately needed hate bang.

But the bigger plot twist is this – the more time we spend together, visiting the most romantic cities in Europe by day and discovering each other at night, the more I'm forced to face our past.

To let go of the hurt.

To see the man he's become.

And when I do, I wonder if it's too late to write a new happy ending for us?

A HOW TO DATE NOVEL

By Lauren Blakely

To be the first to find out when all of my upcoming books go live click here!

PRO TIP: Add lauren@laurenblakely.com to your contacts before signing up to make sure the emails go to your inbox!

Did you know this book is also available in audio and paperback on all major retailers? Go to my website for links!

MY SO-CALLED LOVE LIFE
BY LAUREN BLAKELY

A Standalone in the How to Date series

1

THE ANTI MEET CUTE

Hazel

Obviously, I believe in love.

If I didn't, I'd be the worst kind of romance writer— the kind who lies to her readers.

But there's something I believe in more fervently than love, and that's the meet-cute. You can't get to the happy ending without the unputdownable beginning.

The start of the story is my writing church, and I worship at the altar of those delicious moments when the hero and heroine meet for the first time.

Or meet again.

Tonight, I'll be researching a new here's-how-they-met possibility as I head to dinner in New York.

I'm one block away from the restaurant. My short, black ankle boots click against the sidewalk on Twenty-Fourth Street as I gaze up at the numbers on the buildings. I pass a tattoo parlor where a goth gal inks a burly man's arm, and then I acquire the target.

Menu.

"It's as trendy as it is annoying," my friend TJ said of the joint when he told me about it last week. "And I promise it'll inspire your next chapter one."

I was sold. I made a reservation right away.

Now, I'm here at the minimalist-style restaurant. Under the sign for Menu are the words *Meet, Eat, Mingle.*

Change your life.

Ambitious, but the way I see it, this place is going to be full of fodder. I can't wait. I draw a deep inhale of the May night air, then square my shoulders. "Cover me, I'm going in," I say to, well, no one.

Sometimes I talk to myself. It's a thing. Whatever.

I head inside, marching to the hostess stand. A woman wearing a black tunic and sporting a blonde undercut shoots me a bored look. Yeah, that's on point for a place called Menu.

"Hello. I have a reservation. Valentine. Party of one," I say.

"It's all parties of one," she says, monotone.

"Old habit," I say with a friendly shrug. "In any case, it's for seven-thirty."

With an aggrieved sigh, she scans the tablet screen, then meets my eyes. "The other party isn't here yet. If he or she is five minutes late, we'll have to ask you to leave."

Okaaaay.

It's a new world order. Restaurants have rigid rules.

But I knew what I'd signed up for. "Works for me," I say. You catch more flies with honey and all.

"Fine," she says, then she nods toward the dining room behind her. It's small and bare, in keeping with the theme, aka *we're cool, you're not*. The tables are black wood, the walls are steel gray, the tiles are white. Everything is ordinary, except the experience.

This restaurant is très chic because it seats strangers together.

As I follow her, I smile, giddy at the thought of an inspired meet-cute. Two sexy strangers happen to be seated together at a hipster restaurant just like this. They hit it off. Get it on that night. Then, oops! The next day he turns out to be her brand-new boss, perhaps?

But who is he? A mafia king? A sexy CEO?

The muses will let me know who the next hero is. Maybe he'll even reveal himself tonight.

Undercut brings me to a table at the back. She waves a limp hand in the direction of the framed QR code on the black wood surface. "We use QR codes. You scan them with your phone. Have you ever used one before?"

I'm thirty-one, missy. I can work a phone, a power drill, and a twenty-speed vibrator. Not all at once though. "I'm familiar with the concept of QR codes. Also, phones," I say.

"Cool," she says blandly, then walks away, her tunic swishing against her leggings.

Once I sit, I rub my palms on my jeans, a tiny bit nervous. What if I'm seated with an over-sharer? An endless talker? A dullsville candidate?

But I'm excited too.

What if my companion is an enigmatic billionaire like in a romance novel? A broody rock musician? A hot tech nerd who's looking for a matchmaker?

Gah. The meet-cute possibilities are endless, and when I write this as the opening of my next book, it's going to be epic.

I just know it.

I'm making some notes on my phone about the vibe when a man's voice interrupts my thoughts.

"Four minutes and forty-five seconds." His tone is a little gravelly and a lot know-it-all-y.

Say it isn't so.

I was already dreading sharing a stage with Axel Huxley at the reader expo I'm doing this weekend. I can't believe fate would inflict him on me any sooner than necessary.

I turn my gaze toward the front of Menu, praying that's not my archnemesis. Maybe he has a vocal twin. Maybe that's a thing now.

But my prayers are unanswered. Standing tall at the hostess stand is the smart-mouthed, glasses-wearing, smirky-faced romantic-thriller writer.

Wearing black because of course he wears black.

And *of course* he's arguing with the hostess. He never met a statement he couldn't debate and dissect into a million julienned pieces, then pepper with disagreement.

He blah blah blahs a little more, finishing with, "So, you have to seat me. It's the policy of the restaurant."

I snort. *Get over yourself, Huxley. I hope they kick you out.*

I feel sorry for whichever sucker is getting seated with King Dick tonight.

Inspired, I make another note, chuckling fiendishly as I imagine my heroine running into her enemy before the clever, charming, hottie hero enters the scene. Then I check the menu options while waiting for my brilliant professor, my inscrutable tycoon, my good guy with a heart of gold in need of a makeover.

Until the sound of footsteps grows louder and closer. I look up.

At a face I want to punch.

2

IT'S BECOMING A HABIT

Axel

A long time ago, in a decade far, far away, I'd been terrified to walk to the front of my eleventh grade English class and present a speech on the dangers of wealth in *The Great Gatsby.*

Speaking in front of a few dozen high schoolers who mostly didn't give a shit was horrifying.

My stepfather told me to picture everyone in the class naked. My brain did some extra credit. I didn't just undress everyone as I opined on Fitzgerald's depictions of the moneyed class. I imagined everyone in my class fucking.

A writer's habit was born.

Ever since then, I've mentally written character bios for almost everyone I've met, detailing traits all the way down to their bedroom preferences. Assigning habits— like if they talk during *The Godfather,* how many cardboard wrappers they could possibly need on a cup of coffee, and whether they like it doggie style or being tied up and taken—has become the way I keep everything in perspective.

The hostess? She only drinks soy chai lattes, and she brings her own cup to the artisan fair-trade coffee shop. She doesn't have a favorite position because sex is boring in the same way everything is boring to her.

Poor gal.

The bartender over there with the goatee? The ring says he's married but the way he stares at the hostess says he jerks it to her when the wife's asleep. That is, after he reads lit fic in hardback.

Then there's the redhead I'd recognize from several football fields away. Too bad I don't have the luxury of yards and yards. Instead, she's seated mere feet from me at the last table at the edge of the dining room. The woman with the long, lush hair, the dangerous green eyes, the pouty lips, and the sharpest mouth I've ever met.

Fuck her bio. I refuse to write one for Hazel Valentine.

Ever.

She'd better not be the other party at my dinner. I came here to research how to hire a hitman for my next book, not to share a meal with a woman who hates me.

But as the hostess walks me to the last table, the inevitable becomes my Friday night, and my brain concocts a bio in spite of my better judgment.

Hazel Valentine:

Emotional wounds—we're going to need a bigger boat for hers since someone clearly has daddy and boyfriend issues.

Coffee—ideally via an IV drip. At all times of the day.

Sex preferences—nope. Stop. Just stop. Don't go there.

As I near, Hazel looks up from her phone. For a moment she seems flustered but then she schools her expression. There's simply flint in her gaze.

The hostess waves to the table without speaking. I thank her and pull out a chair as she walks away, dismissing us already.

Hazel stares at me unflinchingly, as if challenging me to leave.

Won't happen, sweetheart.

I park myself, sliding into the chair across from the redhead, then smile without showing any teeth. I fold my hands and meet Hazel's steely gaze. "Let me guess. You're here to test oh-so-cute opening chapters for your next book," I say.

She tilts her head, smiling slyly. "And you must be researching how your next bad guy will off someone, hoping it will make your latest book more...scintillating."

Well, maybe she will give me some inspiration on how to hire a hitman after all.

3

TABLE FOR TWO STRANGERS

Hazel

It's weird how, in this city of nearly 1.7 million, you can run into the same people all the time. But Manhattan's more like a collection of small towns. Axel returned to New York a month ago, and I've bumped into him twice. First time was at the arcade three weeks ago when I was hanging out with my sister and her fiancé, Milo. The last person I wanted to see then was Axel. But he's friends with Milo so I didn't have a choice.

Some days, it's downright claustrophobic here.

I also think New York, with its twisted sense of humor, loves to play chicken. Well, Manhattan, I won't back down from this challenge you're throwing at me in the form of my once-upon-a-time writing partner sharing a table for two with me.

Oh, New York, you don't know who you're dealing with.

"So, your next book," I continue, crossing my arms,

gaze locked on the man I used to call a dear friend. "Is it? More scintillating? More suspenseful?"

Axel hums, marinating the question, taking his sweet time with it. "As a matter of fact, Hazel," he says, lingering on my name, overemphasizing it like he always does with names. I know why he does it, but I won't let that soften me. "Scintillating and suspenseful is exactly how the *New York Press* referred to *A Perfect Lie*."

Somehow, I manage not to roll my eyes as I give him an almost-real smile. "That's sweet," I say as if I mean it.

With a cocky glint in his eyes, Axel shrugs, accepting the comment at face value. "Thank you. That one meant a lot to me," he says.

I stifle a huge laugh. Of course he loves reviews from pompous news outlets.

"I'm sure it did." I lick my lips and go for the kill, "It's sweet that you're still as obsessed with reviews as ever."

His expression falters, blue eyes flickering with what might be embarrassment. I've hit a sore spot. Good. But then his face goes blank like he's rearranging his thoughts to hide them from me. "I'm not obsessed," he says, defensively.

"Don't you know by now? You can't make everyone happy with a story." I fight off a smile. Hell, it's hard not to grin when I can bust him on the thing he loses sleep over—what everyone else thinks of his words. I tried to help him with this, once upon a time. Look where that got me.

Axel nods slowly, like he's letting my comments sink in. "True, Hazel. That's so true. And you'd know better than anyone. You can't please everyone even if you stuff all the quirky pets in the world into your rom-coms," he says, grabbing his own rusty knife and shoving it into me. I simmer as he taps the Lucite frame that holds the QR code. "Want to order, sweetheart? Or are you ready to walk out?"

I burn brighter, hotter. I stare hard at him. "No, Axel. That's your style."

Without acknowledging my comment, he asks, "So you're leaving then?" His gaze drifts toward the door. He looks so hopeful.

Boo-fucking-hoo. I lean forward. "As if I'd give you the satisfaction."

He laughs. "You're going to stay just to vex me? You'll willingly irritate yourself just to irritate me?"

I stare at him, *pot-kettle* style. "Sound like anyone you know?"

He shoots me a *well-played* nod. "Fair enough. Then, may the most irritating one win." He picks up the frame, then looks back at me, gaze shrewd. "Or do you have more arrows in that quiver of yours to shoot my way?" He sits up straighter, almost spreading out his stupidly firm chest. "Go ahead. Hit me with it. I can handle it. Get out all your anger, sweetheart."

I clench my jaw, inhaling sharply.

This man.

I can't believe he used to be my confidante. My close friend. My writing partner.

But I won't let him see my hurt. I have to do better. It's only a meal and maybe it'll be good practice for the reader expo we're scheduled to helm this weekend.

"I'm all good," I say as lightly as I can. "And yes, let's order."

I grab my phone, scan the code, then check out the menu, grateful for something else to focus on besides him.

He does the same, scoffing a few seconds later. Haughtily scoffing.

I take the bait. "Don't see anything you like?"

His eyes dart around the restaurant, then he lasers in on me, lowering his voice. "No. I just wish I didn't have to use my phone to order," he grumbles. "I already have to use it for everything else."

I get that. I'm a little phone-weary at the end of the day too. "Why can't a menu just be a menu?" I ask, without any vitriol or irritation, just a little same page-ness that surprises me.

"Is it so much to ask to have my phone off during a meal? But nope. They make us use it."

"Evidently it's too much to ask," I say, agreeing as I read the dinner options. They're limited, but surprisingly...inventive. "I didn't think a place like Menu would have roasted beets with pistachios on a bed of pea shoots."

"Did you think it would be steak and potatoes?" he asks, a little derisively.

And...that detente didn't last long at all.

"No, obviously I wasn't expecting *that*, Axel," I say, overemphasizing his name, like he does to me. "I just thought it would be minimalist food too. And as stark as the decor."

"Or the company?" he asks, but it's not biting. He

sounds truly curious.

I don't give in though. "Your words," I point out.

"They are indeed."

He flips his phone so the screen's facedown, pushing it to the side of the table. I tuck mine into my purse as a man in a tailored shirt and sports coat swings by, flashing a *barely there* smile.

"Welcome to Menu. I'm the restaurateur. We hope you enjoy the experience of dining here and making new friends just as much as we intend to enjoy serving you," he says, like a robot. "Can I start you out with some wine? We have a Shiraz from Uruguay. The grapes are harvested under a full moon."

I blink. Is he for real? Also, who says *restaurateur*?

"I'll have a beer, please," Axel says.

"A martini for me," I say. "Thanks."

The man's brow furrows. We've flummoxed him. "Are you sure? I mean, the full moon."

Axel smiles. "And what does the full moon do for the wine?"

I knew he wouldn't be able to resist asking. Truth be told, I was gearing up to inquire too.

"It's how the grapes are harvested," the owner answers, speaking in a circle. "And what about food?"

"Is it harvested under a full moon?" Axel asks, and I snort, wanting to kick him to shut him up but wanting him to keep going too.

"No. It's foraged. My chief forager does it himself."

"Ah, of course," Axel says, then looks to me. "Ladies first."

I wait for Axel to pull the rug of the comment out

from under me with a barb about how I'm no lady. But he doesn't, so I give the owner my order—the beets and the mushroom risotto, while Axel opts for seared salmon with rosemary and asparagus.

"Thank you. And may I wish you the best interaction with the real world."

He turns and goes.

I cock my head, watching him, trying to get a read on the guy.

Axel stares too, then turns back to me. "Do you get the sense they're trying too hard?"

"Just a little bit. I mean, foraged food?"

"And *restaurateur*?" he asks with an eye roll.

"Not to mention full moon grapes."

"Also, does this restaurant not know what the other hand is doing?"

"Right?" I say, enthused he keyed in on that too. "On the one hand, it's all *let's be digital and read the menu online*, and on the other hand, it's *let's go forage and experience people.*"

"It wants you to love its quirks, even though they make no sense. I knew this was going to be a mistake." Axel leans back in his chair, huffing, but also giving me a view of his annoyingly handsome face.

Why are jerks so hot?

Seriously? Who decided that sexy jerks could ever be good-looking? With freshly fucked hair, and undress-me eyes, and those goddamn black glasses that get me every time, Axel Huxley is the sexiest jerk of all.

The worst part? When I see hints of the man I used to know in his clever remarks, his sly observations.

The way we once got along.

But I won't be fooled again. Hurt me once, shame on you.

Hurt me twice, and I'm going to write my own damn name in Sharpie at the top of my whiteboard list of people who've pissed me off that week.

I've made my own shit list plenty of times.

I put my self-protection back on, so I'm not fooled by the banter. "So, what's the story with you kicking the tires here tonight, Huxley? Is this how the Nefarious Ned hires a hitman to take down Brooks Dean?"

The corner of his lips curves into a grin. "You know my new hero's name."

I roll my eyes. "Obviously I know who Brooks Dean is." Only the former-lawyer-turned-avenging-bounty-hunter-for-hire who traipses around Europe, solving heists and retrieving precious stolen goods as he falls in love. "You did mention twenty million times he'd be your next hero," I remind him.

"If you say so," he says.

"Oh my god, what do you think I do? Read your publisher's blurbs that far in advance before the book comes out?"

He smirks, then points at me. "Don't you? You can't resist keeping tabs on me."

I scoff. "You wish."

"But Nefarious Ned? C'mon, Hazel. Give me credit. My villains have better names than that."

I wiggle my fingers. "All right. Serve it up. Your next villain. What's his name?"

Axel's grin turns wicked. More wicked than I've ever seen from him. "Hazel. Her name is Hazel."

Damn it. I walked right into that one.

But I'm saved by the restaurateur. The man in the sports coat returns with our drinks, depositing the beer in front of Axel, and the martini in front of me. Then he frowns. "I'm so sorry, ma'am. We're all out of beets tonight. Pea shoots too."

Bummer. I do love a good pea shoot dish. "No big deal. I'll skip the apps. Just mushroom risotto then?"

He winces. "Apologies. Our chief forager canceled the dish. The mushrooms made him mad. We have chicken with kale picked from our rooftop garden though."

"She doesn't eat meat," Axel cuts in. "What do you have for vegetarians?"

The man's eyes pop. "Um…I could bring you the kale and some pistachios on the side?"

Gee, that sounds filling. But I can eat edamame at home later. "I'll just have the drink. Thanks."

Another cringe. "Sorry. We can't let you sit here with just a drink."

I blink. "Really?"

"Truly. It's a rule," he says, apologetic, even though he's likely the one who made that punitive rule.

But even though he and his chief forager ran out of beets and pea shoots, I'm not going to bolt. I won't let Axel have the satisfaction. I'm about to ask the owner to bring me the kale when Axel says, "Can't you make her something with vegetables? You don't want to be one of those places that discriminates against someone for their beliefs, do you?"

The restaurateur gulps. "No, of course not, sir," he says, then scurries off.

I look at Axel, begrudgingly appreciative. "Beliefs? Are we allowed to do that?"

"Sweetheart, it's a fucking pretentious restaurant. And the lawyer in me could argue it's a belief with full conviction."

The lawyer in him could argue anything.

But is his vegetable defense an argument for an argument's sake? Or does he *want* me to sit here with him? That would make no sense. I study Axel, trying to figure him out. "All right. What's your deal, Huxley? Why are you trying to get me to stay? That was a perfect chance for you to let me walk away and have the table all to yourself."

"Ah, but what fun would that be? Especially when I have to see you on Sunday. This is like a little unexpected dress rehearsal."

Ah yes, I'm a game. Got it. "Thanks for the reminder. I'd tried to erase that from my head."

"Same here. But the more you shoot arrows at me, the tougher my villain will be."

This time I don't walk into the comment. I march straight through it. "And that'll make it more satisfying when your hero kills her."

He grins, slow and devilish. "He won't kill her. He'll just tie her up and turn her in to the authorities."

I lean back in the chair. Yup. I'm not leaving.

* * *

An hour later, the meal is mercifully over. I leave the city's most pretentious new restaurant, with Axel holding open the door.

Wish I could say that was fun and inspiring, but mostly it was like a boxing ring. One I escaped from not entirely unbruised.

"Tell me something, Hazel," he says to my back. "Who's Kendall or Avery or Bethany going to meet at the seated-with-strangers restaurant? A cocky chef who smells like cedar and snow? A grumpy professor with a beard that's just so...*rub-able*? A single dad with a heart of gold and a big dick?"

I grit my teeth as I toss a glance at the man with the heart of onyx. Then I let go of the annoyance bubbling inside me, doing my best to seem unaffected. "I've decided to write romantic thrillers too. At the dinner with a stranger, she'll meet the guy she's about to double cross. And he won't even see it coming."

Axel rolls his eyes. "Good night, Hazel. I'm sure no one will be able to tell how you really feel on Sunday." With that, he turns and walks down the block.

Wait.

What?

Am I that obvious? And *are we that obvious?*

Of course we are. We spent the whole evening throwing darts at each other.

But I can't be obvious in front of an audience on Sunday. The Romance Reader Expo chose six romance authors from across the genre for a VIP Reader Q and

A. If Axel and I act like little shits onstage, we'll steal the spotlight from our colleagues. That's tacky and gross, not to mention rude to the readers.

I stare at his silhouette retreating into the New York night, wishing I didn't have to do this but having no other choice. I shove the past aside. Time for a temporary olive branch. "Axel," I call out.

He turns back and waits. "Yes?"

I have to go to him. What a shock.

With my shoes clicking loudly, I cover the twenty feet between us, drawing a fueling breath as I go. When I reach him, I'm painfully blunt. "On Sunday, we can't let on we feel this way," I say seriously, reinforcing his throwaway comment about hiding how we feel. We simply have to.

He's quiet for a beat, maybe weighing the public stakes of our feud. "True. No one likes spoiled brats," he says, begrudgingly.

"And we can't do that to TJ, Kennedy, Mateo, and Saanvi," I add, naming the other authors who'll be onstage with us.

"Right, right, of course." He sighs in resignation, but nods. "We'll have to fake liking each other."

I'm relieved he's willing to play nice. "Exactly. We'll pretend we get along. Like we used to," I say, and that's what hurts the most. We used to get along famously.

"No one will know," he says.

No one *has* known since we split. That's purposeful, keeping the details on the down-low. I don't like to air my dirty laundry to the world. Hell, I can barely stand my own dirty laundry.

Axel takes a step closer and extends a hand. "To faking it on Sunday."

"To faking it," I say as we shake.

His hand wraps firmly around mine. A strong grip. A warm grip.

If this were one of my books—or one of his—there'd be a slo-mo spark. A zing as we connect. And all sorts of wild ideas about hands on bodies, hands on skin.

But life is not a book, so I drop his hand before I can feel a single damn thing.

With the connection severed, Axel flashes a too-broad smile. "We'll get on like thieves, Hazel Valentine. Just you wait till you see how nice I can be."

Is he one-upping me? Like he can fake it better than I can? "You think you can be nicer than me?"

He smiles savagely. The *eat 'em alive* kind. "I do."

"Then I can't wait to see your nice side. I bet I'll get along so swimmingly with Nice Guy Huxley that we'll be like copy and paste."

"We'll be a plot and a twist," he adds.

Damn. That was good. I've got nothing, so I'm going to need to let him have that last-word victory. "See you Sunday, Mister Nice Guy," I say, then I walk away first, wishing it didn't hurt to see him.

I don't like to hurt. I leave that to my characters.

Me? I need all the protection from pain I can get.

4

MISTER NICE GUY

Axel

The thing is, I'm not known for being a nice guy.

So I might need a little help for the Q and A.

Fortunately, I happen to know a certified nice guy very well. My little brother. The next day, after Brooks Dean evades capture in Vienna then saunters into a nightclub and asks the brilliant and sexy owner to make it a double, I save the scene I'm writing in my next book, and hunt around my apartment for my phone.

Now that I've hit my word count, I can't put off dealing with how to face Hazel any longer.

Where is that stupid device?

It's not on my writing couch, under pillows, or on top of the piles of notebooks stuffed with ideas. Or on my living room table, which is stacked with research books.

I march into the kitchen. Nope. It's not here on the counter next to the unwashed coffee mugs.

Fuck. Why can't coffee be self-cleaning? Why can't kitchens be self-cleaning, for that matter?

I stalk through my apartment, heading to the bedroom. It's pristine in here because who wants a messy bedroom? That's rude to me and to anyone else who might see it.

I spot the phone right away. Perched on the night-stand. I grab the device from where I charged it overnight. I haven't looked at it for a while since phones are usually messengers of doom.

When I open the screen, there's a note from Max blinking up at me. I bristle when I see his name—Max at Astor Agency—but I've bristled for a while when Max has reached out. A quick scan tells me it's a report on sales for *A Perfect Lie*, and he's using exclamation points, so that's good. I barely skim it. If I get caught up in sales, I won't write, and if I don't write, I can't pay the bills.

I also won't pay the bills if I don't help promote my books.

Which is where Carter comes in. As I leave the bedroom, I dial my brother in San Francisco.

He answers on the second ring. "You do know that text messages exist?" he says by way of greeting. Pulse-pounding pop music plays in the background, accompa-nied by the sound of machines grinding. Carter's at the gym. Naturally.

I scoff. "You still want me to text you before I call? I refuse to do that," I say, returning to my living room. But I don't flop down on the couch. I just…walk.

I need a game plan for tomorrow. And I won't find it sitting down.

"Of course you refuse. But a lot of people do it. You know, in case the other person can't pick up but wants to talk soon. It's a courtesy, you know. It's a thing," he adds.

"A thing I won't do," I say. "Because the phone has a built-in device for letting someone know you're calling. The ring. And a built-in way to avoid calls. The old-fashioned 'don't answer' trick."

"God, I miss you," he says sarcastically. "Anyway, what's cooking?"

Dragging a hand through my hair, I pace back and forth. "I have to do this thing tomorrow. A Q and A. With a bunch of authors and..." I take a deep breath. "Hazel."

Her name is a raw scrape in my throat.

"Ohhhhh," Carter says, full of insight. "That should be interesting."

I swallow roughly. A little uncomfortably. "But I can't let on that we...have a history."

"Euphemism," he coughs out the word.

"Exactly." I knew Carter would understand the spot I'm in. "I need to be nice to her onstage. How do you do it?"

My brother cracks up. "Oh, Axel. How much time do you have?"

I roll my eyes as I reach the window, then stare out at the streets of Gramercy Park ten floors below. It's a Saturday, so young families pushing strollers crisscross the block, alongside joggers with dogs. "Look, I'm sure a lot of natural charm has to do with the fact that your dad's not a flaming liar."

"That is true," he acknowledges.

Carter's five years younger than I am. We share a mother, a woman who thankfully realized her first husband was a dish made from charm, lies, and fiction.

I'm glad she got out of that toxic marriage to a grifter. I wish I could have gotten out of having the scam artist as my dad. At least my stepdad's a good guy. Hence, Carter's the consummate good guy.

"So, gimme some tips. You know public appearances are not my favorite thing," I say.

"It's hard to live down the broody, grumpy, stick-up-your-ass image you've created for years, isn't it?"

"Damn straight it is," I say, proudly. That image has served me well. It's safe. It protects me.

The reality is my job comes with public appearances. Sure, readers don't seem to mind if I'm a little salty.

But there's salt and then there are bitter lemons. I prefer to be the first.

"Well, have you read her latest book?" Carter asks.

"Of course," I say, incredulous. "Read it the night it came out. I even read it on my phone because the paperback wouldn't arrive till the next day."

Carter laughs.

"Why are you laughing?"

"You hate her, and you read her book?"

I huff. "I used to write with her. Obviously, I think she can write. It's a good book. She's a good writer. Plus, one should know their enemy."

"Right. Sounds like that's why you read it. Anyway,

just pick two to three things about her story to compliment. And when the desire to throw rocks at her like she's Johnny the Jackass from next door who called you a twerpy nerd overcomes you, remember—"

"The pen is mightier than the sword, and you can always make him your villain," I say smugly.

And I did. Johnny the Jackal was my first villain. And it felt *gooood* to use his name, though like any good writer I varied it a touch.

"Also, Axel?"

"Yes?"

"Just smile," Carter adds. "It takes less muscles to smile than to frown."

"Actually a study debunked that," I say. "Several leading plastic surgeons found it takes more but—"

"But men who smile get laid more often. And on that note, *smile. Just fucking smile.*"

That kid gives damn good advice. "All right. If you insist."

"Nice! You sound like less of an asshole already."

* * *

Twenty-four hours later, I've kept it up.

I've been smiling in the shower, smiling on the street, smiling as I do yoga with my buddy Bridger who lives in my building.

"Yoga makes you that happy, man?" he asks as we leave, mats on shoulders.

"The happiest," I say with a grin. Practice makes perfect after all.

I refuse to lose this *who's nicer* battle with Hazel.

I smile as I walk into the hotel, as I head to the auditorium, as I enter the greenroom backstage.

I smile as I say hi to Kennedy and Mateo and Saanvi, mingling by the coffee urn. Then I smile wider to TJ, who's chilling on the gray couch next to the redhead I'm going to vanquish.

Hazel looks sharp in a red twin-set cardigan with black buttons, and a stylish pair of jeans and boots. Damn. She's mastered the pretty-but-approachable-and-quirky look so damn well.

I glance down at my black polo and dark jeans, paired with my black glasses. Well, black is easy to match.

But I'm a romantic thriller writer, so I'm allowed to look dark.

Except today, I'm going to be dark and smiling. "Hello, Hazel. Lovely to see you," I say.

With a laugh, she just shakes her head. "Nice to see you, Axel," she says, then turns her focus back to TJ.

A few minutes later, Luciana strides in. She's one of the publicists for the Romance Reader Expo. The olive-skinned brunette waggles her phone triumphantly, flashing gleaming white teeth. "The auditorium of the Luxe Hotel is packed with more than one thousand fans," she tells the six of us.

Huh. That seems impossible to believe. That's just... too many. "Are there really a thousand people here?" I ask.

Hazel whips her gaze to me, and I swear she's holding back an epic eye roll.

Maybe I sounded like I'm in a courtroom. "It's just a lot," I explain, since I don't want to look like I'm contradicting Luciana. But I guess I sound like I'm questioning her.

You can take the lawyer out of the law practice. But you can't take the cross-examiner out of the lawyer.

But I didn't mean it like I doubt her. I'm more than four co-written books and eight solo books into my career, and I still haven't wrapped my head around the fact that I have readers. That people choose to read, or listen, to my words.

It's surreal.

I'm convinced someone is going to jump out from behind the curtain at any second and say they're punking me.

Then take my career away.

"Actually," TJ cuts in, deadpan, as is his MO, "It's probably one thousand and five. That's what the auditorium seats. But don't worry, I'll make sure no one charges you, Huxley."

"Thanks, appreciate it," I say, dryly. "Anyway," I say, recalling Carter's words as I fasten on a smile, sending it Luciana's way. "It's all good."

With a nod that says the size of the auditorium convo is closed, she walks us through the event. "I'll do a quick intro. Then it's showtime. The focus is on the readers. They're here to ask questions. But I'll moderate and make sure the questions are acceptable. You've all sent me your list of off-limits topics, so we should be good to go." She looks around, checks her watch. "Shall we head backstage and mic you up?"

"Sounds great," I say with a smile.

See? This old dog can learn new tricks.

We leave and head to the wings. The crowd is buzzing with chatter. The noise and hubbub drift back here, and it's heady.

And still hard to believe.

I peer around the wings at the packed room. There's no way they're here for me. Maybe everyone else. But not me. Not the guy who's shitty with names. Not the guy who embarrassed himself at his first signing when he got the name of the bookstore owner wrong.

It's one hour. Then you'll see your friends, play some pinball, and grab a beer with the guys.

I head onstage, and Luciana introduces us, then points to the woman queued up at the front of the question line in the audience.

Ah, shit. She's wearing a *Ten Park Avenue* shirt. She leans into the mic. "I'm dying to know what happens to the next couple at *Ten Park Avenue*. Will you and Hazel ever finish Lacey's book?"

You don't even want to know how painful that last story was to try to write. Trust me, you don't want to know.

But Carter's words flash before me.

Smile. Just smile.

My father's snide comments flicker as they sometimes do. *Have you ever considered, I don't know, trying a little harder to help me pull this off?*

And I smile, and I try. "We're both really busy. Have you read Hazel's latest sexy romantic comedy? The antics of sunshine Kelsey and broody Brayden when they're stuck sharing a flat on a non-refundable trip in *The I Do Redo,* are so terrific," I say, deflecting.

And multitasking too, as I heap on the praise.

Score one for the guy who's picturing how the woman with the *Ten Park Avenue* shirt takes her coffee as she strips naked to screw some dude.

And just like that, no one will know who I really am.

5

HE LIKES TACOS

Hazel

Warring thoughts rush through my head as I sit straight and tall on the emerald-green dais in the middle of the stage, Axel on one side, TJ on the other.

Wistful ones like, *I was dying to finish writing Lacey's story. That plucky doctor had some bad luck in her past and needed some good loving.*

Then, badass babe ones along the lines of *Two can play at this praise game, Huxley.*

And finally, kick-myself-in-the-pants ones such as, *Why didn't I put our previous writing partnership that went up in spectacular flames on my no-fly list?*

Well, because I didn't want to signal to my publisher, any of the publicists, or the entire Romance Reader Expo organizers, that it's still a sore spot.

I try to erase Axel from my thoughts, but it's hard

with him so close. Harder still after he made that kind and witty comment about my new book.

I fight my own mind as audience members line up to ask questions about inspiration, writer's block, and whether "you've ever gotten so turned on while writing a sexy scene that you had to take care of business?"

Dodged a bullet with that last one—the questioner addresses it to Kennedy. My fellow rom-com author, who looks the part with the artfully messy bun and red cat-eye glasses, blows out a long breath, then says, "That's an occupational hazard of writers working in coffee shops, let me tell you."

The crowd laughs.

Whew. Axel's tactic worked. We aren't stealing the spotlight with our private war spilling onto a public front.

When Kennedy finishes, Luciana fields a new question from a woman near the front. She's sporting a T-shirt that says *I claim all the book boyfriends.* I like her already.

"Hi. I'm Melissa," the woman says as an expo crowd runner hands her a mic.

"Welcome, Melissa," Luciana says, then eyes the reader's shirt. "And we might have to keep a schedule of book boyfriends, because I've got some claims to make too. But go ahead. What's your question?"

Melissa dives in, gesturing to all six authors onstage. "First, I've read all your books, every single one, and I have a question for TJ."

"Hit me up," says my bestie. TJ and I write together a

few days a week, on our own stories. He's my work husband and he calls me his work wife.

"In *Manhandled,* one of your heroes hates musicals," Melissa says. "And I know—since I'm a big fan of your books—that you don't care for them either. I would love to know what other personal traits you give your characters." Her wide-eyed enthusiasm hints that she's been dying to ask this question for years. She quickly adds, "And I'd actually love to know that from everyone here today."

Oh, the book-boyfriend claimer is clever, sneaking in a question for everyone. I like her even more.

"Good idea. Let's go on down the row, and everyone can take a shot." Luciana looks to TJ. "And you can go first."

My friend flashes an easygoing grin. He leans forward, almost conspiratorial, then stage whispers into his mic, "You want to know, Melissa? You really want to know what traits I put into a story?"

"Yes!"

"All right. Here you go," he says, holding up his hands like he's saying *you asked for it.* "Some of my heroes have a thing for guys with British accents." He finishes with a wink.

I pat his shoulder. "Gee, I *always* wondered where that came from," I say dryly. His husband is an Oscar-nommed English actor, and TJ was in love with him from afar for years before they got back together.

Melissa points to me. "What about you, Hazel?"

"Of course I love English accents too," I say, but that's a chicken's answer.

There are so many ways to answer this truthfully. Many of my heroines are terrified of true romance. They're scared to pieces of getting hurt. They don't trust love. And they're convinced they choose badly.

Well, just look at their track records of terrible exes.

But no one wants to hear that on a panel. Or, honestly, at all.

Quickly, I cycle through the details I'd be willing to dole out.

Do I tell Melissa I like to shop at thrift stores? And that yes, one time I did in fact make out in the dressing room with a hot guy I met at Champagne Taste, inspiring a scene in *Sweet Spot*? Or that at another time, my phone decided to spill all my secrets when it acted like an asshole and began playing a dictation file of mine while I was on the subway?

Yeah, that was a good one.

"Melissa," I say, leaning closer, even though she's many feet away, then I reveal a little behind-the-scenes detail. "Remember when Colby's audiobook started playing at the silent auction?"

Melissa's jaw drops, then she closes it to speak, a little awed. "Right during the *get on your knees, pretty baby, and take it deep* scene in *Plays Well With Others*?"

"That's the one," I say, then I shrug, owning my foible and the inspiration it provided. "Happened to me while I was on the subway one afternoon. Only it was with the dictation file for a sex scene I had *spoken* into my phone earlier that day," I say, giving them a little piece of me—the piece I'm willing to share. The one that makes me seem human. But never too human, never too raw, never too wounded.

This is just enough, I hope.

And *enough* works, since laughter ripples through the crowd, then Luciana chimes in with, "Show of hands. Has that happened to you with your audiobook?"

Hands fly high.

A throat clears from right next to me. "Hazel, are you leaving out an important detail?"

Tension slams into me from Axel's question. Is he going to dress me down onstage? "What do you mean?" I ask carefully.

He shoots a *c'mon* smile. "Tell them the rest of the story."

Shit. Fuck. What am I leaving out? Dread crawls along my skin. I part my lips, but I've got nothing to say.

Only, he does. "That happened when you were on the subway at three-thirty, and it was filled with school children."

I breathe a thousand and one sighs of relief.

But I'm also shocked. I'd nearly forgotten that detail.

I stare at him, a little amazed he remembers that. He wasn't even with me on the train that afternoon a few years ago. Now that he's mentioned it though, I must have told him the story the next day. Maybe when we were plotting our second forbidden romance in the *Ten Park Avenue* series. I told him all the little details of my days then—like the woman who walked her German shepherd past my apartment each morning as I was leaving for my run. Soon, she started wearing the same color workout clothes as I wore. We decided she was trying to steal my identity, so we called her The Hacker, and I wrote her nickname on my whiteboard.

I blink away the fond memory then focus on the here and now. There's little an audience loves more than an embarrassing tale, so I pick up the conversational baton as smoothly as I can. "And if you think having a sex scene from an audiobook play out loud is bad, imagine if it's *you* dictating a rough version of the sex scene," I say.

Axel fake coughs. "And it was…*very* rough."

Holy fuck.

Axel is a fantastic faker. He's got the whole poke and prod playfully down to an art.

I better up my game. "That's what she said," I add, and the crowd pretty much goes wild.

But it's time for the Axel and Hazel show to end. That's the point, after all—we don't want to hog the limelight.

"What about you, Saanvi?" I ask, helping steer the question to the others.

She answers with a comment about how she's always been drawn to bad boys, like her heroes and heroines are. After Mateo and Kennedy answer too, Luciana strolls to the edge of the stage, picking a new audience member.

A question about what everyone's working on next keeps the focus on the others, and when I steal a glance at the time, I want to pump a fist.

We only have fifteen minutes left of this Q and A, and we've been pulling this off.

Soon enough the clock winds down, and Luciana

wraps up the session, thanking the audience. "And don't forget, these authors will be signing books starting in thirty minutes at the publishers' booths, so get your paperbacks ready."

It's clear the session's over, but a strong, brash voice pipes up from the front row.

"But Axel never answered the question," a woman with purple hair points out. She stands, grabs the nearest audience mic. She looks familiar, and I'm pretty sure I've seen her face on my social media feeds. She's a popular BookToker who's made a mark for being provocative. "About what part of him he puts into his books."

Soft murmurs float through the crowd, a sound loosely translating to *I want to know more about the handsome guy with the glasses who never says much about himself.*

Luciana will probably let him off the hook since the time is running out, but she checks her watch then says, "We've got thirty seconds left. Axel, can you answer Melissa's question and help quench Tracy's need-to-know thirst? Did you ever accidentally play a sexy dictation on the subway or fall for someone with an English accent?"

He laughs, the kind of laugh that somehow manages to say *Oh, Luciana, I never talk about my private life.* He squares his shoulders and faces the crowd, squinting through his glasses at the woman who asked the question.

But before he can answer, Tracy asks another question. "For instance, your last hero was a former lawyer turned vigilante-for-hire. Is he a little of you?"

Axel narrows his brows and nods thoughtfully. "I can see the similarities, Tracy," he says. "I definitely look like a badass vigilante that underground associations would hire to retrieve priceless stolen goods. But... sadly, I've never rappelled into a museum to retrieve a work of art belonging to someone else."

It's a good answer, but I can tell that won't be enough for Tracy. She likes to push buttons. She wants a real answer. Everyone else gave one, but Axel isn't offering any nibbles.

"But the law school bit? The reason he didn't practice? Was that based on you?" She presses, digging deeper into the character's psyche, trying to draw comparisons.

Axel's face goes blank, and he's quiet for a few seconds.

I look to Luciana. Shouldn't she be stepping in? But a stagehand is whispering something to the moderator, so Luciana's not available for swooping.

Ah, hell. I don't want to save him, yet I hate to see anyone backed against a wall. Also, I do want the points. So, I jump on the grenade. "His heroes like tacos," I add with an *I'm sharing a secret* smile. "And this guy's addicted to them," I say, pointing my thumb at Axel.

A flash of relief passes across his blue eyes. Then he's sharp again, confident again, when he says, "She's right. I'm a taco lover."

I cup the side of my mouth. "Taco Tuesday is a religion for him."

"Tacos are holy," he adds.

"Look, he's not wrong," Saanvi contributes, and for a few seconds the audience turns into a congregation singing the praises of tacos.

When the Q and A ends, my sister texts me to come find her in the greenroom. Thank god Veronica's here. I know she came for the signing we're doing next—she loves Kennedy's books. I feel a little exposed after that Q and A, hoping the attendees couldn't see through Axel and me. I need a safe space for a few minutes, and that's my sister.

She's waiting for me by the greenroom, leaning against the doorframe, wearing a red polka-dot top, with brown wisps of hair framing her face. When our eyes meet, she waves me over, grabbing my wrist when I reach her.

"Why didn't I know about the sex dictation? We're sisters in mortification now."

I smile, loving that she can laugh about her own snafu. A year ago she accidentally sent her anonymous sex column to her entire company and lost her job. But it was kind of her cat's fault. Quirky pets can be so dastardly.

"Because no one should ever have to hear me dictate a sex scene. *Ever.*"

"Try me. Do one right now as we head to the signing," she says, and we walk in that direction.

"No way."

She pokes my side. "C'mon."

"Fine, fine." I clear my throat and adopt the most monotone tone ever. "He unzipped his jeans, comma, his thick cock springing free, period, my mouth watered, comma, and I said, open quote, your dick is a delicious summer sausage, close quote."

She laughs. "You're right. You're exempt from ever dictating sex scenes in front of me again."

"Thank you. Anyway, was I okay?" I ask nervously. "I felt extra sweaty today."

She pretends to sniff me. "You don't smell sweaty."

"I'm being serious. Did I sound like a bitch? A know-it-all? A ding-dong?"

Her brow knits. "What? None of those. Why?"

"I always worry."

"You were great. And I'm sure no one could tell you secretly want to bang Axel."

I roll my eyes harder. She's harped on this before. "News flash. You're still wrong."

"We'll see."

"No, we will not see," I answer, drawing a clear line in the sand.

She smiles wickedly at me, then mouths *I'm right.* She's such a stinker, but I'm still glad she's here. "Thanks for coming. I know you came to see Kennedy. But I appreciate it nonetheless."

"I'm here for you too. Let's grab a drink after? Meet me at Gin Joint later?"

"I'll be there," I say, then I head into the signing

room, energized from seeing readers and my sister, even though she's still so dead wrong about me wanting to bang my archnemesis.

* * *

Later that night, when the signing ends, I grab my purse and leave the hotel solo, ready to head to Chelsea to meet my sister. When I reach the revolving door, I spot Axel standing outside, leaning against the glass facade of the hotel, looking cool and broody.

Well, at least from the backside.

Is he waiting for me?

I might have reached my weekend dose of faking it with the enemy. I don't know if I can handle another run-in with the man. But as I walk outside, I steal a glance at him. He's chatting with someone. I tense, wondering if that's his agent. But a better look shows a tall, older man with a thick beard, a shiny bald head, and tortoise-shell glasses, and I sigh in relief.

His editor, not his agent.

"And we'll have that lunch with Stein later this week," Linus is telling Axel.

"Looking forward to it," Axel replies. They're focused on each other. Excellent. All I have to do is walk past, smile vaguely, and head downtown.

Wait. I don't even have to do that.

I turn the other way, but as I wheel around, Axel calls out, "Hazel."

I groan but turn back. "Yes?"

Axel motions to Linus that he'll be a second. The

editor waves to me, and I give a professional grin and a nod. It's a small world, after all. Then Axel heads over to me, the corner of his lips curving up. "Tacos?"

It comes out curious but approving. For a second there, I thought he'd be annoyed I made up the taco thing.

"I improvised. Don't tell me you hate tacos too?"

He laughs. "Who hates tacos?"

"No one," I say. I expect him to say something cutting and leave, but he stands looking at me, silent.

My brow knits. "What is it, Huxley?"

He sighs, as if dreading what he's about to say. "You win," he mutters. "You were nicer."

Oh, right. The Be Nicer contest. We didn't even establish stakes though. "What were we playing for?"

He glances at the cabs streaking by on the street, then back at me. "I don't know. Except, I guess, keeping things private still. So, um, thanks."

He extends a hand once more. I take it and shake. Only this time, I hold his hand for a second or two longer. Maybe five.

But then I let go. What's the point in lingering?

We're just former friends, former partners, former confidantes.

We are former.

We're dead to each other now.

There's no prize for behaving like an adult.

"Maybe the prize is we won't have to see each other again," I offer. That's probably for the best—playing to keep the status quo and staying far, far away from each other.

That's easiest.

He purses his lips and then nods. "Good night, then," he says, and it sounds like we both agree on something.

I turn around and head to meet Veronica at Gin Joint. Too bad I don't feel like I won anything today.

6

WINEDAY

Hazel

The next morning in the shower, the muses of opening chapters deliver my next hero's profession. Because all good book ideas originate when you're naked and wet.

The winner is—wine guy.

My hero will own several vineyards.

Which means wine's now a write-off for me.

Once I'm not naked and wet, but not fully dressed either—because why be fully dressed at home?—I reach out to one of the city's top sommeliers and schedule a time to see him next week.

I *might* be counting down the days.

When next Wineday—I mean Monday—rolls around, I leave my apartment, texting my friend Rachel in San Francisco as I take the subway uptown. She's a wine lover, so I'm required to make her jealous.

Hazel: Guess where I'm off to…Hugo's!

Rachel: I hate you. Also, steal me a bottle of his best cab.

Hazel: I'll stuff it down my jeans.

Rachel: Don't get me excited while I'm heading to work.

Hazel: Speaking of, how's the new jewelry shop going?

Rachel: It's day by day but I'm hopeful. I'm heading to Paris next month to check out some artists to possibly carry!

Hazel: Ooh, la la! (That's, um, the extent of my French).

I'm almost at Hugo's, so I wish her well then head into the fancy restaurant on Amsterdam Avenue, where I soak up the ins and outs of different grapes from the wine expert named owner.

The lumberjack of a man offers me a cab. "And this one is from my favorite region in California. The grapes are big and fierce," Hugo says without a hint of snoot in his voice. He's the wine everyman.

I lean in and draw a hearty inhale of the glass of red. Makes my senses tingle. "Mmm. Smells rich," I say.

"The grapes were harvested at just the right time," he says, patting the label on the bottle next to him like he's praising the winemaker.

"Hugo, I have a very important question."

"Ask me anything," he says with a warm smile.

"Would you ever harvest grapes under a full moon?"

"Why?" It has five syllables.

"That's exactly what I was wondering. *Whyyyyy?*"

I tell him the story of the full-moon wine. Hugo shakes his head the whole time, amusingly perturbed. "Everyone has a gimmick. Before you know it, someone will market sweet raccoon wine."

"Is there such a thing?"

"Not really, but one of the ways you can tell grapes are ripe is when birds, raccoons, or bears show up. They like the grapes when they're sweet," he explains.

That just makes wine even more delightful. "I *must* find a way to put Sweet Raccoon Wine in my next book," I say.

"I agree. You must," he says.

When I leave a little later—without a bottle in my jeans, sorry Rachel—I'm dying to tell someone about the raccoon wine. As I hit the bustling sidewalk, I open my phone to text TJ, but annoyingly, my brain whispers someone else's name.

Axel.

Tell Axel.

I scoff at myself. As if I'd tell Axel, I argue back.

But he was there for the full-moon wine harvest.

So what? TJ will still get it.

But you know you're dying to tell Axel you dispelled the Tides of Wine theory with him.

Enough! Just enough!

As I weave through the afternoon crowds on a

spring day, I write to my bestie. Once I hit send, my phone trills. The number is the main line at my publisher, Lancaster Abel.

"Oh," I say to no one. A familiar mix of nerves and excitement pings through me. Usually it's good news when the publisher calls, but you never know. What if someone canceled me online while I was visiting Hugo? Worse, what if my publisher is dropping me because I've been canceled? Have I done something to get canceled? I'm not a dick. I don't say stupid things. But oh god, I hope I didn't fuck up.

I swipe answer so fast.

"Hey there, it's Hazel," I say as I duck down Eighty-Second Street, where it's a touch quieter than the avenue.

"We know it's Hazel!" the twin voices of Aaron and Cady, Lancaster Abel's publicists, chime in. "We called you!"

Like most good publicists, they speak in exclamation points.

"What are you doing?" Cady asks next. She's the peppier of the two, which is saying something since Aaron ranks a ten out of ten on the cheer scale.

"Just leaving Hugo's Wine Bar. Research for my new book," I say, hoping to impress them, because I'm always hoping to impress everyone at Lancaster Abel since I need them to love me forever and ever and then some.

"Oh my god. So fun. I can't wait to hear all about it," Aaron says, then clucks his tongue. "Sooooo…"

I brace myself. *Doom is coming.* "Yes?"

"We had the best idea," Cady tag-teams, just as a

furniture truck rumbles down the block. She says something more about this best idea, but I can barely hear her.

"What did you say?" I ask, covering my other ear.

"Wait. Hugo's. You're at Hugo's? Why didn't you tell us? The office is five blocks away," Aaron says.

Sure, I know that. But why would I tell them? I don't want to be clingy. "I didn't realize you'd want to see me," I say, honestly.

"We always do," Cady says. "Wait! New idea! Can you come by? It was someone's birthday today. We have cake."

"Oh my god, girl. Don't offer her someone else's cake," Aaron says, mortified. "Hazel, hon. You deserve your own cake."

I blink, trying to make sense of these two. "So, you want me to come in for cake?"

"Cake and news," Aaron adds. "Cady, we need to get Hazel some cake. Like, now. Go to that shop—"

"Actually, you don't have to get me cake." They don't need to roll out the red carpet. "I'm happy to come by cake-free. I'll be there in ten minutes."

We say goodbye, and as I march toward their building, I text TJ, trying to figure out why they want me to visit.

TJ: Maybe the hot guy on the cover of your last book wants to show off how he grew his six-pack into an eight-pack.

Hazel: And the answer is no cheese and no fun.

TJ: I believe in cheese and abs.

Hazel: And I have a time-share in the sea to sell you.

Soon, I arrive at the skyscraper, giving my name to security. Up I go to the twelfth floor, and the second the elevator doors open, Cady and Aaron squeal. Aaron's blond. Cady's blonder. They escort me into a conference room, pawing at me the whole time, asking about Hugo, my favorite wine, how my day is going.

I love their enthusiasm, but I don't want to be touched this much. I don't say a word, though, except *great, everything is great.*

Once I take a seat in the room, my editor, Ramona, pops in the doorway, tucking her stick-straight brown hair behind her ears as she beams at me. "They told me you were coming by. Are you excited?"

"Um, sure. I love coming by," I say, even more confused.

Ramona shoots the publicity twins a *seriously* look. "You didn't tell Hazel on the phone?"

Cady has the good sense to look chagrined. "She was

around the corner. We wanted to tell her in person. You tell her!"

Ramona tuts at them then turns to me. "It's every writer's dream. We want to send you on a special book tour. If you're amenable," she adds, a diplomat in a way the publicist pair is not.

Tour the country, meet with readers, sign books, and chat about stories? That *is* the ultimate fantasy. "Amenable? Of course I'm amenable," I say. Inside, I'm elated. I haven't been canceled. I've been...*continued*. "Whatever is involved, I'm game," I say, but wait. That's not true. "Unless it's a bungee jumping tour. Or, say, one of those tours where you have to walk across rickety bridges with roaring rapids one thousand feet below."

Cady's jaw drops. "There are tours like that?"

"People like to be scared, hon," Aaron says, sagely.

Ramona cuts in. "We won't be sending you bungee jumping. But we had this great idea that, since *The I Do Redo* is set in France, we'd send you on a week-long luxury train tour across Europe with several lucky VIP readers. You'll stop in various cities and do signings and events along the way, and you can show readers some of the locations from the book. How does that sound?"

Like a premise for another book. Like fodder for a train romance. Like...gah.

I can picture it now, all elegant and Orient Express-like. Maybe they even want me to dress up in a velvet evening gown, with jewels and satin gloves, and offer toasts to old-fashioned luxury as we rattle along the coast. Then when I go back to my sleeper car at night, I'll plot a swoony story where our heroine meets a handsome stranger on the train, perhaps somewhere in the French Alps.

No, wait. He'll be a billionaire from a small French village. He'll step on the train wearing a tuxedo, and his dark gaze will be full of dangerous secrets. When he seduces her, they'll have the kind of sex I've never quite experienced but want to—*book sex.*

Well, it's the best kind. The lady always Os. Usually two or three times. I'm seriously jealous of my heroines.

"I can leave this weekend," I say.

Cady and Aaron chuckle, then clap. "I knew she'd say yes," Cady says.

Ramona laughs briefly then gets down to business. "Great. There's a brand-new luxury train service that just launched. We'll be partnering with them. JHB Travel," she begins.

"Oh! I heard of that endeavor. It's owned by some reclusive billionaire who made his money in green energy," I say. Perhaps Mr. B will be the billionaire I meet on the train. Yes, life imitating art, indeed.

"Exactly," says Ramona. "It's perfect for VIP tour groups and such. We want to start in Rome, have you make a stop in Spain, then a few stops in France. Paris, of course because of *The I Do Redo.*" Immediately, I hope the trip aligns with Rachel's, "And then we'll finish in Copenhagen."

Copenhagen isn't a common setting in romance, but I do love a Viking hero too, so...*yay.* "I'll get to check Denmark off my bucket list," I say.

"We need to get everything set up, but we'd like to

send you in a month. If you'd like any basic lessons in any of the languages, we can arrange for that too."

"That sounds great." Like pinch-me level great. I can say a few French words, including *bonjour,* though, like Belle in *Beauty and the Beast*, I usually sing it. I can't say anything in Danish. And I can only say *ciao* in Italian.

"Perfect," Ramona says, then takes a beat before she adds, "Oh, and there are a few other authors doing this too. It'll be a group tour."

Makes sense. That's expected these days. Maybe TJ has been asked. He's written a few books set in London. We'd have the best time.

Only, he has a different publisher. Lancaster Abel probably wants to send someone from the same house.

"We'll send Kennedy too," Ramona says. "You two comp so well."

I brighten. She's always up for adventure. Can this day get any better? "Pretty sure she's my long-lost twin," I say. "Plus, her last book has the Danish hero. So, Copenhagen makes even more sense now."

"That's what we were thinking too," Ramona adds.

Aaron squees. "I knew we had to tell you in person, Hazel," he says, then grabs Cady's shoulder. "Right?"

"So right," Cady seconds.

"And," Ramona continues, "Axel Huxley will be on the trip."

My world grinds to a halt. "Axel?" I croak out.

Ramona's gaze turns serious. She doesn't know the details of our split, but she knows we didn't finish our last book. Well, everyone knows that.

She tactfully explains their thinking rather than

addressing the elephant in the room. "Most of his romantic thrillers are set in Europe."

Damn my overeager brain. How did I miss that *city in Spain* hint? That was an anvil-sized clue that Axel would be a travel companion. His heroes have traipsed all over Barcelona and Madrid, not to mention Italy. The hero of *The Perfect Lie*—Jett—foiled the villain's plot to hack into an international bank in Rome then captured the bad guy in the Trevi Fountain itself, tackling him in the water. Of course Axel will be going on a trip to Europe. Axel loves Europe. He took off for the fucking continent the day he walked out of the coffee shop when our partnership fell apart.

"Will that be okay?" Ramona asks with genuine concern.

A concern that tells me I can't say no.

Yes, I do understand why the publishers are sending Axel, but I don't understand why they'd pair us, knowing we've split. An hour-long Q and A at an expo is one thing. A seven-day, close-quarters train trip is entirely another.

Still, it's not my place to say, *It's not okay because I can't stand his smug face, and I also can't stand how much he's not smug.*

"Totally okay," I say, faking it once again.

Cady cheers. "I knew it! You two are just so fun together. Since the expo, everyone's been talking about how well you two get along. It's all the rage."

"People are talking about us?" I ask.

Ramona nods, clearly enthused. "Readers kind of went wild over your...*chemistry*," she says. "We surveyed them online, and the overwhelming consensus was they wanted the three of you together on a book tour. And since all three of you are with the same parent company, it seems like a fantastic mix."

Great. Just great. Axel and I faked liking each other so well we're now stuck together for seven stinking days on a train.

In Europe.

Can this day get any worse?

7

A HORROR VALENTINE

Axel

I. Freeze.

There's no way my editor just said Hazel's name.

I'm holding my cup of coffee at Doctor Insomnia's Tea and Coffee Emporium, midair, imitating a statue. Am I fucking living in an alternate reality?

I stare at Linus like he's not making any sense. Because he's not. "Hazel…Valentine, as in the romance author?" I choke out, like there could be any other Hazel Valentine. Like there's a sci-fi Hazel. A horror Valentine.

My editor nods in that serious way he always has. "The tacos. The subway ride. Readers dig it, Axel."

That was a survival game so we wouldn't spew vitriol onstage. But instead, we won a prize of hosting a VIP reader trip together?

Talk about being careful what you wish for. "Are you

sure?" I ask, hoping he can read between the lines of my question.

As in…

Hello? We abandoned our last book like a patient left on the operating table, so why would you pair the two of us?

But *they* don't entirely know what went wrong.

Hell, *she* doesn't entirely know what went wrong.

We played nice then too. We didn't let on. We didn't tell anyone.

"You don't want someone from Dunbar and Loraine instead? Like Saanvi," I offer, thinking on my feet as if I'm in court. "Wouldn't that make more sense to send me with someone from the same imprint?"

That's a damn good argument. Linus has to be swayed by my logic.

"Dunbar and Loraine and Lancaster Abel are all owned by the same parent company," he says, and that's publishing for you. Hazel and I might be with different houses, but we have the same corporate big media parent, so we're riding the choo-choo together in Europe.

Fun. Just fucking fun.

But I've never met an argument I won't turn inside out as I hunt for holes. "I'm not that great with public appearances," I say, but it sounds like a feeble protest even to my ears.

Linus shakes his head in a firm, clear *you've got that wrong* style. "I beg to differ. You're actually quite good at them, Axel. You're smooth, sharp, and just the right kind of sarcastic. It works great in front of a crowd," he says, and damn him for the compliment. Damn him too for catching me in my attempt to slither away from the tour. Damn him most of all for saying something nice.

"Thanks," I say, though it's more like a grumble. I'm busy searching for another tactic. "It's just I worry readers are going to ask about our unfinished book."

I offer that nugget like I'm trying to be helpful when I'm really trying to save my own ass.

I can*not* travel with Hazel Valentine and play nice for a week. I just can't. Besides, she can't stand me, and neither one of us is an actor, last time I checked.

No, we're *over*-actors, since that performance at the expo got us into this stupid predicament.

"You handled it so well at the expo," Linus points out. "And it makes good business sense to send you and Kennedy and Hazel. All of your recent books are set in Europe. And as for you and Hazel, you two get along so well. Tacos. Am I right?"

"Yeah, tacos," I say, leadenly.

Fucking tacos.

At least there's Kennedy as a buffer.

I cling to that as he tells me the rest of the details about how I'm supposed to spend a week with Hazel. The woman is still too hard for me to be around.

I've got a long list of regrets that I update regularly.

I don't want to forget all the shit I need to fix in my life, so I write each misdemeanor on a digital Post-it note tucked away in a folder on my laptop labeled

Naked Photos of Mom. Just another alligator in the security moat, after my ninety-five-character password.

The list includes but is not limited to: *Taking mock trial in high school, asking out the sexy brunette in tight black pants at the bar that night a few years ago even though tight black pants are my weakness and wow, did Sarah ever turn out to be a heartbreaker or what,* and *helping my dad with any of his cons, not that I had much of a choice at age seven.*

Now, at T-minus-three days before the Trip to the Bottomless Pit of Torment begins, I click open the file on a Monday afternoon. I'm in my apartment, my brother's newest playlist blasting in my earbuds, draining an afternoon coffee as I add another regret.

Taking Spanish in college.

I close the laptop, turn off the music from my phone, and finish the last dregs of fuel.

Here I go again.

Four weeks of twice-weekly language lessons end today. I've learned how to say in Danish and Italian: *please, thank you, nice to meet you,* plus *why yes, that's where my hero Jett raced against the clock to solve the crime like the rock star he is,* and *no, you can't run through the Trevi Fountain, unless you're vanquishing the worst kind of bad guys and then it's totally okay.* But we've spent the last two weeks on French, since we'll be in France half the time. If only I'd taken that language in school, I wouldn't have had to spend these extra days with Hazel. Kennedy, too, but Kennedy doesn't shoot death rays from her eyeballs into the center of my heart.

Or at my dick.

Though honestly, I'm not sure Hazel even looks my

way anymore, but still I've got my emotional Kevlar on whenever I see her, so I fasten it tighter before I go.

I take off to meet the French tutor, dropping on my shades once I leave my building. I still don't have a survival plan for this train trip, and I need one badly. I really should ask Carter how he handles cornerbacks barreling at him on the field every Sunday when he plays football before millions. Surely that's similar to the kind of hard defense I'm up against now.

As I walk, I fire off a text to that effect. He answers immediately.

> Carter: Fleet feet. Nerves of steel. Also, pads. Those football pads fucking work!

I laugh as I reply.

> Axel: Noted. I'll invest in shoulder pads for the trip.

> Carter: Consider a cup too.

I wince in sympathy, then text goodbye as I bound down the steps to the subway, hopping on. As the train slaloms through the tunnels, I survey the passengers. A college-age dude with huge headphones and a goatee is bopping his head. Bet he likes craft beer and playing guitar with his buds. The harried mom with one kid in her lap, and two hermetically sealed to her death grip hands, probably needs a stiff drink, but not a stiff anything else.

I write some more character bios in my head, feeding possible supporting characters in my current book. When I reach West Seventy-Second, I've got a headful of backstories for the museum guards, Interpol agents, and crooks that Brooks Dean will face.

Damn, I admire that guy. That steely-eyed bounty hunter of stolen goods who's got a sharp sense of humor, a chip on his shoulder, all the moves with the ladies, and a dead-set determination to right the wrongs in the world. He uses his law degree for good. To help him solve puzzles.

Maybe he'll be my shoulder pads. Maybe I'll pretend I'm one of my heroes on the trip and that's how I'll handle Hazel.

Then I laugh at that ridiculous idea.

I suck at pretending.

Although, maybe I want to relocate Brooks's upcoming story to Antarctica. Just in case. Pretty sure Hazel, even though she's a helluva word wizard, couldn't pull off a sexy romantic comedy in the tundra.

Eh, who am I kidding? She'd write hot igloo sex and then melt all the penguins' hearts and cocks.

With no game plan in hand, I head into Big Cup where Angeline, the French tutor our publishers hired, likes to meet. These twice-weekly sessions have helped me learn some basics. I do understand the value of knowing some key phrases since I write stories mostly set in Europe. It's just fucking polite to try to speak the language when you're abroad, at least when you order a meal or buy a train ticket. I speak Spanish and that knowledge came in handy when I researched and wrote my last book hunkered down in Barcelona, stuffing myself with Gaudí and paella.

I survey the shop for the stern, silver-haired, no-nonsense French woman at the sea of tables. Angeline's not here, but my pulse shoots higher when I spot a woman with waves of red hair piled high on her head, her supple neck exposed. Hazel's tucked into a corner booth, tapping away on her laptop, lost in the world in her mind. Her gaze is fixed on the screen, her fingers flying, nothing else happening but her imagination.

It's just how she looked when we'd work together, and I'd find her in the back of a coffee shop, having started early. She'd apologize, saying, "I just had this idea…"

Then she'd share it with me, and invariably, it was a good idea. I'd build on it, and together we'd make something…electric.

A persistent part of me wishes I could go back in time to that day in Chelsea when we blew up and find her like this again. I could say something different. Say a lot of things different.

But you can't go back. You can only go forward and learn to live with your regrets.

I gird myself for the knives she'll deservedly throw at me as I grab the chair across from her. She doesn't look up for a few seconds, then she startles when she does. "Oh. Shit. I didn't see you."

I hide a smile as best I can. That's familiar too. Her reaction. Then I wipe the grin all the fucking way off. "That's clear," I say.

With an eye roll, she looks at her screen. "I guess this is a good stopping point anyway. And Angeline should be here in a few minutes."

"But she's always late," I say.

"True. She is," Hazel says, sighing, then tapping on her keyboard. She's emailing her work to herself, making sure it's stored in Dropbox too. She shuts the silver laptop.

"And what shenanigans are Hudson and Laini up to today?" I ask because I'm a jackass poking at a bruise. "Wait. Don't tell me. He answered the door with only a towel on right after he showered. That clean, masculine scent drifted into her nostrils, lighting her up. Then her eyes popped wide open as she salivated over his six-pack, then she dropped the—hold on, give me a second —the cupcakes she'd baked to give him. To welcome him to the building. He's her new next-door neighbor." I take a beat, savoring the annoyed look in her eyes, since, well, I'm still a jackass. It's easier, this Kevlar. "Am I right?"

The death rays she shoots from her stunning green eyes tunnel into the center of my heart. Possibly, she's charred that organ to a crisp.

She lifts a brow. Takes her sweet time. "Axel," she says, then laughs. "He has an eight-pack."

And I laugh too. Occupational hazard with her. "Touché."

"And of course he smells freshly showered. He just got out of the shower."

"Either freshly showered or woodsy or spicy," I say. Those are the three main scents for romance heroes. We made a list one day, while we googled the sexiest scents for men and women.

"Just like you write 'em too."

"Double touché."

Then, we're both laughing, and that feels deceptively good. So good, I lower my guard. "And in all fairness, this morning Brooks sewed up the laceration in his shoulder all by himself using only fishing wire he found on the dock in the dark and numbing the pain with whiskey."

"That's what whiskey's for. It numbs the pain," she says dryly, and it's like we're right back to the boom-boom rhythm we once had. But there's a note of wistfulness in her tone that's new, that almost feels like she's talking about something else. Something beyond the power of whiskey. Something about pain, but maybe I'm reading something into nothing. Wouldn't be the first time. She's tucked the same rogue red strand into her bun three times between hopeful glances at the door. "Kennedy's usually early. It's weird that she's not here."

Hazel's probably eager for our buffer too. Maybe Kennedy should get hazard pay for this trip. "She'll be here any minute," I say, hopeful Kennedy shows soon. At least, I think that's what I'm hoping for. But I shove any uncertainty away, choosing wit perhaps for this round. "If she arrives before the tutor, maybe we can form a united front and ask Angeline to teach us the most important French phrases today? Like, how to say, *Can the bar car stay open late?*"

The corner of her lips twitches in a smile. "And how to order the best wine?"

I relax into the chair more, stretch my arm across the back of it. For a second, her eyes flicker down my chest, then up. Like she's taking a lightning-fast tour of my body.

Wouldn't that be fun if she were?

But nope. I'm not her type. She likes slick guys in tailored suits, with expensive watches, and silk ties. Whatever. I'm over it. "Look, here's the thing. I figure as long as you can say *please, thanks, where's the john*, and *can you give me something strong to drink* you're good to go."

With that smile staying intact, she nods. "Words to live by." Then her eyes light up. "I should make a cheat sheet. I can't believe I haven't done that yet."

"Yeah, I can't either. You're the queen of prep," I say.

"I can't help it. I have to prep. I hate surprises," she says, and I know that. I definitely know that.

"Including when guys with eight-packs answer the door unexpectedly wearing only a towel?" I tease.

She taps her chin, like she's seriously weighing that one. "That has yet to happen in real life, but I might be okay with that unexpected delight," she says, a hint of a smile on her lips.

The conversation is interrupted when her phone buzzes on the table. Mine vibrates in my pocket.

"Twin buzzes," I say.

"Probably Angeline," she says.

I take my phone out. She swipes hers open.

A message from Kennedy blinks up at me. But it's to both of us. Before I even read the message, the mood at the table shifts and turns heavy. A photo of Kennedy's leg in a blue fiberglass cast stares up at me.

I groan as I read the text.

> Kennedy: Rats are my enemy! There was a rat chasing me down the stoop of my building. Chasing me, I swear. It's like they've become even more powerful and evil. I tripped and fell and THIS is what happened. Is there anything worse than rats?

Another message lands.

> Kennedy: Oh, in case it wasn't clear, I'm drowning my sorrows over not being able to go to Europe in hospital Jell-O.

Then one more.

· · ·

Kennedy: Also, hospital Jell-O is the worst. I think it was made by rats.

For a few long, shocked seconds, I try to picture seven days with just Hazel and me, on a luxury train, hosting a VIP reader tour.

But I can't picture it. It's the great and terrifying unknown.

With a heavy sigh, I set the phone down. So much for the buffer. I meet Hazel's green irises, trying to read her emotions. But she's blank. Maybe from the surprise. She must really hate this one.

She's quiet longer than I'd expect. What is there to say though? Except the obvious. So I fall on the obvious sword, saying, "I guess it's you and me, sweetheart."

She looks like she's about to answer when a flurry of flouncy skirt and jangly bracelets rushes through the coffee shop. Angeline hurries over to us, checking her watch. "Je suis désolée," she says when she arrives. "I am late. I apologize."

"No worries," Hazel says to our tutor. "But if you could teach us to say, *Can you open the bar car at midnight?* that would be great."

We're definitely going to need that translation.

8

UNDER-EXAGGERATING

Hazel

As I zip up my suitcase on Thursday morning, I sniffle. Then, I sniffle a few more times for emphasis.

"Did you hear that? I think I'm coming down with something," I call out to TJ, who's toasting bagels in my kitchen. Since bagels are good any time of day, we're having a send-off lunch before my trip. The flight's at seven, but I'm leaving for the airport a little after three, just in case.

"You sound just fine," he says.

I touch my throat then sniffle again. "Gosh, I hope I don't have a cold. I'd hate to give anyone a cold."

TJ's shoes slap against the hardwood floorboards as he strides toward my bedroom, filling up the doorway with his redwood-tree-size frame, holding a mug of coffee. He stares down at me, one eyebrow arched. "Then don't kiss anyone," he says, ominously. He doesn't have to say Axel's name for me to know who he means.

I wrinkle my nose at that preposterous suggestion, then pop up from my now-closed luggage, stroking my throat again. I force out another cough. "I'm dying. Doesn't it sound like I'm dying?"

"Dying of pathetic attempts to get out of a trip," he says.

I sneer at him, then shake a finger. "This is all your fault."

He cracks up, lifts his cup, takes a drink. "How is this my fault?"

"It's not! I'm just freaking out," I blurt out, then I let my shoulders sag. My stomach twists with nerves. "I don't know how to handle being with Axel for a week. Help."

My friend closes the distance between us, wraps his free arm around me, and squeezes. "Let's get you a bagel, and we'll come up with a game plan."

I nod, feeling a little better for the moral support. We head to my tiny kitchen, where I blow out a heavy breath. Try to shake off the past. "Sorry. It's just that seeing him is tougher than I'd thought."

For so many reasons.

"You miss him," he says gently, and it's not a question. It's just the truth.

I desperately miss the friendship, the camaraderie, the way we understood each other.

"I do," I say, sad and wistful. Then I shake out my shoulders, like I can shimmy away the emotions. "But I'm just going to...adult my way through this trip. I'll focus on the readers and the agenda, and then I'll snag some girl time with Rachel in Paris."

"Good idea. Make that your reward for adulting with Axel," he says. "Tell yourself you only get to see her if you've been good."

"Oh, I do like rewards," I say, excited now.

"I know, Hazel. I know."

"All right, Rachel is my reward and adulting is the plan. I can do this."

TJ slugs my arm. "You've got this. And for the record, you've always adulted with him."

Have I, though? That day in Chelsea when Axel blindsided me was not my finest moment. Yes, I was surprised, but I didn't handle the news well that he was leaving the book, the country, and me.

I said some things.

Things I wish I could un-say.

Maybe this trip is a do-over. A chance to *adult well.* "I need a bagel for strength and sustenance," I say.

The toaster answers my prayer, popping up with a nicely browned sesame bagel. I grab some butter from the fridge, then smear it on. "I hate cream cheese," I explain, though TJ knows this, because we wrote cream cheese on my whiteboard shitlist the day he learned of my dislike for it. It was listed under Axel, and also *me.*

"How do you hate cream cheese again?" he asks.

"Have you tried cream cheese?" I counter, then shudder.

"Yes. It's too good. Which is why my bagel is naked." He pats his flat stomach.

I pat his belly too. "Because you like giving Jude your abs."

His knowing smile says I understand him perfectly. Then he adds, "I like abs."

I laugh, then an image flashes before me from the other day at the coffee shop. When Axel leaned back in his chair and his shirt rode up the slightest bit, giving me a peek of his stomach, lean and toned.

A tiny shiver has the audacity to slide down my spine.

But that's the last thing I need as I head to the airport to meet him at the gate when boarding begins.

Because of course we're sitting together.

Since our publishers think we're former writing partners who simply split amicably over creative differences but managed to stay friends.

That's the true fiction.

* * *

I'm nearly at the airline counter to check my suitcase when my phone buzzes with a text.

> Axel: File this under 'only in New York.' A delivery truck just jackknifed by the access road. Boxes spilled out. There are satin Yankees jackets strewn all over the street. I got out of the Lyft. I'm walking the last mile.

He's sent a photo of the spillage. Holy mountain of shiny pin-striped blue. That's very New York.

> Hazel: Or just order another Lyft on the other side of the exit?

> Axel: I considered that. But it's a bit of a free-for-all. I'm taking my chances walking.

> Hazel: TO JFK? YOU'RE WALKING ALONG THE ROAD TO JFK? It's practically a highway.

Photographic evidence lands once more. A five-second video of his motorcycle boots as he's walking along the access road to the terminal.

> Hazel: That's a death trap.

> Axel: You won't get rid of me that easily, sweetheart.

> Hazel: That's not what I'm saying.

> Axel: Sure it is. You sent that truck to foil me.

> Hazel: Give me more credit. If I'd sent that truck to foil you, it wouldn't have contained Yankees jackets.

> Axel: Fair point. I guess you're not the culprit. But Brooks Dean wouldn't give up, and I won't either. I'll be there to vex you. Anyway, I'm closing in on the terminal. But if you're still in line, can I piggyback and join you?

I glance up. There are five people in front of me. I might as well help out. That's adulting, after all.

> Hazel: Yes, but you'd better move fast.

> Axel: Be there in three minutes.

How the hell will he be here so soon? But as promised, three minutes later, the man in glasses, motorcycle boots, and a tight gray T-shirt wedges past the sea of travelers in the snaking line, saying *excuse me* and *thank you* as he goes.

He might not be nice to me, but at least he's nice to strangers. I'll give him a decency point.

He arrives at my side when I'm one person away from the counter. Axel hardly looks worse for the wear. I half wonder if he made it all up, but he offers me a dark blue shiny piece of fabric from the messenger bag slung across his chest. "As a thank you," he says.

"You stole a Yankees jacket from a delivery truck accident?"

"Spoils of war," he says, like it's no big deal.

"Seriously?" Thievery is not his style.

He huffs, relenting. "I hitched the final mile with a cabby. He had some. Gave me one."

I scoff. "So this is a regifted Yankees jacket that had spilled out of the truck onto the road that your cabby absconded with and you're giving me?"

"And you thought I wasn't a nice guy," he says with a too-big grin.

"Don't worry. I wasn't suffering from that delusion," I say as the counter agent calls out, "Next."

Without taking the jacket, I stride up to the counter. "Hello. I'm flying to Rome," I say to the woman with the cinched-back, blonde ponytail.

"Wonderful. And you're here with…" She looks to Axel in question.

"My nemesis," I say plainly.

The woman blinks in confusion.

Axel snorts, then holds up a thumb and forefinger. "She under-exaggerated. Tell the truth, Hazel," he says to me.

"Fine. Archnemesis," I correct.

The agent pulls a face. "Should be a lovely flight then."

The flight is only the beginning.

* * *

Twenty minutes later, we make it through the first lava pit of travel—security. I grab my red backpack from the other side of the conveyor belt while Axel snags his messenger bag and slings it across his chest.

We head down the concourse toward our gate.

I've survived a half hour with him. I only have six days and...

I don't want to go there. I simply want to get through this trip without any bloodshed. While we weave through the throngs of travelers, I swallow past the discomfort in my throat, then say, "I had this wild idea for how to make it through the trip," I offer.

"Headphones the whole time?"

Why does he make it so hard to be nice? "No, Axel," I say.

"Pretend we don't know each other," he offers.

"You make it so easy to want to throttle you," I say dryly.

He smiles, the cocky kind. "It's my special skill."

I take a deep breath and try again. "My idea is—why don't we just behave like adults?"

His brow creases. Perhaps I've made the strangest suggestion in the world. "Like, just move on?" he asks carefully, but hopefully too.

But I'm not sure if we can just move on. I think for now we just need to deal. I try to work out the best way to phrase that when I spot a far-too-familiar profile. A square jaw. Slicked-back hair. A tailored shirt.

The most confident grin I've ever seen.

Why, universe, why?

I wish it were anyone but him.

"Ex alert," I mutter, like I'd say to TJ, or Veronica, or any of my friends.

"Sarah? Is it Sarah?" Axel asks, tightly.

I shake my head at the mention of his ex-girlfriend. That witch broke his heart nearly two years ago.

I swallow uncomfortably, and say, "My ex."

Axel looks to the right, then straightens his shoulders, saying nothing when he spots the guy I was once in love with.

My ex is walking toward us, smiling like he's so goddamn happy to see me. "Hazel," he says when he's ten feet away, as if nothing's better than running into the woman he screwed over.

By screwing others.

Axel tenses. His shoulders bunch up. His jaw clenches. His eyes narrow.

That's a strange reaction—this level of loathing.

My ex then deals a smile to the guy next to me, followed by a chin nod. "Hey, Axel."

Axel doesn't soften. He just nods, his lips tight as a drum.

Maybe this is a good time to practice adulting. "Hello, Max," I say, coolly, biting back all the things I want to say to my ex.

9

SEPARATE-ISH

Hazel

I met the sharp-dressed Max more than a year ago at a book party. I'd heard about him from Axel over the years, since agents were up there on the wheel of regular conversation topics after *coffee is life, how I procrastinated today,* and *why didn't I come up with that brilliant idea that's at the top of bestseller lists.*

At our writing sessions, there were a lot of *Max says this,* and *Max says that,* especially since their working relationship was newer. Axel's first agent had retired right around the time when we started writing together, so my agent, Michelle, had handled the deal for both of us for the *Ten Park Avenue* series. Shortly after that was inked, Axel signed on with Max for his solo projects.

But I'd never met him. There was never a need or an opportunity.

Until we went to a launch party one evening at An

Open Book. Axel snagged me from the post-reading crowd and said, "All right. Let's do this. For four years of writing together, you've avoided meeting Max, but that ends tonight since he's here."

I nudged him playfully. "Yes. I've been darting and dodging him all this time," I'd said.

You didn't often meet your friends' agents unless you all happened to be at the same industry fete together. Stars simply hadn't aligned till that night.

Axel draped an arm around me and steered me to the man in the suit. His back was to us while he chatted with a guy wearing a vest and a cowboy hat. Another writer, Axel whispered. The writer's name was Vince Caine, two short syllables that immediately set off *pen name* bells in my head. As we waited for an opening, Axel and I made small talk about Vince's ultra-manly moniker.

When vest-and-hat Marlboro Man and *GQ* agent were done, Max turned around.

And Max was all kinds of wow.

Those warm hazel eyes.

That scruffy jaw.

That delightfully arrogant grin.

Most of all, that tailored suit that hugged his thighs, his arms, his chest.

I like all sorts of styles on men, from the rough-and-tumble, leather-jacket-and-jeans look to the workout-casual, polo-wearing style, to this moneyed three-piece wardrobe. I like men; it's easy for me to write delectable heroes because I'm a woman who enjoys the male form a lot. I just wish I could have what my heroines are having—toe-curling, sheet-grabbing sex. Maybe someday I'll have great sex. So far, I've only ever had just the slightly-above-average kind. Perhaps that'll change for me soon.

"Hazel, this is the infamous Max," Axel had said as he'd introduced us.

Max extended a hand. "Then you must be the notorious Hazel."

Notorious? I'd take it. Nicknames were fun in my book. "The one and only," I said, taking my turn with the flirting baton.

Axel dusted one hand against the other. "My work here is done," he said, then with a flicker of relief in his eyes, he walked away.

For the next several months I dated Max, fell for Max, and nearly moved in with Max. During our coffee-shop writing sessions, I told Axel little details about his agent. How sweet he was for sending me tiger lilies, how fantastic the meal was at the new vegetarian restaurant he found, how clever he was for his double word score in Words With Friends (even though I'd nabbed a triple-worder).

Axel would want to know those details, I'd figured, since he'd introduced Max and me. Besides, when Axel had started dating a woman he'd met at a bar the year before, he'd told me the honeymoon details about how taken he was with Sarah. She was sexy and sweet, everything he'd wanted.

Well, until she left him, saying she'd grown *bored*.

The worst fear of a creative person was being dull.

Anyway, because I'd heard all about Sarah when Axel

was falling for her, I did the same about Max. I couldn't shut up about how the man loved to give gifts. From flowers to chocolates to restaurants, Max was the ultimate winer and diner. For months, the cynical writer in me hibernated while the romantic allowed herself to be hook-line-and-sinkered.

The first night we had dinner, he ended the meal early to tend to a client call overseas then sent me truffles in the morning.

The truffles worked.

The part of me that doubts everyone, including myself, the part that *knows* that we are all drawn to those who can hurt us because it's familiar, ignored all the circumstantial evidence over the months I spent with Max.

It took a photo of Max kissing another woman at a nightclub in Barcelona for me to see the truth. Max was there entertaining Axel and Vince at an international book festival. Axel was in the foreground toasting and Max was in the background kissing another woman.

I'd been fooled from the start, since the dinner and the truffles.

I kicked Max out of my life ten months ago, putting him at the tippy top of the whiteboard.

And there's absolutely no need for me to chat with Max at the airport today. Except, for the little matter of adulting.

Max *is* Axel's agent. I made a vow to behave better. No matter how sleazy Max is with love, he's magic with books. Axel needs this guy in his life, so I grin and bear it, smiling painfully as I say, "Hello, Max. How are you?"

"Better now that I've run into the two of you. How the hell is everything, Notorious Hazel?" He asks it without a care. Like I want to chat casually with the guy who snookered me.

"Can't complain," I say brightly, so damn brightly. "After all, we're heading to Rome to start the book tour."

He knows that, of course. Just like Michelle knows where I'm off to.

Max tilts his head, his brow knitting for a second before he says, "Right, right. A book tour is bank, and with the way *A Perfect Lie* is selling…" He trails off then mouths, *Whoa.*

Gross.

This man is such a show-off. How did I miss this? Was he hiding his personality along with the cheating? I hope so. I hope my taste in men isn't as terrible as my track record says it is.

"And those reviews. I could kiss those reviews," Max adds, and I want to roll my eyes. But I won't. I am an expert at throwing the perfectly blank smile at unpleasant people.

"I'm sure the reviews would love a smackeroo," Axel says in a surprisingly dry tone. He doesn't spare even his agent from his sarcasm.

Max turns to me again and beams. "And Notorious Hazel, you are the queen. That final chapter in *The I Do Redo* was just…" He pauses like he's hunting for just the right words. "Refreshingly surprising. The kind of heart-stopping plot twists we turn to a Valentine story for."

That compliment feels familiar, like he's parroting a

review, trying to co-opt it for himself. But TJ made me stop reading reviews. He promised me he'd show me all the potential hot guy cover photos he found online if I'd stop reading reviews. His carrot-and-stick worked—my current cover photo is one he shared as a prize for *keeping my head in the sand.*

So, I can't call Max out on it. Instead I say, "There's nothing like a plot twist. Especially when you're so sure a character is a good guy and he turns out to be otherwise."

Axel's lips twitch, but then he's stony-faced.

Max turns to Axel. "And you, have an amazing tour. It's going to ignite your backlist." Then he shrugs happily. "But your backlist is already blazing. Just the way I like it."

And I like that Max never makes a dime on *Ten Park Avenue.*

Axel smiles once more, but it looks as if he's getting an appendectomy at the same time. "Me too," he says, almost choking out the words.

Max checks his watch. "Well, just got back from Los Angeles, and I already have calls to Los Angeles to make. The day is young and I'm busy, busy. Safe travels."

He leaves, and I want to take a Silkwood shower to get rid of the scent of that smarmy jackass. But he's in my head now, along with the reminders of how stupid I was to get involved with a guy like him.

Just what I need before this big trip. A reminder that I'm a dumbass with romance.

"Let's go to the gate," I say to Axel flatly, so I don't let on that seeing Max has knocked me off my confidence game.

But it's hard to stay chill as I walk closer to Gate Eighteen.

It's hard, since I've tried my best to keep the whole Max debacle separate from the Axel debacle. They're separate things, after all.

Well, separate-ish.

But as I walk, the annoyance in me heats up. I can't believe Axel would work with Max, knowing what he's like. The fact that Axel barely blinked just now proves Axel and I were hardly ever friends in the first place.

Maybe I barely knew Axel. He supposedly hates liars. He supposedly hates cheaters. He supposedly hates men like his father.

But he hired an agent who's just like his dad. A con artist.

The annoyance bubbles up to the surface. But I fight it off. I have to remember my game plan from earlier—be an adult and move on. I swallow down the gobstopper of self-righteous irritation and say, "I'm so glad your book's doing well."

Axel gives me a side-eye. "Thanks. You too," he says, his tone suspicious.

"And that's what we should focus on during this trip. Just the stories, the books, the fans," I say, soldiering on as a pack of harried travelers practically charges us. We part, letting the group of suits march their way down the concourse.

"They're in a rush," he says with a huff.

Wow. We're making shitty airport small talk. So fun.

But you know what? This is what we need. Bullshit small talk. That's what we'll discuss in Europe for seven days.

"They sure are," I say, peppy, like the adult-er I am.

"So you were saying something before we ran into Max?" Axel asks, prompting me as he rewinds to several minutes ago when I was starting to say we should behave like adults.

I draw in a breath. This is it. *Just do it.* I turn to my traveling companion, trying to erase any remnant of resting bitch face. In my head, I practice the next thing I want to say: *"I was just saying 'Let's try to just get along on this trip.'"*

But those aren't the words that come out of my mouth.

The ones that do make landfall? "I can't believe you work with that lying, cheating, two-timing scum."

Axel stares at me with wide eyes that almost, *almost*, twinkle with something like wicked delight.

But before he can say a word, his phone trills. With lightning reflexes, he reads the name, then swipes up. "Hey Mason," he says, then walks away from me toward the nearby coffee stand.

Great. Just great. This trip is going to be so much worse than I'd thought.

10

SCHADENFREUDE

Hazel

I'm an asshole.

I need to apologize for my big, stupid mouth.

But that's a little like asking a dog to meow. It's not a natural skill for me.

I'm still working through how to do it when Axel returns from his call ten minutes later, slumps into a seat across from me at the gate, and drags a hand down his face.

My throat tightens. I messed up badly. I shouldn't have said that to him. I crossed a line, and now I'll have to uncross it.

As the gate agent barks announcements, I rehearse options this time.

Sorry I was rude, but I thought you'd want to get as far away as possible from a lying pig. My bad for not realizing you'd stayed with him.

Sorry I said your agent's scum. Of course you're not scum for working with scum.

Sorry. You can work with whoever you want, but how could you stay with him when you knew that about him? Oh, right, because romance is bullshit.

But none of those will work. Because they aren't real apologies. They're un-apologies.

Why is saying sorry so hard?

"In five minutes, we'll begin boarding our flight to Rome. We will board by group. Please check your boarding passes so you can board when your group is called," the agent warbles.

Okay, I know this plot device. It's the ticking clock. I have five minutes to choose a path to apology. I should apologize before we board, especially in case we die on the plane. No one wants to die with apologies on their tongue.

But apologizing is like learning French. It's complicated and requires new neural pathways, and new emotional ones too. When I was in grade school, my father would lash out at my mother when he came home from the local university after teaching English all day. He'd tell her she was toasting the bread wrong, slicing the cucumber wrong, cleaning the sink wrong.

The next morning, he'd say he was sorry for being such a perfectionist, but he just liked things done the right way. She understood, right? He'd kiss her and that was the end of his apology.

The English professor in him was a perfectionist with Veronica and me too. He wanted his two daughters to learn the difference between among and between, affect and effect, peak and peek and pique.

If we didn't nail them, we'd have to write the correct usage down one hundred times.

There were no morning apologies for us.

Never. Not one.

I'm so glad my mother left him before I became a total asshole.

"And now we'll begin boarding our first-class passengers," the agent says, and the crowds at Gate Eighteen stretch and rise.

I grab my backpack, and Axel hoists up his messenger bag. We head to the gate kiosk, but I don't say a word to him, and he doesn't seem keen on speaking to me. This is worse than I'd thought. The silence cloaks us as we line up, like we're marching down the gangplank.

With no real map, I'm going to have to wing this apology. Once the attendant scans our boarding passes, I draw a fueling breath. I'll do my mea culpa as we walk along the jetway. I turn my gaze to Axel, ready to say *I'm sorry*, but he's chatting with the guy next to him. "Oh, that's a good one. Your mind will be blown."

A forty-something guy in khakis and a corporate polo—that's my best guess since the insignia on the chest reads *Aviano* and that sounds tech-y—is clutching a hardback of *The Girl in the Hotel*.

That's Vince Caine's latest thriller, which has been climbing the charts for weeks now.

"Good to know," the tech guy says gratefully,

waggling the book. "But hopefully not too good. I need to sleep on this trip."

Axel laughs. "Then you're going to have to switch to the news, my man. This is a page-turner," he says, pointing to the tale.

The man curses under his breath, but it's *aw-shucks* style. "Oh, well. What's sleep for anyway? I'll sleep when I'm dead."

"Until then, there are books," Axel says.

And damn, it's cute how Axel talks to fellow readers. Like he's just another reader too.

As we shuffle down the jetway, they chat more behind me, trading recommendations on favorite romantic thrillers until the guy asks, "And have you read *A Lovely Alibi*?"

I smile at the mention of one of Axel's books. But I fight off the urge to spin around and point at him gleefully while shouting, *That's his! He wrote it! Remember the scene at the gala in Barcelona where the hero dances with the heroine while she's still wearing a knife in her garter like the badass she is?*

I stay quiet while Axel hums doubtfully. "Hmm. I'm not sure I have."

"Oh man, you have to. That's the one where the hero commandeers a Jeep in Barcelona to chase down a thief of rare antiquities. He nabs him, then takes his woman out dancing after. He's so smooth," the guy says, admiring a fictional hero that my friend—ahem, former friend—crafted artfully.

"I'll have to check it out," Axel says.

"Huxley. Axel Huxley. But don't blame me when

you're up too late," the tech guy says as we reach the galley.

"I won't," Axel answers.

I step onto the plane first as a flight attendant in a red pantsuit greets me. When I show her my boarding pass, she says, "Right this way, Ms. Valentine." She gestures to the second row, then turns to Axel. "And Mr. Hendrix-Blythe, you're in the second row too," she says to my companion, and we slide into our seats, me by the window, him by the aisle.

When the man walks past Axel to the last row of first class, the fanboy nods at Axel without knowing who the guy next to me really is.

I have a hunch as to why Axel didn't tell him. Only, as much as I want to dive into his motivation, now's not the time. I put a pin in the *you still don't believe your success* convo.

A girl with a big old apology chip on her shoulder has got to do what a girl with a big old apology chip on her shoulder has got to do.

"Axel," I say quietly, stripping any residual snark from my tone. I'm tempted to reach out and touch his hand. His arm. His shoulder. But I refrain.

Like a mistrustful dog, he turns to me, blue eyes guarded. "Yeah?"

Just do it. Just say it. No conditions. No justifications. The opposite of your father. "I'm sorry," I say quickly.

He blinks. "For what?"

"For what I said about Max," I say, nervous. I hope I'm not making this worse.

He scoffs. "Max?" he asks, incredulous. "You're sorry about Max?"

I wince. This is so much harder than I'd thought. I'm going to have to repeat my snide comment. "That was shitty for me to say I can't believe you're working with him. Just because I have issues with him doesn't mean you should stop doing business with him. He's a great agent."

Axel smiles, easy and confident, like a superhero shedding his mortal origins, donning his cape, luxuriating in his new powers. This smile is Axel at the hipster restaurant. It's know-it-all Axel. It's Axel who silently corrects people's grammar. "Max is a great agent. He's also a great jackass." Somehow, that superhero grin grows impossibly wider. "I left him ten months ago."

Seriously?

I sit up straighter. Study the guy next to me like he's under a microscope. "You left him?"

"Mason Stein reps me now, but Max will always be in my work life. He's a soul-less, money-loving bastard, enjoying all his last laughs since, obviously, he makes money off my backlist. But at least Mason makes the fifteen percent on my new deals."

Mason.

That's right. Axel mentioned Mason's last name to Linus outside the hotel after the reader Q and A last month—*lunch with Stein.* He said Mason, too, a little while ago when he picked up the phone. I know Mason. He's fantastic. He's TJ's agent. A sarcastic, Ari Gold-esque, will-go-to-the-ends-of-the-earth-for-you agent. He's perfect for Axel.

"He's terrific for you. He's great," I say, meaning it completely.

"He is," Axel says. Then his expression goes blank before he turns serious. "Appreciate you saying that. And listen, Hazel, I agree with what you were saying before we saw him. For this trip, we'll do our best just to be...writers touring together."

He extends a hand to shake. I take it. It's the first real handshake we've had since I ran into him again. It feels good to hold his hand. There's a zing, a little shiver down my spine.

That's just because I love a good handshake.

Not because his dark blue eyes hold mine for a long beat.

Not because his touch feels both familiar and new.

And not because I'm still thinking about him with his shirt off.

I let go of his hand. "Does this mean we're friends?" Because someone has to end the moment, return to barbs and stings.

With a laugh, he says, "Oh Hazel. Please."

I smile, relieved to be enemies again. "Don't worry. I didn't think you had it in you."

"Good. You wouldn't want me to relent that easily. If I know one thing about you it's that you love a challenge."

"Oh, I do? And you're a challenge?" I ask.

"I'm your Everest, sweetheart."

I lean my head back against the leather chair, scoffing at his analogy. "You know I can't stand outdoor sports."

He snorts. "Who said climbing *this* Everest was an outdoor sport?"

I smack his arm. "You dog," I chide.

"You know you want to plant your flag," he says, crossing his arms, so defiant, so familiar. So entertaining.

"You think I want to plant my flag on my archnemesis?" I ask.

"I'm still your archnemesis?" He uncrosses his arms, delivering a hard stare through those black glasses. Hmm. Have those glasses always looked so sexy smart on him?

Wait. Nope. I can't go there. I backpedal to enemyland. "Of course you're my archnemesis. What could possibly have changed?"

"You apologized. Doesn't that make me a mere nemesis now?" he asks, intensely serious.

I nearly break first, but I hold my laughter. "You want a demotion from archnemesis to mere nemesis?"

"Sure. I thought we were regular...*nemesises,*" he says, attempting to make a plural of that word and failing. "Shit, what's the plural of nemesis?" He grabs his phone as if world peace depends on the answer.

But before he can ask Google, I answer with, "*Nemeses.*"

He checks the dictionary still. Understandable. I'd do the same, since there's no better way to drill home a word. As he reads the definition, he cringes, bemoaning his own mistake. "*Nemeses,*" he repeats as he bangs his head against the back of his seat.

"You know what this means," I say, far too pleased.

"I do," he mutters.

A vocabulary sin requires repentance. It's a game we invented when I told him about my dad's Draconian grammar rules. We took Dad's ruthlessness and turned it into fun.

"Lunch is on you," I say, delighted to celebrate this schadenfreude as I'd expect him to do if the tables were turned.

The last time we played was more than a year ago, when we were working on Lacey's story. The brilliant and pretty ER doc was arguing with her annoying co-worker Noah, before she went home to prep for her date with her sexy new neighbor.

I wrote *another thing coming* in chapter three instead of *think*. Oh, the pain. The terrible pain I felt.

"You've got another think coming if you think I don't know that about lunch," he says.

"I do know that," I say.

"Good. You understand the rules," he says.

And I understand him too. Because ten months ago was when I broke up with Max. I don't think it's a coincidence that that's when Axel split with his agent.

"You left Max ten months ago?" I ask, wanting to be one hundred percent sure.

"I did," he confirms.

"Because he's a jackass?"

"And a liar," he adds.

I take a few minutes and let this new understanding of Axel fall into place, like a room rearranged. A table's in a different spot. A couch is up against the wall. But this new room layout makes so much more sense. It aligns with the man I knew.

It makes sense—intrinsic sense—that Axel would leave Max.

It makes me feel understood too. Like maybe we're...*frenemies*.

I meander back in time to thirty minutes ago. To Axel's dry mic-drop—*I'm sure the reviews would love a smackeroo*. To the smart dig in those words. My heart gives a happy little squeeze.

A few minutes later, as we prep for takeoff, I close my eyes then say quietly, "Thanks, Axel."

"For what?"

"For leaving Max."

He's quiet at first, then, barely audible above the hum of the plane, he says, "I couldn't stay with him after that."

Maybe, just maybe, I can make it through this trip.

11

A TIDGE RUGGED

Axel

That was a close call.

But at least we only talked about the end of things with Max. Not the beginning of his romance with Hazel.

I'm happy to tell the truth about the demise of my business relationship with him. No interest in digging into that damn book party when I introduced the two of them.

They say hindsight is twenty-twenty but I may need to get my glasses checked, since I'm still fuzzy on what I should have done that night.

But what's done is done.

At least Hazel and I buried a sliver of the hatchet. Maybe a sliver is enough. Sure seems to be, since we make it through the next few hours of the flight with occasional small talk, questions like *do you want a beverage* and *excuse me, I need to step over you.* Fine, I *might* watch her ass as she climbs over my legs. But the view. Dear lord, the view.

Hazel Valentine does not possess a writer's butt. She's got a peach rear, and I want to bite into it like a piece of fruit.

Which is not a helpful thought, so I return to the book I'm listening to for another few minutes, turning it off when the meal comes.

Hazel's more quiet than usual as she bites into her penne pasta, then stabs another piece with her fork. "Did you know this is airline code for vegetarian?"

"Pasta?"

"Yup," she says, then pops it into her mouth.

"Were you expecting the wild beets, sweetheart?" I ask as I slice a piece of the roasted chicken, then take a bite.

"Of course," she says. "It's my greatest hope. But you know what else is?"

"Your greatest hope?" I ask.

She sets down her silverware, then looks me square in the eyes. "For you to talk to that guy."

My brow creases. "What guy?" I'm not sure what she's getting at.

She tips her forehead behind us. "The guy you were chatting with as we boarded, Axel," she says, a bit of a plea in her voice. "He likes your work. He'd be really excited to know it's you he was talking to."

I frown. "Nah. That ship has sailed."

She arches a brow. "Has it though? There's no reason

you can't go back there and say you wrote *A Lovely Alibi*. He's a fanboy. He'd be excited."

My stomach churns, and I wish I knew why.

But maybe Hazel does, since she sets a gentle hand on my arm, "You think you don't deserve your success for some reason. But you've earned it. Through hard work and talent. The guy likes you. You'd make his day."

Would I though? "It's so presumptuous," I say, but my argument sounds woefully weak. Like, it's such a weak argument I'm embarrassed I made it.

I lean back in the seat, run a hand through my hair. "I just don't want to come across like…I'm too big for my britches."

That's what my dad did, for all intents and purposes. He hoodwinked people. He pretended he was someone he was not. If I go talk to that guy, am I going to sound like my dad, pumping up my own ego?

Hazel shakes her head. "You won't sound too big for your britches."

"But maybe I'll sound like I lied. Better to leave sleeping dogs alone."

"It's not too late. This is your chance to tell him the truth. Just say *hey, I'm Axel Huxley, and I'm excited you like my books.*"

Hmm. That doesn't sound too tough. That doesn't sound like a con either. Since, well, it's not.

And maybe it'd be a con to say nothing.

Once the food is clear, I stand, shake off the nerves, and head back to the fourth row. The man is deep into *Girl In The Hotel*.

I clear my throat.

He looks up. "Hey?" he says, kind of curious.

"So, I'm...Axel Huxley. I'm excited you like my books," I say, giving him the line Hazel fed me. That was weird, like stretching muscles that have never been worked before.

But when his eyes pop and he says, "No kidding" with utter delight, the stretch is worth it. We spend the next twenty minutes chatting about stories, and it feels incredibly fucking good.

I don't feel like a grifter one bit.

* * *

When the plane lands around eleven on Friday morning, I feel like jet lag has nothing on me. I slept a solid six on the flight, barely even rousing for the quick layover in Paris.

I am raring to go.

My travel companion is another story. Hazel's yawning. *Again*. They're super-size yawns and they're unstoppable. "You going for a record? I can call Guinness and see if you're close?" I ask as we shuffle off the plane.

Hazel sneers. "Not all of us are world travelers who hop off to Europe at the drop of a hat," she says.

"Ouch," I say. That hit close to home.

But I deserved that.

Still, she mutters, "Sorry."

This woman is on an apology roll. But the runaway to Europe situation? That's all on me. I owe her a plateful of sorries, but I'm not ready to dig into my reasons for that matchstick choice.

And honestly, maybe we've tackled enough of the past. Hazel seems keen on moving forward. "No apologies needed. But you can apologize for falling asleep on me on the car ride to the hotel."

"I'm not going to sleep *on* you, Axel. I'm going to sleep *on* my fabulous king-size bed in my hotel room overlooking the Spanish Steps," she declares as we reach the gate, weaving past other travelers.

"Question. If you're asleep, how are you enjoying the view?"

That earns me another sneer. "Who cares? I have a date with my mattress in about an hour," she says as another yawn takes her hostage.

Oh man, I hate to break this to her, but someone has to do it. "Actually, Hazel, if you crash now, you're going to be a mess the whole trip."

She turns to me with no snark or sneer, just confused alarm. "What do you mean?"

There's no mincing words when it comes to jet lag. "You'll never get on track for the trip if you crash this afternoon."

Her plaintive whine sounds ripped from her soul. "But napping is supposed to be good for you."

"Not on the first day on another continent," I say, as we head through the bustling concourse on the way to customs and immigration. "The best thing you can do is get out, see the sights, kick around town. You need light —natural light—then go to bed early. That'll help you get on the schedule here in this time zone. You'll enjoy the trip much more with your sleep cycle in sync. Trust me."

She trudges beside me toward the immigration sign in the distance. "But my bed," she whimpers as we pass a souvenir shop selling sweatshirts with sayings like *Grab Life By The Meatballs* and *Less Drama More Pasta*. She cups her ear. "Can't you hear it?"

"What's it saying?"

"It says: *Hazel, come to me, be my love.*" For a second, she brightens, full of energy. "I want to marry a bed. That's what I want. A big, fluffy king-size bed. What better groom for a romance writer than a bed?"

I shake my head, amused by her slide into the land of the over-tired. "You are seriously exhausted. Did you sleep on the plane?"

She winces. "A little. But in my defense, I was reading a really good book. This memoir of a child actor. It's so wild, the things she went through. It's giving me all sorts of ideas for new emotional wounds."

"So you worked the whole time?" I chide.

"I read," she says, insisting.

"*It gave me ideas for emotional wounds,*" I parrot. I'm not letting her get away with that. "That's work, sweetheart."

"It was pleasure," she retorts, and it's fucking adorable how she argues with me. It's so damn cute how she wants to be right. Shame I'm attracted to women who like to go toe-to-toe.

But every man has an Achilles' heel. At least I'm aware of mine.

"You have no respect for mornings," I say, tsking her.

"Or jet lag. But here's the thing. You can't be a tired wreck this trip. Want to know why?"

"Why?" she asks suspiciously.

"Because then I'll be left holding the bag," I say as we weave through the airport crowds, with Italian accents and phrases floating past us as we pass signs flashing in foreign languages. "While you faceplant in the sleeper car or, worse, on the streets of Nice, I'll have to play tour guide all by myself."

"And that would be unconscionable?" she counters.

"Yes. Yes, it would," I say, sternly, holding my ground. Don't want her to know that jet lag sucks, I don't want her to feel it, and I don't want her to miss a single second of what I suspect will be a trip she loves.

Better for both of us if she thinks I'm still a cold-hearted jerk. If I let down my guard around her more than I already have, I'm bound to let it down more. To reveal secrets that ought to stay locked up.

This descent into friendship with her is decidedly dangerous to my mental health.

"Well, far be it from me to make you suffer unconscionably," she retorts as we near the immigrations checkpoint.

She's yawning less. She's walking faster. Good. My boot camp technique is working.

"Exactly. And that means you're going to jet lag school today," I say, the drill sergeant in me strong.

She starts to yawn, but she shakes her head vigorously, like she's exorcizing the demon of yawns from her very soul, wrestling it to the ground, and defeating it.

"There. I'm better," she says.

"Good," I say. "That's all that matters."

"Since this way no one will know your secret—that you need me as your co-tour-guide," she says, with a deliberately haughty lift of her chin.

"Yep. That's exactly what I need."

* * *

An hour later we make it past the checkpoint, then head down to baggage claim. Once I find my bag and grab it, she spots hers bumping along the conveyor belt. She heads its way, but I catch up, reaching for it.

Fine, I may not be a nice guy. But I'm still going to grab her luggage.

"Thanks, Axel," she says, then in a whisper, she adds, "And don't worry. I won't tell anyone you were nice enough to grab my bag."

It's scary how easily she can read me.

Let that be a reminder. "It was there," I say, gruff. Deliberately gruff.

She gives me a long, overdone nod as she says, "Right."

"Don't make a thing of it, *Valentine*," I say as I pop up the handle on her bag so she can wheel it.

"I won't, *Huxley*. Or should I call you Mr. Alexander Hendrix-Blythe when we travel?" she asks, using my legal name, the one I changed to when I went to college, ditching Dad's surname at last, and taking on a new last name—my stepdad's and my mom's.

"Not all of us were born with pen names," I counter, handing her the checked bag.

"I'll be sure to send Daddy a thank you note for mine," she fires back as she takes the handle. "And hey, you scored a pretty decent writer's name too, even though you don't use it. Hendrix is cool. Rugged. Mysterious. Tough."

"Aww, you think I'm rugged, mysterious, and tough," I tease.

She adopts an evil grin as we wheel our bags past the other carousels, heading toward the exit. "Did I say you were those things?"

I sigh heavily. "Why did I help you with the bag?" It's a rhetorical question.

But she jumps on it, the speed demon. "Aha! So you admit you did help with the bag? It was deliberate? Not just because"—she stops to sketch air quotes as she deepens her voice—"the bag was there."

Damn. She sounded just like me when she said that. That's scary, how well she can imitate me, intonation and all.

What's scarier though is that she's too damn good at turning my words all the way around and against me. *Note to self: watch the fuck out with Hazel. She's a virtuoso villain when wielding your favorite weapons—words.* "You should have been an attorney," I say, begrudgingly.

"Thanks. That's high praise from you," she says with a proud lift of her chin. Then, she stage-whispers, "And fine. You're a little rugged." She holds up her thumb and forefinger an inch apart. "Like, a tidge."

"I'll have Dunbar and Loraine put that on my next dust jacket. *He's a tidge rugged.*"

We leave the baggage carousel, pass through customs for the bag check, then enter the zoo of any airport—the waiting area where drivers and runners and handlers and friends and relatives wait for travelers.

I scan the sea of people holding placards or brandishing tablets, looking for **Huxley and Valentine**. But I blink when I spot a screen reading: **Mr. and Mrs. Huxley.**

Oh, fuck.

Hazel's going to flip a table. Maybe I can get in front of the screen while she's fighting off the latest yawn attack.

No such luck.

Hazel spots the curly-haired woman holding the offending sign, then points at the names.

"Why doesn't it say Mr. and Mrs. Valentine?"

This woman. She kills me. "That's my feminist," I say, laughing.

Fueled by her righteous rage, she marches to the woman. I'm not worried she'll make a scene—that's not her style. Instead, she says, warm and kind, "Hi. I'm Hazel Valentine." She pats my shoulder when I catch up a second later. "He's Axel Huxley. We're not married, but if we were, he'd take my name."

I stifle a laugh, then say dryly, "She's marrying a bed anyway."

Hazel laughs.

The woman stares at us like we're bananas.

Well, we're writers, so…Yeah, that shoe fits.

* * *

On the drive to the hotel, I point out a few sights as we pass. She's never been to Rome, so she stares with wide, eager eyes, taking it all in. But somewhere around Vatican City, her eyelids start to flutter and her head begins to bob. Then, she's drifting off, her cheek introducing itself to my shoulder.

I close my eyes, squeezing them shut, balling my fists. I should say something. I should *do* something. Move her. Gently wake her.

But I don't.

Instead, when she slides further and further into the land of nod and closer and closer to my lap, I just let her.

Jet lag be damned.

She's asleep, her head in my lap, her red hair spilled across my legs. I'm careful not to rouse her as I take out my phone to text my brother, telling him I'm going to win an award for being nice.

> Carter: What did you do? Hold the door for a little old lady? That's baseline nice, dude.

> Axel: O ye of little faith. I am next-leveling it. I am being nice to Hazel.

> Carter: I don't believe this is you. Say something Axel would say.

> Axel: I hate people.

> Carter: It's you, brother! It's really you!

We text some more as Hazel sleeps. It's only another fifteen minutes to the hotel. Letting her doze is the nice thing to do.

Except, I'm not doing it to be nice.

When we reach the hotel, she wakes up with a jolt. Straightens. Blinks. Then mutters a *thanks* when we step out of the car, like her face wasn't just in my lap.

12

GRAB LIFE BY THE MEATBALLS

Axel

After dropping off our luggage, Hazel and I trek to the Piazza Navona and snag a table at a sunny sidewalk café with a view of La Fontana dei Quattro Fiumi. The afternoon sun paints the fountain with a rosy hue.

Hazel breathes it all in with a blissful expression.

"No wonder you have fountains in your books," she says, appreciatively. "They're gorgeous."

Aesthetics aren't the reason, but no need to unpack the real motivation. I'd rather eat, then eat up the rest of the day so we're ready for tomorrow.

"I like fountains," I say in an understatement.

"Me too," she says. Maybe sleepiness softens her up, since she's warmer with me than she's been on the trip so far.

Or maybe it was the car nap.

As we settle in at the table, she opens the menu with a flourish, spreading it across the red and white checkered tablecloth. "It's my *nemeses* lunch," she declares.

"Enjoy it, sweetheart. Because it'll be the last time it happens," I say.

"Everyone trips on their words sometimes," she points out.

"I don't," I say smugly.

"I can't wait for your next fumble," she says, then stabs the menu. "And I already know I want my next lunch here. Check out the pastas. Trenette al pesto, pasta alla norma, mushroom ravioli, pasta puttanesca." She looks up, her green eyes glittering with culinary lust. "No wonder you spent so much time here researching books over the years. I'd have stayed in Italy just for the pasta."

For a few seconds, I brace myself for a dig about my escape to Europe. But it doesn't come. Now that I think about it, I'm not even sure she was referencing my pants-on-fire departure to Europe when she made that comment at the airport about some of us jetting off to Europe on a whim. She might have just been talking about the fact that I've visited Europe a lot for story research. Her *sorry* then was probably just about the general comment and her worries of how it might have come across, not because it was a low blow. Since it wasn't a low blow.

I relax my shoulders.

She salivates over the options for another minute then snaps the menu closed. "It's official. Nemeses has earned me two lunches."

I shake my head. "Nope. One lunch only."

"Maybe I'll order two dishes then," she says, always wanting the last word.

But when the server arrives, she orders only the puttanesca. I choose a pizza, because...when in Rome. Then I ask for two espressos.

After he leaves, she lifts a questioning brow.

"I have to caffeinate you," I explain.

She taps the veins on the inside of her wrist. "Just inject it right here please." Then she takes a deep breath and looks around the piazza, bustling with tourists snapping pictures throughout the square. "So why'd you drag me a mile away instead of someplace closer to the hotel?"

All part of my plan to keep her busy. To enjoy some vitamin D. "I figured if we were outside in public, you wouldn't dare fall asleep on me again," I say, then grin.

She narrows her eyes, and I gird myself for an arrow dipped in poison. But instead, like she's blameless, she says, "Look, you have a nice lap. It's soft."

I roll my eyes. "Great. Just great. I want to be known for my soft lap."

Her lips twitch. "I won't tell a soul it's like a pillow."

"I'm so glad I'm helping you fight jet lag," I say dryly. The server swings by with the espressos. I ask for one more with the pizza.

"Of course," he says.

After he leaves, she lifts her little cup in a toast. "To staying awake by the fountains."

"I'll drink to that."

We clink and down our espressos.

She sets her cup on the table and nods toward the fountain attracting flocks of tourists. "Since you've plied me with espressos and sunshine, maybe we can take a quick tour of all the piazzas and fountains today?" She sounds so hopeful, and it tugs on my locked-up heart. "That one is gorgeous."

"That's called the Fountain of the Four Rivers. Designed by Bernini. Commissioned by Pope Innocent X," I say as she gazes at the baroque beauty in the middle of the square. I can't help it. I love history.

Hazel turns to me. "Seriously. I've never been to Rome. Can we fit in a few?"

I smile. "Eat fast, sweetheart."

* * *

The first fountain I take her to is located in an alley only a few steps away from the Piazza Navona. The Fontana dei Libri, or Fountain of Books, is a smaller fountain, carved into a brick wall. A stone deer head rests in the center, flanked by huge stone books that spurt water.

I tell her the story of the fountain that pays homage to the universities in Rome, then the deer head with its religious origins. "But mostly I think the point is knowledge flows from books," I say, gesturing to the water pouring from the stone pages.

She sighs contentedly. "Then this is a perfect fountain for me to make a wish at."

I scoff. Hazel makes wishes? "Seriously?"

"You don't believe in wishes, Huxley? C'mon. You're not *that* grumpy."

Wishes are so not my thing. Actions are. But that sounds douchey, so I keep it to myself. "I only wish upon stars," I deadpan.

With a smile, she reaches into her travel purse and plucks out a few coins. "Here you go, then. This wish is on me."

"So generous," I say as I take the penny, then flip it over a few times between my thumb and index finger. "You really want me to make a wish?"

"Yes!"

"For real?"

"We're at a fountain," she says, then scans the alley, which is surprisingly quiet. "I won't tell a soul you made a wish. I'll protect your grumpster rep."

"Thanks," I say, then fiddle with the coin some more, unsure what to wish for, unsure *if* I should even wish.

Fountains and me, we have a complicated history.

But then, so do Hazel and I.

She tosses her coin into the water with relish, like she enjoys the plink of the metal against the liquid.

"What'd you wish for?" I ask.

She gives me a look, like *don't try to pull that*. "I can't tell you or it won't come true."

"You don't really believe that, do you?" I ask, with a doubtful rise of my eyebrows.

"Of course I do," she says, adamant. Huh. She *does* believe in wishing rules. Who would have thought?

"Hazel Valentine, are you...*superstitious*?"

"With some things, yes."

Holy shit. This is excellent fodder. I can use this to

poke and prod her. I need new ammo. "Do you avoid black cats, ladders, and opening umbrellas in houses?"

"Why would I need to open an umbrella in a house? It's never raining inside."

Fair point. "But the others?"

With a smile, she shakes her head. "No. I only believe in wishes," she says, soft, almost under her breath.

Like she's embarrassed to admit it.

This is going to be so good for me. I push on. "What about eyelashes? Do you wish on eyelashes that fall?"

"I do," she says with a genuine smile.

"And dandelions?" I ask, delighted by this charming fact.

"Yep," she says in that same vulnerable tone.

And dammit.

That tone makes it impossible for me to tease her about wishes now.

Especially since it's too hard to look at her right now, with that softness in her lips, that warmth in her eyes.

Instead, I turn to the gurgling water, and I flick the coin into it, making a wish for the trip—a wish that's entirely in my control. I can make this wish come true all on my own.

"What'd you wish for?" she asks as we leave the alley.

"You told me not to tell a wish."

"I know. But it's a natural human impulse to ask what someone's wish is after they make it."

"When you tell me yours, I'll tell you mine."

She huffs. "Fine. When mine comes true, I'll tell you what it was." She offers a hand to seal the deal.

Once again, we shake hands.

Once again, I wonder what it would feel like to yank her against me.

If she asks again about my wish, I'll lie.

Once again.

13

THE LONG CON

Axel

We visit the Fountain of Neptune next, then the Piazza Colonna. Finally, we trek toward the Trevi Fountain.

The day hurtles toward evening. Hazel yawned only a few times during the afternoon. I might have logged a few too. I am looking forward to bedtime more than I usually do. Sleep is awesome, and it'll be more awesome tonight.

As the sun dips low, we reach the popular landmark made famous in *La Dolce Vita* and every travel guide ever created for Rome.

A tourist trap? Yes.

But landmarks become unmissable for a reason. The Trevi Fountain is a stunner. When we arrive at it, Hazel draws a big, satisfied breath then stares at the sight in front of us. She doesn't snap photos of it. She simply inhales the moment. I can appreciate that even as throngs of tourists surround us, a far too familiar experience for me.

One that takes me way back in time.

To days and years I'd rather not remember.

I try to shake off the unpleasant thoughts. So far, this tour guide routine is a decent way to survive being with her on day one, so I launch into the history of the fountain, how it took thirty years to build and the architect died before seeing its completion, how the fountain's more gorgeous at night when there are fewer people and it's illuminated, and how more than three thousand euros are tossed in the fountain daily.

When I'm done, Hazel levels me with a curious stare. "All right, Huxley. What's the story with you and fountains?"

Whoa. Talk about diving into the deep end with her cross-examination.

"Since I noticed a theme," she adds.

"Because I took you to fountains after you asked to see them? That's a theme of mine?" I ask, both reminding her why we're following this travel route today and deflecting from her insightful question at the same time.

She's undeterred, though. "You have fountains in a few of your books. There's usually something *noble* that happens at one."

She's like a fucking microscope zooming in on all my baggage. It's not fair. But life's not fair, so I have to be smarter, faster, and nimbler than anyone I encounter.

Life lessons from Pops. Some of the only useful things I learned from him.

"Fountains are cool," I say evasively, but that's not a smarter, faster, or nimbler answer.

It's a stupidly obvious one. No shit fountains are cool, and that answer won't throw a bloodhound like Hazel off the scent.

"Like in *A Lovely Alibi*," she continues, clearly not giving a fuck that I'm avoiding answering her. "After a chase scene, the hero catches up with his buddies at a fountain in Vienna. In *A Beautiful Midnight*, he meets the heroine at the fountain at Lincoln Center. And of course in *A Perfect Lie*, there's the climactic scene right here. You like fountains and you use them for good in your stories." She sweeps out her hand like she's presenting all the evidence—the evidence of seeing right through me.

That won't do.

I scratch my jaw as casually as I can, like everything is no big deal. "Water is good. Rome is a city of fountains built on a series of aqueducts. This whole city is an ode to H2O," I say, and hey, maybe that'll fool the opposing counsel.

She shakes her head. "I don't think this cigar is just a cigar. I think fountains are special to you, like wishes are to me. Want to know why I like wishes?"

Oh, shit. It's the old secret-for-a-secret game. It's a classic con. *I'll tell you mine, you tell me yours*. I should say *nah, I'm good*.

I don't.

"Sure," I say, I'm fascinated by her obsession with wishes. It seems so out of character for the Hazel I know. Or that I think I know.

"Veronica and I used to wish upon stars," she says, a small smile shifting her lips. "When we were growing up, we'd climb up to the roof and make wishes. The skies were bright in Wistful at night."

"Yeah?" I ask, liking the story of her and her sister far too much.

"We'd make wishes for lunch the next day. Mac and cheese, and sandwiches. And for bigger things. Like being a rock star or an astronaut or president."

I latch onto the last one, kind of digging it. "Which of those did you wish for?"

"All three."

"Naturally," I say.

"I wanted to be everything," she adds. "Now I just get to write about everything."

"Best job ever," I say.

"It is. I make my characters' wishes come true. When I was younger, though, I just wanted a tree fort so Veronica and I could read and make wishes in it."

There's a note of sadness in her voice now. I prompt gently, "That didn't happen?"

"Not at first. My dad refused to build us one. Said we needed to learn some grammar rules first or whatever. A few years after my parents split, I taught myself how to build one. So I made a tree house for Veronica and me," she says, squaring her shoulders, lifting her chin, damn proud of her accomplishment.

She's never mentioned any of this before. Not that she told me everything when we worked together. Not by a long stretch.

Still, this is the old Hazel here today. The one I worked with. The one I wrote with. The one who shared stories with me. But she never shared *this* story. I don't know what to make of this openness, or how to trust it.

"Why are you telling me this?" I ask, cautious.

She meets my gaze, looking tired but guileless. "Honestly," she says, stifling a yawn, "I wanted to share something, so you would too. I just really want to know about your fountains. I saw the puzzle pieces in your books. I know the fountains mean something. To *you*. Just like wishes do for me." With a helpless shrug, she says, "I'm curious about you."

Yeah, it's the time-honored tit-for-tat con.

And it works like a key in a well-oiled lock.

My childhood memories play out in sepia tones as I stare at the fountain. "My dad always said fountains were perfect spots for cons," I begin, diving into the deep end.

"Oh," she says, her back straightening, her tone surprised, like she didn't think I'd go there. "He did?"

"Yeah. He honed his pickpocket skills at fountains." I hold up my palm like my dad did when he'd teach me a con. "He told me, *See how everyone's looking the same way? They're looking at the water and their wallets and purses are loose since they're taking them out to grab coins to make wishes.*"

Hazel clutches her purse closer. Smart move. I'm sure the square is teeming with thieves.

"Then he said: *They're usually on vacation, so they're happier. Happy people and lonely people are easy marks for a short con.*" I draw a deep breath and finish the heart-warming tale, "Then he looked at me, all fatherly, all teacherly and said, *Don't ever be a mark.*"

Her green eyes flicker, perhaps with sadness, maybe even empathy. She has a shitty dad too. But she also looks like she's adjusting to this new information. It's one thing for her to know my dad's a grifter; it's another to know he taught me to follow in his footsteps.

"That also means—don't be happy, Axel," she says, heavily.

"Dad's motto," I say heavily, then since I've unlocked this door, I kick it open. "Then he told me: *Alexander, you have to remember to always be suspicious. Be wary. Question everything. Otherwise you're a mark.*"

There was nothing worse than being a mark. A mark was a fool.

"That's a tough thing to hear," she says, then she reaches for my bicep, squeezes it.

Fuck, that feels good.

I keep talking even when she lets go of me. I can't seem to stop. "He taught me how to pickpocket at Lincoln Center. Then he helped me refine the technique in Florida when I went to visit him. *So many fountains in Boca, Palm Springs, Miami Beach. So many old people, so many marks. They're either happy or lonely,*" I say, and even though I'm trying to strip the acid from my tone, I can hear it in my voice.

More so I can feel it in my throat as I speak of my father.

"What was that like? Growing up with that?" she asks, with no agenda other than concern, it seems. "You must have been so young."

"Six, seven, eight," I say, recounting. "See, I was more valuable to him then. I could play on people's sympathies. Prey on them, really. I was the kid lost from his parents, asking for help, for money. He'd teach me the script, make me practice it, then send me out into the world of marks," I say, letting the light shine on my whole damn story.

"You were in grade school and he made you grift?"

"He did," I say, tightly.

"Axel," she says, my name full of sympathy. But a new kind, one perhaps born from this new understanding she was so damn curious about.

I heave a sigh, then shrug. "What can you do? We all go through stuff. You just figure out what to do with it," I say, since I can't open the door any farther. It's off its hinges.

"Is he still conning?"

"He lives in Florida. Land of the scam. He's graduated to online scams for the most part. But they work well enough for him."

"And now you rewrite fountains," she says, shifting the topic as she gestures to the water.

"I'm sure if he read my books, he'd laugh at me. He'd see through me. He'd know what I'd done."

She shakes her head. "Don't give him so much credit," she says, in a strangely protective tone. "What you did is clever. And cathartic. I don't think anyone, especially a con artist, could see it. It takes someone who knows how to look, to really look, and to really want to know."

Like you? I want to ask. *Someone like you? And do you really want to know me? Is that your goal?*

But I don't ask any of that. That's a recipe for rejection.

Instead, I reach into my pocket for another coin. Flip it in the water. Add to today's Trevi Fountain haul. "Want to know what I wished for?"

"Tell me," she says eagerly.

"Gelato."

"Now it won't come true." She pouts.

"Oh, but it will." My gaze drifts to a gelato cart on the other side of the fountain. "Want some?"

"Yes."

I make my way to the cart as I keep my real wish private.

The same one I wished for earlier—to pull off the long con of this trip.

I make the wish again as we eat the gelato, then as we head to the hotel, and once more as we take the elevator to the third floor.

We step out together.

This is the moment when I have to bang that wish into my skull. Because everything—*every single thing*—about this moment reminds me of the things I once wanted.

When she reaches her room, she heaves a weary sigh, one that says *that was a long day, but a good one.*

"Thanks for taking me to jet lag school. I guess you're a smidge rugged after all."

"And a smidge is more than a tidge," I say.

"It is." Her brow knits. She's deep in thought for a few seconds. "You know, this is going to sound weird. I kind of can't believe I'm about to say this," she says, then takes a beat, gearing up, "But I had a good time today."

I *could* do something with the compliment, return it with a legitimate one of my own like *I did too.* Instead, I say, "Don't worry. I won't tell a soul you had fun with me."

I'm home safe like this. Just a few feet to my room and I can shut the door and escape from her for the night.

I turn to go, but she blindsides me.

Her arms are holy-fuck fast. They wrap around me. I tense. I don't know what to do with my hands. I don't know what to do with her.

"Thanks again. But you still owe me double lunch," she says into my shoulder, her hair brushing against my neck, her breasts against my chest.

It's like a dream.

And just like that, I know what to do with my hands. I wrap my arms around her waist, taking what I can get, even though it's risky.

Even though it probably makes me a mark.

I close my eyes. Breathe her in. *Imagine.*

Picturing the rest of the night in her room.

Then I break the embrace, almost jumping away from her. "Night," I say quickly. Then I wheel around, head down the hall, and unlock my room in record time so I don't do something stupid, like tell her what I wished for—that she'd never know why I walked away from our partnership.

That I left because spending every day with the object of your unrequited love hurts like hell.

14

SYMPTOMS OF A ROMANCE HEROINE

Hazel

He was right.

I wake up ridiculously refreshed as the sun streaks through the window, luring me out of the king-size bed that I was betrothed to for twelve wonderful hours overnight.

It was a quickie marriage between the mattress and me, but oh so good.

After a shower, a fruit-laden breakfast from a nearby outdoor market, and a cup of coffee from an espresso stand, I'm ready for the book tour to begin this afternoon.

I head toward the Spanish Steps, mentally reviewing the day ahead.

First, we have a signing at a popular bookstore in the city that carries lots of English language titles, but also ones translated into Italian—like mine and Axel's.

In the afternoon, we'll meet up with the VIP group that we'll be riding the rails with. Before we go *all aboard* with them in the evening, Axel will take the lead and show the group around the city, visiting some of the locations in Rome from his books. I'll play sidekick as he goes. I'm kind of looking forward to my second fiddle role today. As much as it's fun to be *on* every now and then, it's also nice to lurk in the background.

To observe.

And to take notes on everything and everyone around me. Maybe I'll find unexpected inspiration for another romance. I've yet to write a romance that contains even a single scene in Italy. As I wander up the one hundred thirty-five steps, soaking in the Roman vibe, I decide that just might need to change.

This city feels…romantic.

At the top of the steps I turn around, indulging in the view of the tourist mecca. Then I savor the memories of my day yesterday. I can't see it from here, but I can perfectly picture the nearby piazza where Axel and I ate lunch. I can see in my mind the fountain of books, and I can recall our conversation about wishes and cons.

My chest feels warm, sort of glowy.

Hmm.

That must just be from the weather. I crane my neck heavenward, enjoying the rays from the summer Italian sun.

Yup. This is a sun glow, clearly.

Since it's time for me to get ready, I lower my gaze and head down the steps. I walk across the square then into the hotel so I can freshen up before the signing. When I push open the door, my pulse sprints as Axel steps out of the elevator several feet away.

He hasn't noticed me yet.

But I definitely notice him.

He's wearing those black glasses, of course. But today they somehow make him look not only sexy smart, but sexy *smarter*.

Then, I check out his clothes—the trim jeans that hug his legs, the black button-down that's nice and tight in the arms.

Huh.

Does Axel have strong biceps I never noticed before? How is it possible I've never noticed them? I'm an arms woman. Surely, I'd have checked out the guns before. I'm checking them out now for longer than I probably should. When I realize I've been staring—okay, gawking —my gaze snaps to his face.

I try to rearrange my expression to *I was not staring at you* while I do just that, taking in that just-the-right-amount of stubble, the soul-deep blue eyes, the full lips.

That warm, hazy feeling in my chest kicks up a few notches.

Turns into something hotter.

When he spots me looking at him, he flashes me a crooked and cocky grin as he stops in front of me. "Sleep well, Valentine?"

"The best," I say, trying to school my voice so I don't sound like I was just purring over his trim, toned physique.

"Told you so," he says, a little pointed. Like he *has* to land a dig.

But I don't dig back. "Yeah, you did," I say simply. I'm too busy trying to figure out what to do with Axel being ultra-sexy today.

My pulse spikes. Has it spiked with him before?

My skin buzzes. Is that new too?

Wait. Just wait.

I know what this cacophony of foreign sensations in my chest is. This must just be the residual effects of yesterday's jet lag.

Whew.

I'll be fine. "I'm going to get ready for the signing. I think Amy with Chandler Publicity is taking us together?"

"Yup. Amy said she'd be here at twelve," he says, then nods toward the revolving door of the hotel. "I'm going to kick around the Eternal City. Maybe do some book research for a little bit. Catch you in an hour."

With a casual chin nod, he's off. A little swagger in his step. A coolness in his stride. As I watch him go, I study him intensely, the shape of him, the swoop of his hair, the set of his shoulders.

Yes, I know what this shivery feeling in my body is. It has to be the jet lag burning off.

It just has to be.

* * *

A twenty-something brunette with an eager smile hands me a paperback of *The I Do Redo*.

"Who should I sign this to?" I ask in my best attempt at Italian.

"Very good," she says in that language, then she shifts to English. "To Andrea, please. I just love Brayden and Kelsey so much," she says as I flip open the copy. I'm at a table in the back of the bookstore, next to Axel, who's chatting with another reader.

"Aww, thank you. I'm so happy to hear that," I say to Andrea, then I grab my purple Sharpie and sign the book.

As I hand it to her, Axel reaches for a pen, brushing my wrist as he stretches his arm to grab it.

A tingle sweeps down my chest.

What the hell?

I jerk my gaze to him, like I can find the answer in Axel. In his playful eyes.

But the only answer he gives is a wink. "Pen ran dry."

My mouth has run dry.

My breath catches as I look at him again, but I try to shake off these sensations. It's hard, though. With him only a foot away, my nostrils get in on the action, sniffing Axel like he's a fine wine. Wine with top notes of sage fading into the afternoon and something deeper, woodsy and dark like a forest at night.

Oh, god. No. This can't be happening.

I'll just ignore this blooming feeling.

Surely I can do that.

Right? Of course I can. I'm an expert at avoidance. That's what writing is, after all. Avoiding reality.

Tra la la la. I'll spend some time in my imagination.

Except...what did the blonde now standing in front of me just say?

When did she show up in line? Her friendly eyes crinkle at the corners, her hair is looped into a swingy ponytail, and she's wearing a *Book Besties* shirt, dark blue against her pale skin. She's standing next to a woman with glasses, who's sporting a matching *Book Besties* shirt.

"I'm Jackie. I make dog bandanas and I love romance novels more than I love potato chips," the blonde says, sounding like she's straight out of Jersey.

"And Jackie—we call her Jersey Jackie—loves her chips," the woman in glasses adds. She taps her heart. "I'm Alecia. I don't do anything nearly as interesting as making dog clothes. I'm in data analysis." She shudders. "But who cares about that? We're here for the swoony men, the fabulous women, and the escape. Your books are pure five *Calgon Take Me Aways*."

I beam. "That's all I can ask for."

"That's our book rating system. Five *Calgon Take Me Aways* is the highest for our reviews. We're the Book Besties! And we won the trip with you and Axel," Jackie says.

"But no Kennedy," Alecia says with a frown. She sounds like she's from Minnesota perhaps.

"But we'll have the best time anyway. We won the trip in a publisher giveaway. We entered a gazillion times. We loved *Ten Park Avenue*," Alecia says.

Uh-oh. They're going to pepper us with questions about Lacey's story the whole time.

But I can handle that. I've been answering and

evading *Ten Park Avenue* questions for more than a year. "I'm so glad you won the trip," I say honestly. They seem enthusiastic, and enthusiasm is the best reward from readers.

Plus, I want to hug them in gratitude for saving me from the spate of zingy feelings taking over my bloodstream.

Maybe those feelings won't dare to reappear.

Maybe I'll just immerse myself in readers, and travel, and imagination, and I'll somehow survive this trip like that.

Sounds doable.

"And," I add, "I want to hear all about the dog bandanas, and the data."

We chat for a few minutes about how their friend Maria is going to join them on the train ride tonight, how the three of them run a blog, a social media feed, and a TikTok channel, and how they love all our books.

But especially *Ten Park Avenue*.

I hate disappointing them. I wish I could give them more of what they want.

"Can we take a picture of the two of you?" Alecia asks, her voice pitching up. "You and Axel. I want to use it for a cookie design. I'm learning how to make cookies."

I frown in confusion. "You want a picture of Axel and me for a cookie?"

That gets his attention. "Did someone say cookie?"

The ladies laugh then shoo us up next to the table, with Jackie scooting in the middle between us.

I'm so thankful for her.

"Jackie, you go on the side. We're bookends. They're the books," Alecia chides.

Nooooo! Don't put us next to each other!

"Right, right," Jackie says, scurrying over, then gently nudging Axel so he's closer to me.

He wraps an arm around me.

Oh god.

His hand on my shoulder feels good.

So good that I steal a glance out of the corner of my eye. That zing wiggles down my chest. I'm dying to turn my face toward his neck and catch the fading scent of the forest at night.

Alecia snaps a selfie, then shows it to us.

As I stare at it, I privately whimper.

There it is in Technicolor.

Me, with flutters in my stomach.

Yup. My sister cursed me. The diagnosis is official—I've got all the symptoms of a romance heroine.

15

TAKE THE PILL

Hazel

Six more nights. I only have to make it through six more nights with this...*infection.* It'll pass. It always does.

I'll take antibiotics in the form of this group of super readers surrounding us.

They're the cure.

That afternoon, as Axel takes the dozen VIP readers on a tour of five key locations from his books in the center of the city, I make it my mission to own the side-kick role like no one ever has.

I'm the tour guide wing woman, hanging by the back of the group as Axel tells a middle-aged couple with matching Nikons slung around their necks, and some college girls by the front, about the scene in *A Lovely Alibi* where the hero sneaks into the Pantheon at night to solve a riddle that'll help him retrieve a lost artifact.

As Axel then guides the group past the famous land-mark, I make small talk with Jackie and Alecia. "How did you two meet?" I ask.

"In an online fan group," Jackie says.

"Then we became book besties," Alecia adds.

And after five years of recommending books as a team, they finally met when they landed in Rome yesterday.

"That's so great that this trip brought you together," I say.

"Book friends are the best friends," Jackie says.

Alecia slings an arm around her buddy. "Love you, hon."

It's heartwarming to see, and it's good medicine. I'm far away from Axel and fighting off the fever of desire with chitchat. If I can just keep this up, I will survive. The early days of illness are always the hardest.

We visit a few more sites, then finish at the Trevi Fountain. Axel walks them through the climactic scene. "And here is where Jett leapt into the water, jumping over the crowds of tourists." He gives a sheepish shrug, acknowledging the fiction physics as he adds, "As one does."

Like he knows you sometimes have to go all Jason Bourne with a thriller hero no matter how unlikely leaping over heads is.

I smile back, feeling a little dopey, a little woozy. I understand him so well. I get him. I truly do.

Stop!

That's just the infection talking.

I force myself to think about the stone in the fountain, the coins on the floor of it, the water. Anything external instead of these internal hummingbirds.

The reader questions begin, and the Nikon Man shoots up a hand. "But you can't actually go in the fountain," he points out.

"That's true, Steven," Axel says, and that's familiar, the way he uses people's names once he learns them. Because of his first signing, when he forgot the bookstore owner's name and felt foolish. Now, he repeats names as he speaks to people, to remember them better.

"So how do you deal with that? When Jett jumped in the fountain. Because it's against the rules," Steven adds.

Axel nods like he's considering this quandary for the first time. "Sometimes you have to break the rules," he says.

His eyes roam the crowd and find mine like he's searching for a kindred spirit. Or maybe he just needs a little help. He doesn't always love being the center of attention.

"Catching the hacker was worth the risk," I add from the back.

"Hmm," the man says doubtfully and scratches his jaw. "I guess I just wonder why he didn't go to jail."

Axel shudders. "Jett would have hated jail."

Steven the Nikon Man is relentless. "But...why didn't he take off his boots before he ran through the fountain? He wouldn't have tripped if he'd just used some common sense. This happens in so many thrillers."

One of the college gals near me rolls her eyes. "It's

called a trope," the redhead mutters. "Like how all billionaires magically have huge cocks."

Jackie and Alecia crack up.

I laugh too.

I don't look at Axel. I can't risk another fluttery feeling.

* * *

By the time I get back to my room after the tour, I have twenty minutes before I have to check out of the hotel and head to the train station. Rushing around, I gather my things, but I barely unpacked since I was here only one night. Once I zip up my suitcase, I FaceTime my sister for some emergency girl talk.

Veronica answers right away. She's on the balcony of her Greenwich Village apartment, and I spot her big Siamese walking behind her, sniffing the potted plants as she waters them. "Ciao," she says as she tips her watering can.

"You cursed me!"

She knits her brow. "Sounds cool. Tell me more about this new skill of mine. Because there are others I might like to curse."

"Axel," I mutter, annoyed. Then I'm double-annoyed when my stomach flips at the mere mention of him. "You and your sex talk."

A satisfied grin spreads on her cute face. "You finally admit I'm right."

"Undo the curse. Now." I stomp my foot to get my point across.

"Aww. Lust hurts, doesn't it?"

"It's the worst," I whine, effectively admitting she's right. Or right-ish. "What do I do with this... attraction?"

"Bang it out," she says, too cheery.

"You are such an enabler. Help me for real, V."

She sets down the watering can and strokes her big cat. "Look, he's sexy, and he's working that whole cocky thing that you love."

"I don't love cocky men," I hiss.

She snort-laughs. "You so do. He's like a jackass cat. And you love jackass cats. You always put them in your books."

I stare at her like she's gone mad. "I do not always put them in my books."

Except, hold on. I did have a jackass cat in *Sweet Spot.* And in *Plays Well With Others.* Dammit. Axel was right about that too, when he said I like quirky pets in my stories. But, to be fair, all cats are kind of jackasses. It's endemic.

"Axel is also intensely verbal, and so are you," Veronica adds. "And the two of you talk like it's fore-play. So, um, good luck."

"You were supposed to be helping me," I say.

"I'm dissecting why you're attracted to him. Maybe if you understand it, you won't be so captivated by it. He's all the things you think you don't like but you do. Plus, he's smart. So, just know that's your downfall and focus on other things, like the trip."

She makes a good point. I can't give in to this lust. I

can't act on it. I'm here for work. Not to act out a sex scene. "Right. Focus on the trip, the readers, the purpose," I say, reinforcing her very good advice. "Thank you."

"You can do it, Hazel," she says, then swings her gaze to the door. "Milo's home. I love you. And my jackass cat loves you too."

"Have fun with your guy," I say. "And your jackass cat. And thanks. That was helpful."

"Anytime."

I say goodbye then leave the hotel, thinking about books and work—the reasons why I'm here.

They really should do the trick.

* * *

The Roma Termini railway station is like a pill, and I swallow it dry that evening because I'm damn eager for the medicine. This station is not romantic at all.

The city's largest train station is like a space hub.

Digital signs flash arrivals and departures in bright orange overhead, while silver columns and sleek walls scream *modern*.

Thank the goddess.

Plus, there are crowds. Oh yes, the massive crowds. No one can feel flutters when they're surrounded by scurrying passengers and harried travelers.

At least, I'm trying not to.

Amy, the PR professional organizing the tour, escorts Axel and me through the station. "The platform we're departing from is less busy. It's everything JHB envisioned when he designed this luxury train. A hearkening back to another era of travel," she says.

No. That's bad.

Early train travel is romantic.

But how romantic can a reclusive billionaire train mogul really be?

I decide the train won't be that romantic after all.

I listen intently as Amy shares more about the tour's agenda. Amy Chandler is outgoing, welcoming, and capable. We met her at the hotel earlier today—she runs her own PR firm in Los Angeles and one of her specialties is book tours. But I already know *of* her. Through TJ, I met and became close friends with some of his friends who play for the San Francisco Hawks, including the receiver, Nate Chandler. Amy's his sister and Nate adores her. As one should do with big sisters.

"We'll meet up with your readers in the dining car once you're all settled on the train. You'll have some time to freshen up, put your things away, and all that good stuff," she says, guiding us to a quieter section of the station, around the corner and back in time.

This platform is quaint. The crowds have thinned. Classical music plays overhead, mingling with the sound effect of an old-time steam engine. The train itself sits proudly on the tracks. It's modern, I'm told, but the outside of it is straight out of an Agatha Christie novel, with an old-fashioned blue and cream facade and *JHB Travel* in calligraphy along the side of the cars.

"That's a helluva train," Axel says with a low whistle of admiration.

Amy smiles and gestures to the platform-edge doors.

"We have two cars reserved for our group. And we have dinner tonight with everyone, a little on the late side, but that's what makes it fun. We'll do the nine o'clock seating. We have a stop in Florence after that to pick up some more passengers, and then the trip to Nice should be peaceful overnight. Perfect for sleeping," Amy says, then checks her watch. "We'll arrive early in the morning, but you don't have to rush off the train. Take your time."

As we board, Amy says, "You two will be all the way at the end of this car with me, so there's a little buffer between you and the readers. I'll show you," she says, but then a train attendant in a blue suit flags her.

"Ms. Chandler. A minute, please?"

"Of course," she says, joining the Italian man. "I'll be right back," she says to us.

As she chats with him, Axel shoots me a daring look, then whispers, "Let's be scofflaws and check out the sleeper compartments. My heroes never get to enjoy a sleeper compartment."

"Let's go," I say, cheery, and this attitude will get me through the sickness too.

I follow him toward the back of the car, the signs for sleeping compartment our guide. When we reach the compartments, I see two doors. I swing my gaze from one that has a sign with *Ms. Chandler* written on it.

The other one has a sign that reads: *Mr. & Mrs. Huxley.*

16

ELEPHANT BED

Hazel

This can't be happening.

I should be prepared—I've written this story, the one where the protagonists have to share a room—and yet I'm not.

My cells shake as I stare at the sign on the oak door of the sleeping quarters, pronouncing us husband and wife once again.

What's the appropriate reaction when the heroine walks into the small-town bed-and-breakfast and discovers she's been booked into the last room in the inn with Mister McGrump?

I riffle through the plotting notebooks in my head. The heroine should say with a smile, *There must be a mistake.*

But the words that rocket out of my mouth are: "Are women not allowed to be single anywhere?"

It's better than the other things circling through my head, like *oh shit, no way,* and *please tell me there are two rooms hidden away behind that door, with two separate beds, and two separate everythings.*

Axel clears his throat as if he's getting his bearings too. "We can dismantle the patriarchy another time. First, let's straighten out what is probably a simple booking error."

"Right!" I cling to this idea. "I'm sure there are plenty of other compartments on the train. Amy said we have two cars for our group."

"Exactly."

"And I can stay near the readers. I'm sure there's an empty compartment. It'll be fine," I say, so amenable, so willing. Because I can't sleep near him while I'm experiencing these acute symptoms of lust.

"Or I can," he offers, eager too.

I hook my thumb toward the door of the car, where we'd last seen our guide. "I can go find Amy and tell her." I poke my head around the corner and peer down the aisle. She's still chatting with the train guy. "I bet she's sorting it out right now."

I've adopted the cheeriest tone possible. I am going to positive-attitude my ass off on this trip.

"I'm sure that's it." Axel glances at the door of our assigned compartment. "But we should check out the accommodation anyway. Maybe it's a two-bedroom with an adjoining living room?"

There are ten gallons of hope in his voice too. Good. We're on the same page.

"In that case, we won't have to make a fuss," I say.

"Exactly," he agrees. "I don't want to give Amy a hard time with problems this early."

"Totally. I feel the same." Nor do I want our tour group to think anything has gone wrong with the trip.

No one wants to witness their hosts negotiating for separate sleeping quarters or changing up a travel plan. We might look like divas making a scene. If we can manage with this suite tonight, it'll be for the best.

Axel grabs the handle, turns it, and steps inside.

Please, please, please, let that door open into a spacious suite.

With my heart in my throat, I step gingerly across the threshold, then peer around.

We're in a tiny anteroom, maybe five by five. But there's a tiny blue velvet sofa situated under the window. Blessed piece of furniture. I could kiss it. If this were my own suite, I'd imagine lounging on the tiny love seat at dawn, feet tucked under me, hoodie on, working on my current novel while the sun rose.

But instead, that glorious couch is going to fulfill a higher calling. It'll save me from living out a trope. I pat the armrest. "This looks fine as a last resort. I could sleep here if I had to," I chirp.

Ack! My voice sounds like a freaking chipmunk's. Clearing my throat, I try to modulate my tone. Cool Hazel, rather than Helium Hazel. "It's probably a fold-out sofa," I add in a baritone.

Great. Just great. I'm a dude now.

"Yes! Of course!" Axel says, and I'm pretty sure he spoke with exclamation points for the first time in his life. He marches to the sofa and lifts a cushion.

With a wince, he turns back to me, shaking his head. "Just a regular sofa," he says in a strained voice. "But maybe there are two rooms?"

"I'm sure there are!" I flap my arm toward the white scalloped door.

I hold my breath as we head toward it. He flashes me a nervous look.

I've hardly ever seen Axel looking nervous.

We reach for the door handle at the same time and touch each other's hands.

Oh, that's nice.

That's the problem, though. I snatch my hand away. "You go first," I say quickly.

He tosses a *what gives* glance at me. But isn't it obvious why I yanked my paw away? He doesn't want me to touch him, and I don't want to make him uncomfortable. We've made progress over the last twenty-four hours. I don't want to regress.

He slides open the door then mutters, "Oh fuck."

There's. Only. One. Bed.

It's not even a big bed.

It's queen-size.

I stare too long. My mind has stalled on images of Axel whipping off his T-shirt one-handed, unbuttoning jeans, sliding under that white duvet wearing only snug black boxer briefs.

Giving me a *come-hither* look. Growling, *"Ride me, baby."*

Axel is staring at the bed too, like he's caught in a trance. Or maybe he's confused.

Meanwhile, my dirty, filthy, sex-starved brain is

stuck on repeat as I imagine him beckoning me with his finger. *"C'mon, sweetheart, you know you want it,"* he'd say.

I do, I do, I fucking do.

Dammit.

I need ice. I spot a bucket for it on a table in the corner, but it's probably empty, so no point jamming my head into it.

I hunt for words to handle the situation, but the best I can manage is, "Why aren't there any bunks?"

Axel knits his brow. My odd question seems to have knocked him out of his what-the-hell haze. "Bunks?"

Bunks would have been a decent solution. Bunks are for siblings. Bunks are for roomies. Bunks aren't for lovers.

"Bunks. Like one on top of the other." Great, I made that sound dirty.

His lips twitch. "I know what bunk beds are. But you thought the train would have bunk beds?"

This digression is safer than talking about that tantalizing bed calling out to me. "I pictured a little compartment with one bed here," I say, demonstrating with my hand about two feet high, then I move it up six feet. "Then one above it. I was going to put my suitcase on the lower one and sleep on the upper one."

"You had this all mapped out. Your bunk bed fantasy," he says, and he can't stop grinning.

But we need to discuss the elephant in the room— tonight's accommodations. "Anyway, like I said, I'll sleep on the sofa." I need to make it crystal clear that I don't expect this travel snafu to play out like it would in a romance. "We don't have to share a bed like in a book."

This is life and we'll solve it like real life, not fiction.

But he's not looking my way. He's staring out the window. Then he pulls his gaze back to me. "I know that, Hazel," he says, sounding half stern, but half hollow too. "I know this isn't one of our stories," he says as footsteps grow louder.

"Knock, knock." Amy's voice calls out.

"Come in," I say, grateful for her return and certain she's here to tell us she found another compartment.

But her face says *no such luck*. Her face *says I tried and I'm so sorry*. "The JHB Travel Manager was telling me about the error with the booking agency. I'm so sorry, but he assures me we can get it cleared up by tomorrow."

"Oh great," I say, relieved we only have to deal with this problem for one night. "I'll sleep on the couch."

"*I'll* sleep on the couch," Axel cuts in.

Amy stares at the couch, quizzically. "Oh, that's so thoughtful of both of you, but that couch is more like a chair. You'd have to curl up into a Border Collie-size dog ball to sleep on it."

Her dog-size comparison seems spot on as I regard the furniture. I'd have to fold up my arms and legs and wind around myself a few times. Axel's several inches taller than I am. He'd be a pretzel if he slept there.

Amy gives a quick, decisive nod. "But I have another solution." She pats my arm. "Just take my room, Hazel. I'll sleep in a train seat."

"What?"

"It's no problem. A regular seat will work fine."

"No. That sounds miserable."

"I'm a single mom. I have two young kids at home. The second I close my eyes," she says, then snaps her fingers, "I'm down for the count."

I can't let a single mom who's away from her kids sleep uncomfortably.

"That won't be necessary, Amy," Axel says, like a ship captain steering the boat through dangerous waters. "I'll sleep in a regular seat on the train."

He sounds so gallant, so willing. And that's hot too.

I'm unfairly turned on by his offer.

What is wrong with my traitorous libido today?

I've got to get my mind out of the gutter. "Or you and I could share *this* compartment and Axel could take yours?" I ask Amy, but that sounds weird too.

Like we're all just playing musical beds.

She holds up her palms. "Whatever works. I just want you two to be comfortable. And I promise we'll get this sorted out overnight."

I gulp, then look at the couch. Then the floor. "I'll sleep on—"

"—I'll sleep here in the anteroom. Amy, you enjoy your compartment," Axel says. Firm. Businesslike. A declaration.

We'll slumber in separate rooms, elephant-free.

* * *

The next hour is spent in icy politeness in our compartment as we get ready for dinner. Squeezing awkwardly past each other with *excuse mes* and *thank yous*, we navigate suitcases, and the bathroom, and the anteroom that connects the bedroom and bathroom. Alone in the bedroom, I text TJ. I need a distraction, so I update him with the news that my life is so meta, I'm living in a book and will he please press control-alt-delete to set me free.

He replies with gifs of people cackling. He can be such an asshole. I love him to pieces.

But the chat only distracts me for so long. As I button my blouse in the bedroom, behind the closed door, I picture Axel changing for dinner in the anteroom.

Tugging on a shirt. Buttoning it up. Zipping up slacks. I fight off the desire to peek.

Maybe the elephant isn't gone. Maybe it's growing.

17

ACCIDENTALLY ON PURPOSE

Hazel

Dinner could be a scene from a Merchant Ivory movie. I eat with the VIPs in the elegant dining car as the Italian countryside rolls by under the stars. The hum of the engine and the rattle of the wheels soundtrack our meal while servers in old-timey uniforms bring sumptuous dishes on silver platters, presenting them grandly.

It's so turn of the last century, and I adore it.

But I feel like I've gone back in time for another reason—because Axel and I are frosty again.

All the good will from our time in Rome yesterday remained parked in the Eternal City.

We're only two tables apart in the dining car, but I feel like there are miles between us. He's talking to Steven the Nikon Man, his curly-haired wife—who I learned cut her reading teeth on cowboy romances as a girl before graduating to the *red-hot chili reads,* as she calls them—and the redheaded college girl, along with some other travelers. I'm seated with the Book Besties, finishing my meal.

"The sleeping compartments are so great," Jersey Jackie says as she sets down her fork.

"We're all sharing a compartment," Alecia adds, gesturing to their friend Maria, who joined them at the station in Rome. She turns to me, brows lifted in curiosity. "I hear you are too?"

Word got around quickly. "Yes, we are. But we're not together. It's just a temporary thing tonight."

That's the truth, but I also don't want to be shipped during this trip. We'd just disappoint readers with the fact that we are not together and will never be together. Lord knows we've already disappointed them enough, leaving Lacey hanging in our unfinished series. Readers were dying for her to finally get together with the sexy, broody guy in the suit who lived down the hall. Poor Lacey will be hanging on a cliff for all time.

Jackie frowns, patting my hand *there, there* style, like I've shared something sad. "Want to stay with us, hon?"

I'm touched she'd offer. But I don't want to horn in on their bonding time. And I don't want them to think I need to drown any sorrows. "I know how precious girls' trips are," I say. "I don't want to impose."

"Nonsense," Maria says, jumping in. "You'd be an esteemed guest."

Great. Now I'll be a dick for turning them down. But I don't want to put them out. "I truly appreciate it, but we're fine, and it'll all be sorted out tomorrow." Time to change the subject, stat. "The seared tofu tabbouleh is amazing," I say, pointing with my fork to my nearly finished dish. "I might need to put it in an upcoming story."

Then Jackie adds, "And can you have a gal pack named Jackie and Alecia and Maria?"

I give them a conspiratorial grin. "I already wrote them into the work in progress."

Jackie lets out a high-pitched sound.

Alecia rolls her eyes as she pats Jackie's hand. "You are such a squealer."

"I know. I'm just excited," Jackie says, but she doesn't care. She owns her excitement.

"Obviously," Alecia adds dryly.

"Maybe the Jackie in my story can make dog bandanas," I suggest, meeting the blonde's gaze. "You could show me the ones you make, and it might help me with inspiration."

The look on Jersey Jackie's face is pure delight as she grabs her phone.

"Show her the one with the skulls," Maria says. She's the bossy one in the crew.

Jackie nods enthusiastically then shows me a seriously cute design of sassy skulls. We talk more about her fledgling business, and when the dinner service ends, I say goodnight. Axel's already taken off, so as I head to the compartment, I brace myself for more cool politeness.

I knock before I open the door, listening for his voice.

No answer. I head inside, racing though the anteroom and into the bedroom. If I get ready for bed quickly, I can burrow under the covers, pretend I'm asleep when he returns, and avoid any more awkward niceness.

As I grab my toothpaste and toothbrush, the main door swings open with a creak.

So much for my big plans.

"Are you decent?" he calls out.

That's the Axel I know, not wasting breath on *hi* or *hello*. But with all these new feelings jockeying for space inside me, I'm at a loss for a clever response, so I simply say, "Yes."

I head to the anteroom where he's grabbing his toothpaste and toothbrush from his suitcase on the floor. Should I smile when he looks up? Yes, I'll smile. When he rises, I grin stupidly as I waggle my toothpaste. "I need to brush my teeth."

It's the most obvious thing I've said in my entire life.

"I gathered," he says, then brandishes his. "Me too."

"You go first," I say.

"No, you," he says. "I insist."

And we haven't left Too Polite Depot at all. "Okay," I say, then squeeze past him to the bathroom. When I'm done, I leave with an *all yours* right as he passes me, his shoulder brushing mine, sending a dangerous swoop through my chest.

I try to ignore the lingering warmth as I enter the bedroom. But while I root around in my suitcase, I freeze, one hand on my sleep shorts. Do I just put on my jammies then shout *goodnight* from the dark?

That's even weirder.

Instead, I return to the anteroom still in my blouse

and slacks. I wait there so I can say goodnight before I close the door to him.

I perch on the edge of the couch.

Is this made of stone? It's the most uncomfortable piece of furniture I've ever sat on. As much as I can't stand Axel, I can't let him sleep on a cinder block.

Even though I *can* stand him now.

I very much can stand him.

That's my new problem.

But the choice I'm about to make isn't because of the melty, lusty, crushy feelings occupying me. It's because of the friendly ones. When Axel emerges from the bathroom, I act on those feelings, patting the cement furniture. "This sofa is uncomfortable," I begin.

Axel waves a hand dismissively, adopting a too-easy grin. "It'll be good research. My heroes never get to sleep on anything comfortable."

I don't take the writing banter bait. I soldier on, determined to do the right thing. "We can share a bed," I continue, keeping this offer cordial and above board.

Nothing salacious in my tone. No wink and a nod.

And just like that, he's no longer looking at me in a friendly way. He stares like I just suggested we cliff dive into a stormy sea. He seems confused? Or maybe perturbed?

Oh, shit.

I hope I haven't made things worse with my suggestion. "It's only weird if we make it weird," I add quickly. "And we won't make it weird, right? I mean, it's not like we're going to make out." I scoff at that ridiculous idea. That ought to help him feel more comfortable since *he* doesn't want to make out with me.

But he's quiet for a long beat, his jaw twitching. I have no idea what he's thinking. "I didn't think we were, Valentine," he says evenly, and his tone is as impossible to read as his face.

I try harder. Patting the couch. "I mean, c'mon," I say. "Try this out and you'll see you have to sleep in the bed."

Tentatively, he sits and then immediately cringes. "Is this couch a test of will?" he asks, seeming offended by the furniture.

"Pretty sure it's used in reality shows to earn misery points," I add.

"I'd be the first to surrender," he says, and perhaps Axel has let go of whatever was bugging him moments ago.

Good. I want to return to normal. Or find a new normal with him.

I turn the thought over in my mind a few times. Yes, that's what I've wanted lately with Axel—to find a path beyond our blow-up in the coffee shop, past our painful breakup. That's what I've learned on this trip so far. My goal isn't simply to survive him anymore.

It's for us to start over as friends.

I try again to make the night a little easier for him. "So, you'll share a bed with me? Don't worry. I'm not a cuddler. You won't wake up with me wrapped around you. I mean, that stuff only happens in books. Like accidental kisses," I say, lightly. And I feel light for the first time since we discovered the booking agency married us.

"Only in books," he echoes, and he's smiling the slightest bit. On that hopeful note, I glance out the window, enjoying the nighttime view.

It's dark. The train lights illuminate the path as we curve along a bend in the tracks. But neither one of us slams into the other.

"See? We didn't just fall and land in each other's laps, lips pressed together, like we would have in a book." Though, a lot of things that happen in my romance novels haven't happened in my real sex life. Like, say, great sex. Maybe someday I'll have what my heroines are having.

"How does that even happen in stories? We never wrote an accidental kiss," he says.

"I haven't in my solo books either," I say.

"I don't understand how a kiss could be anything but intentional. Even if they're in a cab, and the cabbie slams on the brakes and they wind up in each other's arms, the thing that happens next is always intentional."

"Kisses are deliberate," I say, relieved that finally we're talking again—like yesterday. But also like we did once upon a time, before our blow-up.

"And they should be," he adds as the train swings around another curve.

Faster than I expected.

Before I'm even aware of what's happening, I'm sliding closer to him, my hip slamming against his hip. He grabs my upper arm, holding me tight.

I laugh briefly from the surprise, then look at the shaved distance between us. "See? We're closer. But we're still not accidentally kissing."

Even though I kind of want to be. Even though my heart is beating faster than it was before.

When Axel looks at me, his eyes are darker than I'm used to. "Because someone always has to make the first move," he says.

"Even if there's an accidental-on-purpose kiss," I add.

"Like in a book," he says as he curls his hand a little tighter around my arm. I hope he doesn't let me go.

Since I'm letting go of reason, I let go of the past too. In this moment, I want an accidental-on-purpose kiss.

"Sort of like this?" I ask, then lean in and give him a swift peck on the cheek. I catch the fading scent of the forest after it rains. I let out a tiny gasp.

His breath catches.

I pull back from his cheek, meet his eyes. They're wild. Hungry. Then my gaze strays to his lips. They're plush, pillowy soft.

"Or maybe…" I lean in, and I don't accidentally kiss him. I kiss him on purpose. A soft, barely-there sweep of my lips. "…like this."

"Like that," he murmurs against my mouth.

I linger in the kiss and then take a little more. Another brush of our lips. Another press of my mouth to his.

Another hiss of breath from him.

Then a hand on my face, fingers gliding over my jaw, a touch that sends delicious tremors over my skin.

Axel Huxley can kiss. A tantalizing tease of a kiss like I've never felt before.

This one radiates down to my bones, through my skin. I swear I can feel it in my eyelashes.

And most of all, in the center of my chest where I'm melting.

When the train straightens out seconds later, we break the kiss.

"So," he says, huskily, looking like he's reorienting his reality, perhaps to this new one where we've kissed very un-accidentally.

I'm adjusting to my new world order too—one where I want to kiss him on purpose again and again.

But if I stay like this, hovering on the edge of want, I'll climb onto his lap and kiss him so purposefully it could only lead to the bedroom.

What would happen in the morning though? No idea, and I'm not sure I'm ready to face a morning after.

Maybe he's not either, since he nods toward the bedroom door, then rasps out, "You should get in bed first."

Whatever his reasons are, I vehemently agree. We need some separation.

I head into the room, shutting the door to change into sleep shorts and a T-shirt, then opening it to invite him in. With my back to him, I hop under the covers, my stomach still fluttering, my body still craving.

He comes in a minute later, turns off the light, and heads to his side of the bed. I look away, even though I want to stare at him.

I want to read his reactions in his eyes. In his face. I want to study him to see if he's still wondering what the hell just happened and why it felt so good.

I hear him set his glasses on the nightstand, then he slides under the covers.

We're two stiff logs in a queen-size bed, hustling along the European coast after dark.

I'm acutely aware of how near he is but how far apart we are too.

And how completely deliberate that kiss was for both of us.

"Good night," I say, my voice full of unasked questions.

"Good night," he says, the same way.

Neither one of us falls asleep for a long time.

18

GAME FOR ANYTHING

Axel

That list of regrets I keep on my laptop?

The French Riviera is nowhere near it. In fact, I might need to start a list of un-regrets and this stunning view of the sea will be at the top of it.

We're in Parc de la Colline du château in Nice the next afternoon, after having trekked up a steep hill to this park. It overlooks the Baie des Anges in the sapphire-blue Mediterranean Sea. This is why people work their asses off all year for a vacation—I feel like I am living inside a travel brochure.

As I stare out at the water, I try to focus on *this moment*, rather than on last night.

That kiss has been playing on a goddamn loop in my mind, and I need to stop it.

I try to commit to memory the blazing emerald

colors of the park and the rusty red of the roofs below, along with the salty scent of the sea floating on the summer breeze. Maybe, just maybe, they can fill the space in my head that she's taking up. Possibly, I can use them to block out the new item on my list of regrets.

Kissing Hazel Valentine last night.

But it'll be like scaling a mountain to erase that kiss since she's currently standing at the edge of the park, talking to the tour group about, what else, kissing.

Fucking kissing.

"Once I discovered this park on a European trip, I knew I had to include it in a book someday," she tells them.

I seethe.

Bet she took that trip here with a guy. Was it Max? Or maybe it was Jacob, the musician she dated before him, another guy in a history of bad-news boys.

Jacob was a jerk too, married to his guitar and his gigs rather than to her. The dude left her hanging far too many times, canceling, forgetting, then asking for forgiveness.

What is wrong with men?

Present company included.

But what is wrong with Hazel for picking these awful men? Though, I'm the pot calling the kettle black. My track record in picking women is as bad as Hazel's in choosing men.

Still, I'm sure whatever guy got to take her to Nice, to kiss her, to have her, then to travel home with her, was a dude bro too.

Jealousy claws through me, dragging its jagged nails over my skin.

As she talks about her trip here, I look away, trying to tune her out. I should never have kissed her last night. I know better, yet when I was next to her on that awful couch, the hum of the train seducing us, that wildflower scent of her skin seducing me, I didn't think.

I *felt*.

I felt an infuriating resurgence of all that pulsing, aching want I tried to vanquish when I went to Europe more than a year ago. To get away from her.

So I gave in.

Dumb fucking move, since now I can't get her kiss out of my head.

"And it's the perfect spot for a kiss, isn't it?" she asks the group in that charming, vibrant voice that makes her readers adore her.

She's so perfect for this genre, it kills me.

She has an every-girl charm about her. She's accessible and chatty. She's the woman they want to be their bestie. She's not afraid to show them her real self. When we climbed up the steps earlier, Hazel stumbled on the second to last step, but one of the Book Besties grabbed her elbow, stopping her from falling.

"Guess I'm a clumsy heroine today," Hazel had said to Maria, with a self-deprecating smile.

"I'll save you anytime, girl," Maria had said.

Now, they're enrapt as Hazel brings them behind the scenes to the Nice chapters in one of her most popular books—*Sweet Spot.* But I can't stomach hearing how she crafted that romance. Because I know—I just know—

some other man inspired her. He kissed her here in this park, overlooking the Mediterranean, and I hate him.

"And I thought, *someday*," Hazel continues, all wistful, and hearts-a-fluttering, "*I will write a first kiss scene here, and it'll be epic.*"

"And *the Sweet Spot* kiss was so epic," Jackie chimes in, bouncing on her pink Converse-clad toes. "It's one of my favorite kisses of yours. But I also love the kiss in the alley in Old Nice, just past the market. When Bennett yanks her into a doorway—"

"—and he growls at her, saying, *You are maddeningly beautiful,*" Alecia puts in, hand on her chest, ready to swoon. "*And all I can think about is what your lips taste like.*"

"And she says, all sultry and needy, *So find out,*" Maria says, batting next with their performance of memorized lines from Hazel's book.

Damn. They're something else.

Hazel whistles in appreciation. "Wow. Impressive," she says.

The Book Besties high-five each other.

"It's one of our favorite kisses. It's a top five *Calgon Take Me Aways* kiss," Jackie says.

"What's your all-time favorite? Across the whole romance genre. Not just my books," Hazel asks the whole group. As different people answer, mentioning Kennedy, and TJ, and plenty of others, Hazel listens attentively and once, or maybe twice, I swear she steals a glance my way.

A furtive little stare.

Is she checking me out?

Regretting last night too?

Obsessing over it?

I don't have a clue, so instead, I stare sullenly at the water, inventing character bios for all the people passing by down below. I do my best to keep my brain busy, so I won't linger on that kiss I regret.

I definitely regret it even more after knowing she came here with a guy.

But I can't tune her out since her voice grows louder, a closing note tone to it. "And that's why I'm glad my mother took me on a trip to Nice years ago. When we visited here, I even told her someday I would write a kissing scene here," she says.

It's like a smack upside the head.

I was dead wrong. She came to Nice with her mom, not a lover. As she ushers the group out of the park, I straggle behind, delightedly corrected.

Feeling like the most relieved idiot in the world.

I grin privately as I head down the steps. I maybe even preen. Yeah, no one else kissed her.

You jackass, you didn't kiss her here either.

You're not sharing a sleeper car with her for real.

You're not having a relationship with the woman who has utterly captivated you for years.

And so, I still regret last night.

Because I'm still the jackass who wants another kiss. One that doesn't end.

As she finishes the tour, I stay quiet. I refuse to look at her. I live in my head. That's easy for me. My imagination is rich and vivid, and I have so many stories to tell. Stories where the hero always gets the girl, no matter what.

But when the tour ends, and the readers head off with a local guide for a late afternoon snack (translation —glass of wine), Amy tells us we have a free hour before the early evening bookstore signing.

"I have some calls to make but if the two of you want to wander, we can meet up in an hour," she suggests, checking the time on her phone.

Hazel looks at me, her eyes saying yes before her mouth does. "I'd love to," she says, and I'm not at all surprised. She loves kicking the tires.

I just give a curt nod.

"Perfect," Amy says.

"By the way, did you ever hear from the travel manager about the suite?" Hazel asks, sounding eager. Overeager maybe? It's a kick in the gut, yet another reminder that a kiss can't happen again.

She doesn't even want to share a suite with me. And, really, do I want to share one with her? Well, not like we did last night, playing crime-scene-tape-down-the-middle-of-the-bed.

Amy waggles her phone. "Working on it. I'll have an answer soon," she says, then picks a spot for us to meet in an hour.

Once she heads off, Hazel looks me dead in the eyes. "Are you mad at me? Because the only thing you've said all day is *same here.*"

That's the real smack upside the head.

I am so see-through.

Better add another regret to my digital Post-it—how

I've handled every single irritating emotion I've ever felt for her, then and now.

But I can only move forward, and I won't ice her out again. That means I need to try to act like last night didn't devastate my heart. I'll have to find a way through with something I didn't do when I took off—be honest. Be...*kind*.

"No. I'm not mad," I say, but that's not quite right. "I was sort of lost in my head today," I add, since that's true enough to give her something, but safe enough to protect me.

She takes the answer and nods crisply. "Fair enough. I've been there."

She gets it. She gets me. "But I would love to check out the alley where that maddening kiss took place," I say, since I'm not going to turn down a free hour in Nice. Especially with her.

She rolls her eyes. "Yeah, right."

"No, I mean it," I say, free of sarcasm or acid. I want her to know I truly would like to kick around town. We've only ever hung out in New York, exploring that city together. Never another. This is a brand-new activity for us, for me. Maybe it'll be what I need today to clear my head and my heart.

Her right eyebrow reaches above the sky. "You do?"

I suppose she's right to doubt me. So there's one surefire way to let her know I'm where I want to be right now. "Brooks will definitely have to hunt for treasure here as he evades bad guys," I say with a smile that says I'm ready to plot, and she damn well better come along for the ride. "Want to help?"

"Sure," she says brightly. She's game for plotting anytime, as she's always been.

That's promising. It's a return to what once worked between us. And if we return, perhaps last night can truly be behind us now.

Where it should be.

19

THE PLOTTING GAME

Axel

As she traipses down a cobbled alley, Hazel smacks a weathered yellow building with her palm. "This is where Brooks will chase Nefarious Ned," she declares, upbeat, excited. "He'll slam his shoulder against the brick, taking the corner at full speed. On foot."

"Of course he's on foot. He's a badass. But he'll keep going," I improvise, as I assess the damage the four-story building will do to my hero. "It's only a bruise after all."

"Can it draw blood, please?"

"Damn, you want to make it hurt, don't you?"

"I really do." She mimes grabbing a knife and carving up Brooks's insides. I only know that's what this gesture means since it's a Hazel thing. She does it while plotting, always saying our job is to make it hurt, like a knife through the stomach.

She's vicious. It's the best.

"Fine. I'll make him bleed," I say, like I'm acquiescing, as though I like to torture imaginary people too.

She pumps a fist as we walk past apartment buildings with white shutters and flower planters. "But then Brooks will lose the chase in the rubble."

"I'll be sure to let Brooks know you want him to lose," I say.

"Of course. Because he has to lose before he wins," she says. "That's how books work."

"I know, Hazel, I know," I say dryly, but I'm glad, too, that we said yes to this hour. We're resetting to something like friendship by plotting a book. And as we plot, I don't have to face the aftermath of that kiss. Hell, we don't have to talk any more about how quiet I was earlier today. We've tackled it. We're done.

If I'm lucky, I'll get my fountain of books' wish—I won't have to excavate any feelings for her on this trip.

Maybe we can skip over *that day* and just return to something I can handle—book talk. I've fucking missed it. "Did I tell you Brooks meets his heroine at a nightclub in Vienna? He's very smooth when he picks her up."

She shoots me a mischievous look. "Of course he is. I'd expect nothing less." Then she doubles down on the twinkle in her eyes. "And I fully expect him to break a toe or something while he's banging her over the bathroom sink in their luxury hotel room."

That's a thing in my books. My heroes always get it on with their ladies, but nothing goes perfectly.

Someone usually stubs a toe, or hurts his back, or winds up with rug burn.

Sex is messy. But it's still worth it.

"And he doesn't regret a damn thing about his broken toe the next day," I add.

"Of course not," she says, then stops at a terracotta building at the corner of an even narrower alley. She tips her forehead down the shadowy passage. "Even when that stubbed toe makes it harder for him to commandeer a motorcycle to chase the bad guy down these alleys as he tries to outwit the...evil banker."

I laugh. "Did I tell you Nefarious Ned was a banker?"

She smacks my shoulder playfully. But it's friendly, like two former writing partners should be. It's not romantic, like it could be between two people who got lost in a kiss on the train after dark.

Or, really, one person.

"Hey! You promised you'd make me a villain. I'm holding you to it," she says, sternly, shaking a finger.

"Be careful what you wish for, sweetheart," I say as we wander deeper into the maze of alleys in Old Town.

We're still side by side, but it's a tight squeeze as we walk. After a beat, she says, "Axel?"

I brace myself. "Yes?"

"Why do you call me sweetheart? You started it... *after*," she says cautiously, as she busts me.

I don't want to tell her. I don't want to admit that it helps keep her at a distance. That I can say it with a curl in my tongue. I started it months ago when I had to face her for the first time *after*. It had bite. I needed that bite.

I sigh heavily, saying nothing.

But when she shoots me a sad look, it's clear my sigh said enough.

"Does it bother you?" I ask, a little concerned now. I don't want to backtrack with her now that I've gotten something right with her today—the plotting game.

She shrugs.

I wiggle my fingers. "C'mon. You've never been one to hold back. Just lay it on me, sweetheart," I say before I realize what I'm doing—falling into old habits completely.

Calling her that name again.

She wheels around, fire in her green eyes as she stares sharply at me. "Fine. Yes, Axel. It bothers me because you say it like an insult. And I don't want to be insulted."

Oh, shit. Oh, hell.

I've been such a dick.

She's dead right. "I won't call you that anymore," I say, honestly, looking her square in the eyes. "I promise."

"Thank you."

"Thank you for telling me I was being a dick."

"You were a smidge of a dick," she says.

I laugh. "Better to be a smidge of a dick than…"

But I trail off since sexual innuendo is a bad idea. But also because it hurts to be this close to her, this aware of how much I want to push her up against the wall and call her *maddeningly beautiful*, since she is. She fucking is. So I grab the tool of sarcasm to jimmy my way out of this situation. "Besides, I need to get used to calling you Hazel the Hungry."

"That's my villain name?" she asks dubiously as we resume walking.

"You don't like it? But you like lunch," I point out, so helpfully.

She scoffs. "I would think something like Hazel the Horrible."

I shake my head. "Nah, too on the nose. How about Hazel the Harried?"

"Because I'm too...*busy* to be a good villain?"

"Hmm," I say, tapping my chin as I consider other options. "What about Hazel the Hot-Blooded?"

She nods a few times, digging it. "Works for me."

"Then I'm definitely not using it," I say, as we reach the end of the alley. It lets us into the main drag.

She draws a deep inhale as she looks around, smiling as her eyes travel across the view. "It's good to be here again."

"So you and your mom had a nice trip to Nice?" I ask.

"Yes," she says. "She always wanted to travel here. My dad never did, so I finally took her to France when I graduated from college. I wasn't sure I wanted to travel with her, but I'm glad I did."

"Why weren't you sure?"

She's quiet for a few seconds before she answers. "I was frustrated with her when I was younger. Even though it wasn't her fault, I was still annoyed with my parents' relationship. I didn't like how she let my dad treat her, but then she went to a codependent anonymous type group when I was a teenager, and I did the same, and I think I understood her more. Why she let him control her but also how she wanted to change."

"That's great," I say, genuinely glad she sought the help she needed, and that her mom did too. While she's told me before about her complicated relationship with her father, and how strict he was with everyone, I wasn't aware of how that impacted her connection with her mother. "That you went, that she did, that it helped."

"I'm glad I went too. I think it made it possible for us to be close again. Know what I mean?" She holds my gaze for an important beat.

She's not talking about her mom. She's talking about *us*, and *us* is terrifying. "Sure," I say, sinking back into my protective shell.

We walk in silence for a block, then she turns to me again at a street corner. "This is nice, Axel," she says.

Her remark sends a jolt of warmth through me. Maybe of wistfulness too. I know what she means. *Talking. Sharing.* And I can't be entirely monosyllabic in my replies. "It is," I say, admitting that much. "It's nice to talk to you again."

Please let that be enough, Hazel.

Please don't ask me for more.

I don't want to tell her how deeply I've missed her, how hard the last year has been, how awful I felt when I left.

"Axel," she continues, her tone vulnerable. "I was so mad the day you left me. I still don't think I understand it."

Nope. No way am I going down that path. I made

myself a promise at a fountain. "Hazel. Let's just have a nice day together," I say, fixing on a smile, hoping it smooths over my blockade.

She drops her face, frowning, resigned.

And once again, I've said the wrong thing.

20

BLINDSIDED

Hazel

That morning, more than a year ago

I settled in at our favorite writing table at Big Cup in Chelsea, ready to tackle the next scene in our co-written novel. This was going to be a good one. After I flipped open my laptop, I took a sip of the writing fuel, then tapped away for the next hour, eagerly waiting for Axel to arrive so I could show him all these words.

Lacey had just marched down the Park Avenue high-rise hall toward the hero's penthouse when my writing partner walked into the coffee shop.

At last!

I'd been stealing glances at the door that morning. I was bursting. I had so much to tell him about what I'd planned for our hero and heroine. I wanted to see if he liked the idea as much as I did.

I loved these characters so much—Lacey was the strong and feisty doctor, and Nate was a rich, broody business mogul. Plus, the misunderstanding between these two in the scene Axel and I worked on together yesterday was deliciously brutal.

The makeup sex today had to be passionate, and I'd finally found the perfect lead-in for a guaranteed reader favorite moment—when the hero answers the door wearing only a towel, droplets of water sliding down his pecs, and a towel slung low on his hips.

Yum.

The second I saw Axel round the corner toward me, I vaulted from the table. "I have to show you what I've been up to," I said.

We'd pulled off this kind of hate-sex scene before. Our *Ten Park Avenue* readers loved a good, hard, hot hate-bang.

I grabbed the sleeve of Axel's battered leather jacket and tugged him over to the table before I even realized he hadn't said a word in greeting. It wasn't till I sat down, spun the computer around, and showed him what I'd been working on, that his silence hit me as ominous.

The quiet before everything changes.

In the silence, I quickly studied his face. Those blue eyes were darker, harder than usual. Like they were covering up something.

"What is it?" I asked, concerned about him. Was he okay?

My friend dragged a hand through his messy hair, then shrugged helplessly. "I can't do this anymore."

"Do what?" My pulse sped. What was he talking about? Except, my skin crawled and I knew. I just knew.

He was talking about our work.

After a painfully long sigh, he said, "I can't work with you anymore."

With me.

That phrase cut. It felt so personal. "W-why?"

"I just can't do any of this. Lacey, Nate, the story," he said, barely elaborating.

"You don't like the story?" I pressed, hurt for the characters, but embarrassed too, for me. Had I written my scenes badly? Was this his way of telling me I wasn't good enough to write with him? Had he hated my work all along and only now worked up the nerve to tell me?

The corner of his lips twitched, a little derisively. That wasn't like him. Axel was sarcastic, sharp, and a little acerbic, but in all the good ways.

He'd never seemed mean.

But when he flapped a hand at the screen and muttered, "This hero is such a douche," he was thoroughly cruel.

And I was desperate. I couldn't let our work crumble. We'd written four books and were halfway through our fifth.

"But we can change anything, anything at all," I said, scrambling. "We can make him nicer. We can tone him down. We ca—"

"Hazel," he said, cutting me off, and I'd never heard that *I'm not interested at all* tone before. "I'm just over this romantic bullshit." He flapped his hand at the screen.

The tears welled in my chest. He was insulting my work. *Our* work. *His* work. "So you're just...what? *Not* writing the book?"

He pushed back in the chair, glanced toward the door. "I'm going to Europe. I need to research my next thriller." He looked at his watch. "I should go."

I blinked, unable to move from the shock, as he walked out.

This was not happening.

There was no way this was real.

But then I stared at the empty chair across from me, and the unfinished book on my screen.

This was real and terribly painful.

I slammed my laptop closed, stuffed it into my backpack, and marched out, rushing after him down the street. "Don't you fucking walk away from me, Axel Huxley," I shouted.

He stopped, spun around, crossed his arms, then breathed out through his nostrils. "Hazel, I *am* walking away. I don't want to do this. It's over."

Think fast. Remind him of the practical. "And what do you want to tell our publisher?"

He waved at me like it was my problem. "Tell them we're stuck. We have writer's block. I don't know," he said, and his voice hardened more, an icy shell covering the man I'd known. "They haven't paid the advance yet. Maybe it was meant to be."

I wasn't getting through to him. He was dead set on

leaving. So I took another swing. "Oh, so you believe in fate now?" I countered, like an argument could keep him by my writing side.

His eyes were slits. "I believe it's time for me to go so I'm going," he said, then he snapped his gaze away, like he couldn't stand looking at my face any longer.

That was it. We were over.

I didn't understand it at all. "Why?" I asked again, soft this time, imploring, hoping.

"I'm going," he said softly, his voice threatening to break. "I have to."

"But why?" I asked again, my stupid voice trembling.

"I just do," he said, firmer, like he was pulling up the drawbridge over the moat. Then he gritted his teeth and turned around.

I lunged at him, grabbing his sleeve. "Please."

I was begging, and I didn't care.

His gaze swung in slow motion to my hand on his arm. Then his lips parted. He breathed out hard. With fire and finality in his eyes, he said, "It's done. It has to be done."

That was it.

There was nothing left to be said.

I swallowed my hurt, and I let it fuel me, since I wanted to inflict some hurt on him. "So you're over romance. I guess that explains why you can't keep a girlfriend," I said.

It was a low blow.

Sarah had devastated him when she took off.

But he'd hurt me. It was his turn to feel some pain.

He simply shook his head, said nothing, and left the country.

Leaving me to clean up the mess.

21

STOP TALKING

Hazel

This evening, as we return to the train after the signing, I keep replaying our split. I couldn't figure out what went wrong back then. I still can't figure it out now.

I *should* shut off this loop, but when I open the door to the suite, I'm still stuck on it.

Just like we're stuck in this room, it seems.

Amy said earlier she was still waiting on word of an open suite. "There might be an empty one in another car at the other end of the train," she'd said on the way back to the station.

"That'd work for me," I'd told her.

"Same," Axel had said.

And so, we wait.

And as we wait, I revisit.

Maybe this late dinner will help me stop remembering that day at the coffee shop. How much it hurt.

How much I regret my parting words. How much I still wish I understood him.

But as we dine while rolling across the French countryside hurtling toward Barcelona, I can't stop the loop from playing in my head.

I can't stop it after dinner either, even when Amy pulls us aside after the meal, a sad smile on her face, one that says she has bad news. "I don't have another suite. This route is popular and since the train line launched, JHB has been selling out. Is there anything I can do?"

"Thanks, but it's fine," I say, defeated, then I head to the compartment. But as I unlock the suite door, the words *I can't work with you* play louder in my head.

I have to know. Once he shuts the door to the suite, I wheel around, wasting no time. "Axel, *what happened?*"

He frowns, clearly confused. "Like Amy said, they sold out."

I huff. "That's not what I mean."

That mask I saw cover his eyes the day he took off? It returns, like blinds shuttering. "Then what do you mean?"

"Don't play dumb with me."

"I'm not playing dumb. I legit don't know," he says, but his voice…it's like he's trying too hard to be cool, to be blank.

"You said this afternoon *let's just have a nice day together*, and we did. And let's be honest, we've been having a nice trip, right?" I say, standing in the tiny anteroom, arms crossed, like I'm caging him into this small space. I am not letting him wriggle away again.

He's quiet for a beat too long.

My hackles rise. What the hell? Is this all in my head? "Are you *not* having a good time? I am. Why aren't you?"

"I am," he says, evenly.

There it is again. That...veneer.

Like he won't let me see how he really feels. Fine, if he's going to play it that way, he can see how I truly feel too.

I strip off all the self-protective armor I've worn.

"Axel," I say, fueled by outrageous hope that maybe, just maybe, we can try again to be friends, "I'm sorry."

His eyes widen. "What?"

"I'm sorry for the shitty things I said on the street when we split. I'm sorry I didn't handle it better. I'm sorry I said you can't keep a girlfriend. I'm so, so sorry. I didn't want you to go to Europe. I felt terrible about what had happened to us. Like you didn't want to work with me, and I was an awful writer, and you had to get as far away from me as possible, and I'm just so sorry," I say, my voice trembling as I lay out my own complicity.

He closes his eyes, but not before I see pain flash through them. A deep sigh comes next, almost forlorn as it falls from his lips. Shaking his head, he opens his eyes. "It's not your fault. It's all mine," he says quietly. But full of emotion this time.

I don't feel much lighter though, or exonerated. I still feel shaky, and sad, and so far away from him. But I feel some of this new longing for him too. This want. All these opposite feelings are stirring inside me, jockeying for position. "Why is it yours?" I press.

"Hazel," he says, and it's a warning, like he's borderline begging for me to stop asking. "Can't you just accept it's not your fault? It's entirely mine. And it had nothing to do with your writing."

"But how can I just accept that?" I ask, frustrated he won't let me in. I take a step back from him to get some space.

"Because I think you're a great writer and you know it," he says, pressing his back against the door like he's gluing himself to it.

"How? How am I supposed to know that?"

He scrubs a hand across his scruffy jaw. "Because I've read all your books. Including your last one. Because I fucking love your work, including the fight that Lacey and Nate got into. Including the plans for them to hate-bang," he says, spitting out that confession.

Holy shit. He liked our book. But I'm not any closer to an answer. "So why did you leave? Was it me? Did you just not like me?"

He scoffs, then takes off his glasses, pinching the bridge of his nose. "It was so not you."

"What does that mean?"

"Oh my god," he says, utterly exasperated. "You're so fucking relentless."

I sneer. "So you're mad at me again? For wanting to know what went wrong in one of the most important relationships in my life?"

"No, I'm not fucking mad."

"You sound mad," I counter.

He shoves his glasses back on his face. "Hazel Valentine, can you just get a clue?"

I hold my hands up, letting him know I don't have

one, but I'm also not backing away. "How about giving me one?"

"Fine," he spits out. "You want to know why I walked away?"

"Uh, yeah."

He inhales sharply, on a growl. "Last night."

That makes no sense. I furrow my brow. "What does that mean?"

"Last night. That kiss. That's your clue," he says, but then he mutters, "Fuck it."

He steps closer. That forest rain scent tickles my nose. He showered before dinner and his aftershave is wreaking havoc with my plans to wade through the friendship mud.

"Because I'm so infuriatingly attracted to you and I have been for years," he bites out. "And being around you was impossible, especially with…"

He doesn't have to say the last part. I know what he's referring to. *Who he's referring to.*

But I'm also floored by the admission. I set my hand on my chest. "You're attracted to me?"

He rolls his eyes. "I kissed you last night, baby."

Baby. I'm not *sweetheart* any longer. "But I thought that was an experimental kiss. Like we were testing a scene?" I ask, but my skin's prickling with newfound awareness. My body's waking up again. I wasn't testing anything but my own limits. My own interest in him.

"Maybe you were. But I wasn't," he says, and it's an admission. Of desire. Of lust. Of wicked attraction.

I heat up. "Same," I whisper. "It's the same for me."

His face turns stony in disbelief, then his lips part and he looks awestruck but wary too. "Yeah?"

Nodding, I breathe out hard, my skin tingling. "I'm kind of turned on right now," I say, shocked I voiced it, but glad, too, to make room for this true desire.

His eyes flicker with heat. "Kind of?" he asks, cocky and challenging.

That tone makes me hot.

"More than kind of," I admit. "*A lot* turned on."

After he takes off his glasses, Axel closes the distance, stops talking, and starts touching.

22

MY SO-CALLED SEX LIFE

Hazel

Theoretically, I've had a lot of sex. Every position, every kind, everyplace.

On paper.

And on paper, it's been great.

In real life though, sex has been good enough, mostly fun, and usually enjoyable. But I often have to write my own ending in my head to get over the cliff.

Right now already feels different than anything I've experienced.

Or written.

Axel's hands on my face are better than the feelings I get when writing one of my books.

There's nothing accidental, nothing experimental. This is a full-throttle kiss. He's not playing any games, and I'm so damn grateful. I want to be kiss-fucked, and he must know it.

He crushes my lips like he wants me naked, and *soon*. *Really soon*.

But there's a restraint in him too, coiled, like he's ready to pounce when I give him the word. Like he's waiting for me to unlock the next level of this kiss. I arch my hips against him, grinding against his erection.

He grunts. It's primal, and heat flares in my cells. Then, he cages me against the door, pressing his hard-on against me and answering my move with a dominant one of his own. Like he knows that's how I want it.

And I do. I want to be dominated. I want to be pushed around. I want to be a little manhandled.

He lets go of my face to grab my wrists, lift them over my head, pin them.

Book kiss, here I come. I am no longer jealous of my heroines. I *am* my heroines, but even those lucky leading ladies have nothing on me now.

I'm having what I gave them in all those stories. A kiss that makes me hot, wet, hungry.

As he sweeps his mouth over mine, he moans again, rough and carnal. The sounds of his desire thrum under my skin, between my thighs.

Have me, my body begs.

It's strange to feel this way with him. It's so unexpected that I'm still shocked it's happening, even though it's also the very thing I've craved wantonly since the first night in Rome.

When I roll my hips against him, he drops my wrists so he can slide a hand down my chest. He's not tentative. He's deliberate as he palms my right breast, then squeezes my nipple.

I gasp. The sound turns into a long "ohhh."

He breaks the kiss, stares down at me. His lips are red, swollen. His eyes are blue flames. "Better," he rasps, as if he can barely form sentences.

"What is?" I ask, breathy from being kissed senseless.

"Kissing you is better than I imagined," he says.

My skin glows. My whole body tingles. He's talking my language. I want to be wanted. I want to be craved. I want to be *talked to* in bed.

"Have you thought about me a lot?" I ask, still a little shocked, a little awed from his earlier confession.

He rubs the back of his knuckles over my cheek. "More than I want to admit." But he does just that—*admits*.

I feel…electric everywhere.

Shivery and tingly.

"You're a really good kisser." I'm not trying to be smooth or seductive. Axel simply is, and I want him to know.

"I just really like kissing *you*," he tells me, like he's stripping himself bare, laying all his confessions at my feet. "So I think I'll do it again," he says, finishing in that cocky tone that's irked me so many times before.

Right now? That tone makes me wetter.

This time when his lips come down on mine, he's not as rough. He's almost gentle, a little reverent.

But he's also very, very busy.

Unbuttoning my blouse.

Kissing as he goes.

Another kiss on the corner of my mouth. Another button undone. His lips coast along my jawline. His fingers trail down my chest, over the curves of my breasts.

I'm breathless with longing as he kisses and undresses me. My shirt falls open, and he pushes it off one shoulder then sweeps his mouth along my collarbone. "Can't get enough," he says.

Same here. I grip his arms, running my hands along his skin, so damn eager to explore him.

As I go, I'm amazed that we're doing this. That *we're* hurtling into bed. It feels so unreal.

"Is this really happening?" I whisper. If I talk any louder, I'll break the spell of the train, the rattle of the wheels, the soundtrack to this rampant lust that's driving us on.

"Yeah, baby. You want it to?" Axel asks, and there's zero cockiness now. He sounds...vulnerable. I hardly ever hear that emotion from him. It hooks onto my heart.

"I do," I gasp. "I really do. I think I need to say it because it's just so...unexpected."

"Say you want me," he commands.

Easiest words ever. "I want you."

"Good." He rains more kisses onto my shoulder, then pulls back to look at me again. "Want to kiss you across every inch of your body. Your neck." He swipes his thumb down my throat to demonstrate. "Your tits." His fingers travel down my chest. "Here, right here." He journeys over my belly, then visits the top of my skirt. "Your thighs. The back of your knee. The top of your ass."

I try to breathe. I try to stay upright. But I'm bone-less. I'm on fire. "Do it. All of it," I say.

One possessive hand curls over my ass. He squeezes, then moves his hand to my thigh. "Want to taste you everywhere. Want to kiss you everywhere. Want to fuck you just the way you want to be fucked."

I was already sold, but *that*—ending his soliloquy with an ode to my pleasure—has me gushing. "Now. Please. Now."

He growls, the sound an appreciative rumble. "You have no idea how long I've wanted to hear that."

He's right. I have no idea. But as I gaze at his wet, parted lips, then his darkened irises, I'm getting the message loud and clear. "Actually, I think I do," I whisper.

"Let's make sure though. I'll show you." With a wicked grin, he drops down to his knees, pushes up my skirt, tugs at my panties, then slides them down my thighs.

I step out of them, trembling.

Axel looks up at me, licking his lips. "You are too sexy for my own good."

I don't even know what to say. I've never felt too sexy for anyone's good. I've always felt like I'm having better sex in my head. Like I'm writing sex, rather than experiencing it.

Until now.

"Oh, god," I gasp at the first flick of his tongue.

I rope my hands through his soft hair as he kisses me nice and slow and so luxuriously, like I'm the appetizer, the dinner, the whole meal.

I could get lost in this kind of attention. It's deca-dent. It's pulsing. It's a mix of midnight and starlight and fire. "So good," I murmur.

That spurs him on, and he kisses me even more passionately. I'm dying to come, but I really want him to fuck me. To throw me down, to push me against the wall, to take me. The images send me spiraling to the edge.

"Fuck me now. Just fuck me," I demand, tugging on his hair to pull him up, but I pull him closer instead.

It's too late to stop this climax. I'm coming hard, and holy fuck.

This is book sex, and I'm having it, and it's not stop-ping. Pleasure seizes my body as I tremble all over. Euphoria radiates everywhere, and I want to bask in it. But I want more too.

Seconds later, I tug him up and grab at his jeans, in a frenzy to take off his clothes.

"Now. I want your dick. Just give me your dick." I sound like a madwoman.

Because I am a madwoman.

"You can have it all," he says, like he's won every prize.

In seconds, I've got his shirt off, and he's found a condom in his wallet, and we're both shoving down his jeans and his boxer briefs.

His cock springs free, thick and hard.

But the sight of it jars me.

It's like I'm having an out-of-body experience. Is this really me, on a train, the French countryside rattling by outside that window? Am I truly about to sleep with my once-upon-a-time friend, my former partner, my enemy who's no longer my enemy? My almost lover?

I never thought we'd do this.

Now it's all I want, but am I being impetuous? "This is weird," I blurt out.

Stopping his work opening the condom wrapper, he frowns. His dick is rock hard, aiming at me, as he says, "What's weird?"

But I hear, *Do you not want this? Should I stop? What's going on?*

I reach out to reassure him. His dick, that is. I stroke his cock, thrilling at the velvety smoothness, the pulsing hardness. Touching him sends shivers down my spine. "You and me," I say, breathy and mesmerized at the sight of him in my hand. "It's weird to be naked with you. It's weird to watch you put on a condom. But it's a good weird. Don't you think?"

"Uh…" Speechlessness is rare for Axel.

"Sorry," I say, feeling foolish. "I didn't mean to ruin the vibe by talking."

He shudders. "You didn't. It's good."

"What's good?"

"Your hands on me, Hazel. It's so fucking good," he grits out as I run my hand over the head of his cock. "But if it's weirding you out, we should stop."

No fucking way. I squeeze him harder. "Don't you dare stop."

With a smile, he resumes rolling on the protection. Then he roams a hand up my thigh, hitching up my leg, hooking it around his waist. Slotting his body to mine, he rubs his length against me.

"Oh fuck." He groans like I'm his dirty fantasy.

It's heady, his desire. Especially since it matches all my wild, newly unleashed desire for him.

He notches the head against my entrance and then slides home. Filling me. Stretching me.

He eases out, his lips quirking up. Slowly, luxuriously he slides in, inch by inch. Then he's buried inside me. He takes a moment to breathe, maybe to savor the way we feel, before he says, with a hint of a smile, "Even better."

I meet his eyes. "Yeah, it's even better," I repeat. The words—*even better*—feel like our little secret.

Our dirty, sexy secret as he fucks me against the door, on a luxury train, coasting across Europe, no one suspecting what's happening here in this compartment.

Long, deep thrusts fill me. Jolt me. They make me feel used in the best of ways.

His fingers curl around my hip, gripping me tightly. His other hand loops through my hair. I yelp a little at the pull.

"Too much?"

"Not enough," I whisper.

He pulls harder. I lean my head back, savoring the roughness.

It's demanding.

It's real.

It's raw.

"Tell me what you need," he commands.

The intensity of the order thrills me.

"Fingers," I gasp.

He slides a hand between my thighs. He's rubbing

my clit, filling my body, fucking me hard, slamming my back against the door.

I'm going to have bruises from banging against it, and I can't wait.

I want to be fucked in a way that's not *enjoyable*. That's not *good*.

In a way that is *great*. That's toe-curlingly, sheet-grabbingly great.

Just like this.

As he strokes me, fast and insistent, pleasure coils in my center. I tense, then my orgasm crashes into me, hard and punishing, beautifully brutal.

It's everything I've ever written and nothing I've ever experienced.

I feel savage, and sexy, and very well fucked. I can't stop moaning.

Axel's not done though. He cups my jaw, squeezing it as he pumps, thrusts, then stills and shakes. For a mouthy man, he's quieter than I'd have expected. He says nothing as he comes. Just shudders.

Then he kisses my neck.

I can feel all his held-back words in that kiss.

I don't know what they are, but I swear he's imprinting them on my skin. Things he's afraid to say but he'll speak with touch instead.

Or maybe I'm just feeling the endorphins raging through me.

And for the first time in my so-called sex life, I can definitely say I've had book sex. "I don't feel weird now," I say.

He smiles against me then laughs, soft and husky. "Good. Me neither."

His smile fades though. His gaze turns serious. "Can I sleep in your bed? With you? As in...*with you*?"

"You'd better," I say, and I can't wait to share the only bed in the compartment with him.

23

THE ANTI-CUDDLER

Axel

I've never written a rock-star romance, but I think I could pull one off now.

This must be what it's like to perform an epic concert, bring the crowds to their hold-up-the-lighters feet.

What a rush. What a high. As I savor the view of post-sex Hazel, still sandwiched between the train door and me, her smile dopey, her skin flushed, I feel like a fucking hero.

Because of her. Her reactions. Her words. Her screams.

I'm dying to ask: *Was that the best sex of your life too? Because holy fuck, that was more than the best sex of mine. It was you. I have been crazy for all of you—that smart mouth, that beautiful brain and your-bigger-than-you'd-ever-admit heart for far too long.*

I should gather clothes and get ready for bed. But I can't stop looking at her, searching for the answer in her eyes.

She blinks, then stares back at me, smiling, then laughing a little woozily. "Why are you looking at me like that?"

"Like what?"

She shakes her head. "I don't know. You're not doing it anymore."

Good. Maybe she'll forget I stared at her like a love-struck fool.

After a long exhale, she runs a hand through her lush red locks, "I feel like…"

I wait for her to finish. For a breathless moment, I imagine she says *I feel like I'm falling.*

I'd say *join the club.*

"A shower," she says instead.

Right. Yes. I orient myself to the new task—wash up. "Shower's good," I say.

I dispose of the condom and follow her to the tiny bathroom, but I don't touch her while we shower, and I don't know if that's good or bad, or just practical.

But at least we're clean, so there's that.

A few minutes later, I'm getting into bed with Hazel Valentine. We're half-naked—I'm in boxer briefs; she's in a tank top and undies.

What. Do. I. Do. Now?

Am I allowed to touch her under the covers? When I asked to share the bed, she said *you better.* But on the other hand, she's told me she's not a cuddler. Is the bed a no-touch zone?

This is why friends shouldn't fuck.

It's like doing math without a calculator—a surefire guarantee you won't get the right answer.

I stall, adjusting the pillow, even though I know what I *want* to do next. Curl toward her, kiss her neck, run my fingers down her arm, tease her. Maybe tell her how I want to use *Give me your dick* in a book because it was the best combination of words any person has ever said to me. I could tell her I want to make her feel amazing all the damn time.

She stretches her arms above her head, and I indulge in the still-surreal sight of this woman, including that bare shoulder I'm dying to kiss. But if I kiss her the way I want, will she know I lied when I told her I'd been attracted to her for years?

Fine, fine. It wasn't technically a lie. But it was only the iceberg tip of the truth—this is so much more than attraction for me.

As she settles under the duvet, her ridiculously contented sigh answers one question. The sound is inviting. And hell, I earned that sigh. I drove her wild. I made her come hard.

Enough questions. I'm taking what I can get tonight.

I shift closer, my heart pounding, then I kiss her shoulder. "Don't worry. I'm not a cuddler either." I murmur against her soft skin.

"Good to know I won't have to pry you off me in the middle of the night."

"I'm very well behaved in bed." I layer a trail of kisses down her collarbone. While I'm here, I steal a few more kisses, like I'm stuffing food into my pocket to eat later when I'm cold and hungry. She stretches and moves with me, encouraging me to keep going. That's not helping, her responsiveness. It only makes me dizzier, makes my tongue looser with words like *you feel so good to me,* and *I want so much more.*

But I wished on a fountain that I would make it through this trip without telling her the truth of how I feel.

The truth would ruin us all over again. I'm only now getting her back as a friend. I can't lose her again.

I didn't even realize how much I needed her in my life until a few days ago. Not gonna fuck up this repair job by blurting, *You're the one.*

With that decided, I cease kissing, flopping back on the pillow so I can just enjoy being with her like this. "In addition to being opposed to cuddling, I'm not a cover hog, and I don't snore."

"I *don't* steal sheets or saw logs either," she says, chin up.

I laugh, shaking my head. "You are so competitive."

She nudges me with her elbow. "It's not a competition. It's the truth."

"You're a competitive monster, Hazel Valentine."

"So are you, Alexander Hendrix-Blythe, Esquire." She'd call me that when we were writing and hit a scene that needed legal background, like an annulment or a contract issue. It's nice to hear the nickname again.

"Want me to draw up a contract outlining the terms and conditions of sharing a bed?" I ask.

She laughs and then turns to me, her eyes sleepy but amused. "Do you ever wish you practiced law?"

"Not one bit." Using my law degree for character research rather than a career was one of the best decisions I ever made. "Dad wanted me to be a lawyer. I never did. Didn't realize it, though, till I had that JD in hand. Then *bam*. One of those moments of enlightenment where the heavens open and you get a message."

"From a higher power?" she asks curiously.

"Nah. More like from the gut, know what I mean?"

"I do."

"I just knew I wasn't going to practice. Super useful thing to realize after paying tuition for three years," I say. But that's what work is for—to pay off your past mistakes and prepare for future ones.

"So you joined the ranks of lawyers-turned-writers. It's good company, at least," she says, delivering the silver lining and a sympathetic smile. She knows I used our joint royalties to pay off my last loan. Good thing I went to a state school for that degree I never used.

"Now I can just use my JD to argue about important things." I lean in, plant a hot kiss on her neck, then travel to her ear to whisper, "Like who's a better bedmate?"

She scoffs. "I will win that contest."

"You're on. My bed skills will stun you."

"So, you're good in bed in all the ways," she says with a wink.

And…maybe I puff out my chest. Maybe I beam a little. "I'd be happy to wake you up with my face between your thighs if you require more proof."

"Generous," she says on a yawn.

"Damn. Sex wore you out."

She yawns one more time, bigger and deeper. "I've never been tired like this. I didn't realize good sex would make me so tired."

Wait. What did she just say? I prop my head into my hand. "You've never had good sex before?" That doesn't add up.

She shifts too, turning to meet my eyes. The moonlight from the window spills across the bed, illuminating her bright green eyes and those kissable freckles on her nose.

"It's been good enough." She seems earnest but resigned to her lackluster bedroom life. "But not like that. Not book sex."

I preen inside. I crow. But outside, I keep my cool since I have to go fishing for more intel. "So, all those hot scenes in your books? The go-down-on-her-on-the-desk scene in *Sweet Spot*? Not to mention the elevator, the stairwell, and the kitchen scenes in our first, second, and third books. Those were just…?"

"From my imagination?" she asks dryly.

"Well, were they?" *Because I figured they were real.*

She shoots me a challenging look. "Did you once sew up a wound on your shoulder with fishing wire? Chase a hacker into the Trevi Fountain? Hitch a ride on a zip line to apprehend the evil mastermind behind a sinister plot?"

Damn. She'd make a good lawyer. But she's missing the point. *The point is, tell me how happy my dick makes you.*

"No, but the ones in—"

I cut myself off before I mention Lacey's story, the

unfinished *Ten Park Avenue* romance. Before I tell her that while we were writing that, I was sure she was modeling the hero after Max and it was killing me to hear about it. How I was positive, too, that she was about to write a soul-shattering sex scene inspired by that cheating prick.

"The ones in what?" she presses. Such a bloodhound.

"Just...all the ones you've written." Even avoiding *our* book, I'm unable to strip the jealousy from my tone. "They're good. Hot. And I figured you'd felt that."

Her grin widens with anticipation. "Axel, are you jealous of the imaginary sex you think I've had?"

Ah, hell. I might as well just admit something. I'll burst from all these annoying self-secrets. "Yes," I grit out.

"Really?"

"Like I said, I've been getting you naked in my head a lot."

There. Covered it up *again*. Yup. This guy can wriggle out of any plot twist.

"Let me assure you, sex has always been better in my imagination." Taking an important beat, she locks eyes with me before she adds, "Until tonight."

Ohhh.

Holy fuck.

I preen visibly this time. Rock star indeed.

Plus, I'm learning something fantastic. Max was bad in bed.

That should not make me so happy, but it does. Oh yes, it does.

"Good. You deserve lots of orgasms," I tell her. "In

fact, I bet I could give you two more before you've even eaten breakfast."

Her eyebrows shoot high. "You're on." She sticks out a hand above the covers and shakes mine, then drops a kiss onto my lips. "Like a hero in a book would do," she whispers. A yawn cuts off the last word, and she lies back on the pillow, her eyes fluttering.

"I'll have my breakfast in bed, thank you very much," I say, wishing it were morning already.

Another laugh, and I'll take that too. Bet Max didn't make her laugh like I do.

"And listen," she adds, her words getting slurry. "Since we're doing the only-one-bed-in-the-room trope, this seems like the time for the lay-out-the-ground-rules scene."

Right. Rules. Friends with benefits need sex rules. "Like how long we do this? Whether it's a trip-only trope?" I ask.

"Yes. Ticking clock and all. But I'm too tired. Morning?"

"Morning," I agree.

I'm not looking forward to that conversation. But it's better we have it. It's better if we adult.

Seconds later, she's snoring. The little liar. She does too snore.

Then she's tugging all the covers off me and wrapping herself into them like a little cover piggy.

Ha. She fibbed about that as well.

I don't fall asleep right away. I don't even try. Instead, I just stare out the window, and imagine a new story unfolding.

A feisty woman and a smart-aleck man. He's got a chip on his shoulder. She's been hurt.

They meet on a train, and somewhere, sometime after midnight, he uncovers another solution to his plot problem.

If he can win her over in bed, maybe, just maybe, he can subtly, so artfully she won't even know it's happening, get her to fall in love with him, day by day, until she's as smitten as he is.

But when I settle back into bed with the anti-cuddler, she's turned the other way, wrapped up in the covers and her own sleepy world, and I take that as a sign that the story will be better if the hero stops reaching for the stars.

She's told him, for all intents and purposes, that she wants to be friends again.

Friendship will have to be enough.

24

THE TRUTH ABOUT SIXTY-NINE

Axel

But I can't have that ground-rules talk when I wake up —my mouth is rightfully occupied.

Soon, I can barely breathe, but I'm not stopping. I'll scuba dive without oxygen until she comes.

It's early in the morning, she's grabbing my head in a vise grip, squeezing my face with her thighs, fucking my mouth with her pussy.

There is no air, but who cares if I go blue? Best way to die.

Hazel is seconds away from coming on my mouth as I devour her sweet, hot center. Then, with several concentrated, devoted flicks of my tongue, I elicit a glorious *Oh god, yes*, as she shudders and cries out.

Somehow, she grips my face even tighter as she climaxes. But book heroes are undeterred by little obstacles like insufficient oxygen. I lick her till she gently pushes me away.

"Damn, woman, were you trying to kill me through cunnilingus?" I ask, as I move up next to her.

With a long exhale, she says, "That sounds like something that might happen in one of your sex scenes."

"Please. The hero would get lockjaw, be unable to argue his way out of a situation with Interpol, and wind up in jail."

"But of course," she says, then sighs again as she runs a hand through her hair, savoring her post-sex high. I'd like to take that sound and bottle it. Take hits of it when I need a shot of adrenaline, a boost of extra confidence.

"My heroes' sex injuries always drive the plot." Like the time the pulled muscle from a shower-bang made it harder for the hero to grab onto the back of a rickety old truck absconding with stolen antiques.

"Didn't some reviewer once say your sex scenes are *weirdly realistic and somehow still ridiculously hot?*"

I grin, clucking my tongue. "That's me."

She laughs, then she sets a hand on my chest. "But I guess I'm not such a great villain if you're still alive."

"Alive and horny. Also, feel free to kill me anytime with your pussy."

"Sorry not sorry. I just kind of got into it."

"Kind of?" I ask, arching a brow.

"You really like teasing me," she observes, then pushes up on her elbows. "While you were down there *not dying*, I was almost going to ask you to fuck my face at the same time, but then I remembered something."

"That sixty-nine sucks?"

She beams. "Yes! Sixty-nine is the worst. What is the point?"

"It's selfish," I say, stating the obvious. "Just tap out. Tap in."

"Exactly. Oral sex doesn't need to be multitasked. I don't write better if you eat me while I write," she says.

"Wait. Was that an option? Will you suck my dick while I write? Because I'd be willing to try that," I offer, like the generous fucker I am.

Hazel smiles wickedly. "Get out your laptop and see."

I shake my head. "You know what I really want to see?"

She bites the corner of her lip, a sexy, come-hither move. "Me on my knees, taking your cock deep in my throat?"

I shudder. She is going to kill me with sex appeal. I just know it. She's everything I've craved—a feisty, fiery, smart, relentless woman.

But I can't think about how right she is for me.

I should only think about how right she looks as she slides off the bed, kneels on the floor, and wraps a hand around the base of my cock. Then she licks the head, and I nearly fly off the mattress.

That'll do. That'll definitely keep me in the sex moment.

"That's right, baby. Take me deeper," I urge. I know my girl likes dirty words. She likes a commanding man who understands how busy the freeways are in her head.

And since she's in her head all the time, I'm pretty

sure that's why she needs to *feel* the rawness, the real-ness of sex.

That's what I can give her. "Play with my balls," I tell her.

She obliges, cupping them, rolling them in her nimble hands. My skin sizzles.

"Yes, fucking yes." I run my fingers through her hair, urging her to take more of my dick. "Open wider, baby."

She obeys, lavishing deep, adoring sucks on my shaft. Then she coughs, but she shakes her head to say she won't stop. She'll keep going, and she does till my world blurs away, and I lose my mind to her mouth, her hands, her eager tongue.

Then, on a grunt, I come. It's mind-bending, but a little less surreal than yesterday. Less surreal because it's more real.

More authentic.

We're coming together in the sunlight.

We're not backing away from the intimacy.

We're seeking it again and again.

That brings a new level of risk to our rekindled friendship. It's hard to have sex without feelings messing everything up. We're going to need those ground rules really fucking soon.

But when she crawls onto my lap, wraps her arms around my neck, and kisses me, I don't want to talk. I want to *enjoy*.

She kisses me, a firm, quick kiss. "Sixty-nine sucks," she says.

"We're on the same page," I say, then run my fingers

along her cheek, enjoying this stolen chance to touch her.

"We sure are," she whispers softly.

I want to believe she's looking at me and seeing more than just sex. But I know stories only unfold like that in books.

This is reality, and I can't get lost in these moments. I take a deep breath, steadying myself for a dose of reality. "Let's get dressed and then talk," I say.

But once we're dressed, there's a knock on the door.

"Hey there. Almost time for the reader brunch before we arrive in Barcelona," Amy says cheerily.

Oh, shit.

We need to go play hosts.

Ground rules will have to come later.

25

THE NUTCRACKER

Axel

We power-walk down the train aisle, rushing to the reader brunch like a couple of jerks who keep people waiting.

"We'll just say we slept late," Hazel offers in a rushed whisper.

"We didn't oversleep. We over-sexed," I point out. I mean to be helpful, but she hisses *Axel* at my back. "Just telling the truth."

"If anyone asks," she says, "it was accidental sex." We cruise past high-backed chairs filled with passengers drinking coffee, reading news on their phones, staring out the windows as we near Spain.

Bossy, bossy Hazel. She's too feisty, too busy, too entertaining.

I glance back at her, rolling my eyes. "There was nothing accidental about the nutcracker of your legs."

Her shoulders shake in laughter, but then she tries to swallow the sound so I don't notice. "Do you need a cast for your balls, Axel?"

"Already took care of that, baby. I made one myself."

"That better go into your next book."

I'm glad she can't see how I'm smiling over the accidental sex.

The accidental kiss.

Maybe tonight we'll accidentally sleep together again. A man can dream.

"But seriously," she continues, "just say we slept late."

That's my Hazel. She never lets up.

At the end of the car, I stop by the luggage rack, spinning to face her. "Baby," I say, reassuring her quietly. "No one is going to ask, and the more you say, the more obvious it is you're covering something up."

I should know. That's what I've done, religiously, the last few years, saying zero about my feelings for her. It's worked well enough.

"You think so, Axel?" Her question sounds pointed. Specific to me. Like I'd definitely know the answer about covering up stuff.

"Yeah, but why are you asking?" I ask, half dreading the reply. What if she's got a microscope into my feelings?

She shakes her head. "Just something I thought of, but it's not important."

I should leave this alone, but what if it's about last night? Or tonight? Or ground rules? "What is it?"

If she wants to cut me off, she can do it now. I don't want to wait any longer.

"It was about…" But she stops, annoyed with herself. "It's just about Max, how I found out he was cheating, but that's over, so it doesn't matter."

I draw a sharp breath, irritated to hear his name again.

Or maybe I'm still irritated over how I handled things with Max and her at so many points, including the way she found out. I should have said something sooner, but at least I can say something now. "He didn't deserve you," I say firmly. "Don't give him any real estate in your head."

That doesn't cover everything, but it's a start.

She smiles softly. "Thanks." I'm about to turn around and resume our race to the dining car when she reaches for my arm. It's a friendly gesture, nothing that could be interpreted as more by anyone watching. But I feel the fondness in it. The heat too. "And I'm really glad your balls aren't casted. Because," she says quietly, then checks the scene behind her before she finishes with, "I want you in my bed again tonight."

Fuck yes.

That's enough of a ground rule for me for now. *Another night.*

"I'm there," I say.

I might want more than sex, but I'm nothing if not a realist. I'll take what she's offering, and I'll give her another night of the best she's ever had.

As an attendant yanks open the door to the dining car for us, I wipe the smile off my face. A man doesn't smile this hard unless he's gotten laid, and I'm not going to sandwich-board my sex life for the tour group—my sex life that just earned a sequel.

I fucking love trains.

Inside the dining car, a man with an expensive haircut, a strong jaw, and clearly custom-fitted slacks and shirt greets us. "Good morning, Mr. Huxley and Ms. Valentine. We're thrilled you could join us."

This dude has *rich motherfucker* written all over him. He must be JHB himself. "Thrilled to be here...Mr. Bettencourt?"

His dark eyes twinkle. "Yes. J. Hudson Bettencourt."

When he gestures for us to follow him to the table, I shoot a look at Hazel like *wow*. Her eyes pop open, and she mouths *oh my god*.

This is unexpected, seeing the reclusive guy himself, but maybe he's one of those billionaires who likes to show up unannounced, though I don't actually know what billionaires like to do.

He's the first one I've met.

"Here's your table," he says, stopping at one full of readers.

"Thank you so much," I say.

Hazel seconds the sentiment.

Then he joins Amy at a table. Shortly after, she pops up and cups her mouth. "And this morning is our special reader brunch where we dive into readers' favorite question—where ideas come from. But first, enjoy your breakfast, everyone."

JHB seems to be enjoying his meal once Amy joins him at the table in the corner. He's attentive, focused on her the whole time.

I catch Hazel's eyes as we eat, tipping my forehead toward them, asking silently, *What do you think is up?*

"Get it, Amy," Hazel whispers, with a crystal-clear answer.

"The billionaire and the single mom," I add.

"Meant to be."

We're seated again with the Book Besties, Nikon Man, and Redhead College Girl, and once we've finished eating, Jackie sets down her coffee cup and declares, "I'm ready for my first question."

After a glance to check that I'm ready too, Hazel tells the woman, "Go for it."

Jackie holds up her hands as if to show she's unarmed before she starts in. "Look. I'm one of those people who doesn't mince words. I don't hold back. I say what's on my mind." Jackie's normally enthusiastic, happy-go-lucky, so this intense side of her is new. "And I want to know if Lacey is ever going to get together with—"

I brace myself for what's coming next. Will Lacey and Nate, the rich dude down the hall, ever get it on? Our readers had been shipping the ER doc and the broody suit ever since we pubbed our first co-written romance.

"With Noah?" Jackie asks.

I did not see that coming.

Noah? The doctor Lacey works with? For real?

Hazel snaps her gaze to Jackie, mirroring my confusion. "Noah?"

With an emphatic nod, Jackie says, "Yes. I always saw her with the cute-but-surly ER doc. Noah's sarcastic, but in a way that you could tell he had it bad for her all along."

What is she talking about? Noah does not have a thing for Lacey. Noah's just her annoying work colleague.

I scratch my chin, confused, looking to Hazel for her thoughts.

Apparently, this character matchmaking is shocking to her too, since she's shaking her head. Then she asks, "You think Noah has been into Lacey?"

Jackie nods, big and long. Maria chimes in next with an *oh yes*.

But Alecia tuts her friends, before she says to us, "I've got a dinner at Ruth's Chris Steak House that says these two are wrong, so could you please, please, pretty please with a well-done ribeye on top write the dang book with Lacey and Nate? So I can say *I was right, I was right, I was right*."

I flash a smile at Hazel, who flings one right back at me. They say in our secret writer code that the readers are wrong but we don't want to be rude to them. We mastered the signals when we worked together.

Funny to be using it again.

Though, funny's not the right word. More like warm, or even…comforting.

"Those are the three most satisfying words in the English language," I say, deflecting for both of us. I'm not going to tell the Book Besties that they're dead wrong about Lacey's love interest. We were writing her with Nate, not Noah.

But Lacey's fictional guy hardly matters since her book is dead.

I'm relieved that Steven the Nikon Man has no interest in *Ten Park Avenue*. He motions me closer once the servers have cleared the table. His wife must have taken off, since he's alone. "Been dying to ask you something. It's about the scene in Vienna in *A Beautiful Midnight* when the hero races through the city center on his Vespa."

"Hit me up, Steven," I say. One table over, the college gals chat with each other, seemingly uninterested in this book dissection.

"Now, I did a simulation on whether it's possible to reach all those locations in ten minutes, like in chapter twenty-two." Steven breaks out his phone and shows me a map of places in my book, then spends several minutes telling me that it's not possible to pull off the chase scene from my story on a Vespa.

He's engaging enough to distract me from Jackie's far-fetched idea. "That's all plausible, Steven. But the thing is," I say, pulling the ace from my sleeve, "his Vespa was souped up."

I'm about to tell him where to find the mention of the tricked-out vehicle when the redheaded college gal —Uma is her name—pipes up with, "It says so in chapter fourteen, paragraph four. That's how he pulls it off."

Damn. She has a steel memory and bionic ears. "Uma's right," I say.

Steven's eyes flicker with *you're kidding me*. "No way!"

"Yessss," Uma says, then since she's done correcting him as he reader-splains to me, she returns to her conversation with her friends, whipping her gaze back to them.

I clap Steven's shoulder. "Yes. Check it out. It's a quick mention but it's there."

Scrambling, he flicks through the book on his phone, and when he discovers the little detail, he whistles appreciatively.

Then, because we've talked about me enough, I ask him what he does for a living.

"I'm a lawyer, but I want to be a writer," Steven says, a little sheepishly. "That probably sounds ridiculous."

"Not in the least," I say, then I pull my chair closer. "Have you started your first book?"

"I finished it, actually. It's, well, it's a thriller. That's probably obvious," he says, and it's funny to see this side of him—the nervous and worried side. He's been such a lawyer all along, fast and sharp with questions.

Now he sounds like a writer.

"Let's just say I'm not surprised," I say.

"It's edited too. I hired a professional editor. I'd like to try to find an agent or self-publish it. It's just..." He stops, winces, scrubs a hand across his chin. "The reviews. How do you deal with them?"

That's his worry? He came to the right guy. With a laugh, I say, "Badly, most of the time."

His shoulders seem to lose some of their tension. "Really? You seem so...impervious."

Glad my facade works. But there are times when I need to let it down. This seems like one of those times.

"Some days I have the thick skin of a rhino. Other days, I'm cellophane," I admit with a shrug.

"Yeah?" He sounds relieved. "That's good to know. Well, that it's hard for someone like you."

I flash back to a comment Hazel made during dinner at Menu, that I was obsessed with reviews. That stung, but only because it was true. Also because that obsession was messing with my mind. "It is, but I'm trying to get better. I used to care about them too much—the good and the bad. The bad ones sent me into a tailspin, but I let the good ones go to my head. I had to get a better handle on all of it."

"How do you do that now?"

"My favorite way is to just ignore the bad ones. As for the good ones, well, I like praise. We all do. But my agent made me a deal. He shares a handful of good ones, along with a promise to send me a bottle of the best single malt for my birthday if I don't Google myself anymore."

Steven laughs. "Does that work?"

"I've abstained from review searching for three weeks. Never underestimate the power of scotch."

He sighs, seeming relieved, then winds himself up again. "I'd be too worried that I got something wrong in the story. Some detail."

Everything about this guy added up. I thought I could write his character bio easily—assertive dude who likes to find flaws, take copious pictures as evidence of said mistakes, and then dissect those errors alone with his wife before she says *enough already, just shut up and fuck me.*

But he's got a vulnerable underbelly. I suppose we all do.

"Look, you'll make mistakes. You won't make everyone happy. But everything you write is a choice. Think about why you want to make that choice, and then when you put your book out there, let it go. Anyone who creates something has to do that—a singer, an actor, a dancer, a poet. Hell, athletes have to deal with this all the time," I say, thinking of Carter. He has to deal with reporters and sports analysts Monday morning, analyzing him week in, week out. "It's part of the job. You learn to listen to the people you trust, and you try to filter out the rest. Or put your head in the sand—the ostrich strategy works too."

Steven nods, taking that in. Maybe that's enough for him, because we shift topics and talk about the best and worst parts of the law until we arrive in Barcelona.

The chat with him keeps Jackie's questions about *Ten Park Avenue* on the back burner.

For now at least.

* * *

Today is my day to shine. Barcelona is my place and Gaudí is my companion. You can't write about the Spanish city without knowing the architect whose work defines it.

In Barcelona, I don't need to play mental tricks like I did in high school, or like I did at the reader expo back in New York. I've spent countless hours researching for the novels I've set in this city. Here, my knowledge is my trick.

But as I show the group around Casa Milà detailing how my hero slipped into an apartment in the private residence at night using the physics of the undulating walls of the building itself, an unexpected, new idea taps on my brain.

It won't let go. Like at the podium back in high school English class, I'm in two places at once. I'm speaking while I'm picturing something else.

I'm talking to the group about how my hero climbed up the side of the building while I'm thinking about another guy.

Someone back in New York.

Someone I just can't get out of my head.

A COMPETITIVE MONSTER

Axel

I'm close, so damn close, to putting all the pieces of the puzzle together, but I can't snag a private moment to tell Hazel as we traipse all over the city with the group. We eventually stop in the Sarrià-Sant Gervasi neighborhood for dinner, eating charred artichokes and drinking wine at a sidewalk café.

Hazel lifts a glass of her rioja red. "Because it's Wineday."

"May every day be Wineday," I second, then take a hearty swallow of a wine that tastes like plums. I sit across from her, but there's no chance to talk at the table. We aren't boarding the train until late in the evening, but maybe I'll grab some quiet time with her on the way back to the station.

At the end of the meal, Amy clinks her fork against

her wine glass, then says, "We have a surprise for Axel and Hazel."

I tense.

A surprise is usually something that blindsides you. Like your dad saying *Surprise, we're going to Atlantic City for the weekend so you can work on some short cons.*

Or, when you discover your love is cheating thanks to a social media post, like what happened to Hazel with Max. She mentioned it this morning, and I wince over that too, and my role in it. That's another reason I need time alone with her. I *have* to tell her.

"Since our train ride to Paris is a short one," Amy continues at the head of the table, "I put together a scavenger hunt for you two."

Well, shit.

Welcome to my Hunger Games.

I don't actually mind scavenger hunts. Carter dragged me on one when he visited me in Vienna in the off-season. My brother loves escape rooms, riddles, treasure hunts, and all that stuff. "Don't care if I win," he'd said. "Okay, that's a lie. I love winning, but this is no-pressure winning, unlike, say, my Sundays."

Made perfect sense. On Sundays, he plays pro football.

Scavenger hunts are fun for him because they aren't part of his job.

But they *feel* like part of mine. Like I'm supposed to

be good at them. That's why they aren't *my thing*. At least, not like this. *With a group.*

As we leave the restaurant, heading toward a nearby square, I try to develop a game plan for clues I don't even yet know. That's how badly I feel pressured to win.

Looking concerned, Hazel tugs on my shirt, pulls me aside on the street.

"You okay?"

Her concern feels good. "Was it obvious?"

She points at my face. "The sour look gave you away."

I go blank, stony. "Better?"

"That's good. But seriously, what's wrong? You hate scavenger hunts?"

I sigh, dragging a hand through my hair. "Yeah."

"Any reason?"

I hate that she's so caring, but I love that she's so caring. "There's no way to say this without sounding like a dick," I mutter.

"It's okay," she says, gently, a little playfully. "I know you're a jerk, and I don't mind."

I love that too. That she knows me, all of me. That she's not afraid to call me a jerk, because it's different to call your friend a jerk than it is your enemy. I can hear the softness in her tone. I welcome it.

And maybe today is one for confessions. I told Steven about the reviews. I can say this to Hazel. "I hate doing them in front of people. Because everyone expects me to be the best," I admit with a sneer. The sneer is for me—I do sound like a big dick.

She nods. "Because you're a former lawyer, because

you're a thriller writer, because you plot for a living." Of course she gets it.

"Yep."

She pats my arm with affection. "Want me to let you in on a little secret?"

All your secrets, especially if they're about me. "Yes," I say.

"It's okay if you don't win. Other people like to win too. Just play for fun. You'll be on my team."

"Where's my competitive monster?" I ask, pretending to hunt around for her.

An impish shrug is Hazel's only answer. "Sometimes my competitive monster likes to have a glass of rioja and take the night off. Yours can join her at the café drinking wine while you and I scavenge." She drapes an arm around my shoulder, squeezes. "Hey! That reminds me of sweet raccoon wine."

As we head along the street toward the nearby square, I arch a dubious brow. "That sounds like a clue in a scavenger hunt, or something the chief forager was peddling."

"Or," she says, holding up a finger, "a new type of wine."

She goes on to tell me about the research she did with the New York sommelier about grape harvests. "I was dying to disprove the *restaurateur*," she says.

"Ah, that's the malcontent I know," I say. "I'm so proud of you for wanting to prove someone wrong."

With a laugh she asks, "And you want to hear the wildest thing of all?"

We're ten feet from the group, so there's just enough time. "Always."

She stops at a street cart, where a vendor peddles fresh fruit. She's using the cart for protection, so we can talk freely before we're with the crowd again. Her face is soft, her eyes tender as she says, "When I found out, I wanted to tell you about the raccoons and the bird and the grape harvest. Isn't that weird?"

My heart squeezes. "That's the weirdest."

"Later that day, I found out about the trip. But even before the trip news, I still thought of you," she says, then knits her brow, like she's sorting her impulse to talk to me then on the timeline of us.

Before the airplane apology.

Before the fountain confessions.

Even before we started stitching our friendship back together, she *still* wanted to talk to me.

I was a jerk then.

Hell, that barely covers it. I was a world-class prick, yet she wanted to share the idea of sweet raccoon wine with me.

That confession doesn't slow the train of my new, unexpected thoughts. It speeds it up. Soon, I'll need to talk to her about them, or explode.

But first, it's time for a scavenger hunt.

* * *

Hazel was right. Other people do enjoy winning, and focusing on that—and them—takes all the pressure off me.

I'm having—gasp—fun. Steven kills it at solving clues leading to locations from my books. No surprise there. He's in first place with his teammate, Alecia, collecting photos at all the locations in the hunt.

While we gather outside a tapas bar with flickering white lights, Amy sends the final clue to our phones.

Beside me, Hazel reads out loud from her device. "*Here, the metal glistened,*" she says, then cuts herself off, shouting, "The Hotel Reyes!"

I laugh as she immediately claps her hand over her mouth, eyes popping like she can't believe she just spoiled the name of the hotel that hosts a glittery gala in *A Beautiful Midnight.*

"Sorry!" she says to the group, but the Book Besties are already laughing, and Redheaded College Girl is too. "It's just my favorite scene in that book."

Amy laughs as well. "No biggie. And we need to catch the train anyway, so maybe it all works out."

A smooth baritone cuts through the crowd. "I can hold the train if you need a little more time for the photo."

That's Bettencourt, who's materialized by Amy's side. Perhaps that's another thing billionaires do. *Materialize.*

"That would be great," she says. "We can get a shot of the tour group outside the hotel." The Book Besties lose their minds at the suggestion.

As we walk, Hazel explains more to the group again. "I just love when Francesca dances the tango at the gala with the knife in her garter," she says, unapologetic in her apology.

I love that she loves that scene.

When we make it back to the train—held by Betten-court, as promised—I put my language lessons to use, ordering drinks in the bar car for the crew.

"Ooh, la la," Hazel says when I return with her favorite—a chardonnay.

We toast, and soon the conversation returns to the Book Besties and their daily lives. Jackie and her husband are raising two teens, including a high school senior with autism, Alecia's wife just returned to work after beating breast cancer, and Maria's going back to college at age forty-five to finish her degree.

We drink and talk about life and all its complications until Jackie says, with a wink in her dark eyes, "So, Noah and Lacey?"

Alecia smacks the table playfully, admonishing her friend. "You are like a dog with a bone, girl. Let it go. I want my ribeye steak reward," she says, determined to win the bet with her friends over the love interest in our book.

But I want something too.

I want to work with Hazel again. Badly.

I turn to my friend—or *friend again* I should say. Even though I've had a few glasses, I won't give wine that much power. *This* is the thought I've been mari-nating all day.

The guy I've been thinking of all day.

The guy we left on the operating table more than a year ago. Lacey's guy.

When our gazes lock, Hazel's wearing her familiar, public grin.

The one that says she'll protect me from the *will you finish your book* question. Like she protected me when I walked away. When I left her holding the bag on the contract. That was such a shitty thing to do. And I hope —I truly hope—she'll take me back.

I'm glad we learned that secret code long ago so I can use it now. I give a shrug of my right shoulder then a lopsided grin. A gesture that's always meant *I'm all in if you are.*

I hold my breath, desperate for her yes, but it comes in no time. Hazel shrieks. "You mean it?"

"I do."

All day, all the good memories have knocked on the front of my mind. I've second guessed myself. I've wondered. I've worried. But I can't deny this ache in my creative heart—I've missed working with her so much.

"Let's do it," she says, bursting with excitement.

I expect Alecia to whoop the loudest since she'll get her steak, but they're all wonderfully deafening. Her friends holler and cheer with her, and the other readers join in too, even Steven, and Uma the Redheaded College Girl, along with her crew.

"Can we put this on our social?" Jackie asks.

It seems fitting that the Book Besties should break the news after their role in bringing us back together. "Works for me if it's good for Hazel," I say.

My train roommate can't seem to contain her excitement. "It's very good for me. You're like fairy godmothers."

Jackie squeals. "Matchmakers, hon. We're matchmakers," Jackie says, then grabs her phone, presumably to make the news official.

Over at her table, Amy's cheering while Bettencourt watches her intently, a smile tilting his mouth.

"It's a train trip reunion," she says, then holds up a glass of champagne. Bettencourt clinks his glass with hers, then clears his throat. "To the magic of trains bringing people together."

It's heady, this midnight celebration as we cross the border into France. Heady and dizzy and scary. Maybe I've jumped too soon. Or maybe I didn't jump soon enough.

Either way, there's no turning back, and I'm good with that.

I'm only nervous about one thing—how Hazel will react to what I have to tell her. The role I played in the end of her and Max.

27

SEX MISCHIEF

Axel

But my thing will have to wait. At our compartment, Hazel grabs my shirt collar before the door has time to clang shut.

She yanks me to her in the dark and covers my lips with hers.

Hazel is a woman who knows her mind.

That is such a turn-on.

She's rough and hungry. A tiger who wants her prey —*me*. I happily let her devour my face. Yes, *my face.* She's kissing me hard, ruthlessly, and she's not stopping at my lips. She's kissing along my jaw, running her cheek against my scruff. "Mmm, stubble," she murmurs, then she reaches my ear and nips on the lobe.

"Do that again and I'll be bending you over the bed in no time," I say in a rough growl.

"Is that a threat or a promise?" she taunts, then pulls

back and looks at me, those green eyes twinkling with utter mischief.

Sex mischief.

"The bedroom is no place for threats, so it's a promise," I say.

With flames in her eyes, she drags her hand down my chest. "Good, because I've been thinking all day about what happens to Lacey."

"Have you now?"

"I think her hero fucks her against the window in the train as the French countryside speeds by."

My sexy romance writer has a filthy mind, and I am here for it.

I turn the tables on her, clasping her gorgeous face and slamming my mouth to hers, tasting her, consuming her.

She wants real, raw, unfiltered passion, and I intend to give it to her that way. As I kiss her with a little hurt in it, I undo her jeans roughly, tug at her top harshly. Soon, I've stripped her to nothing.

She's naked in front of me, the moonlight shining across her creamy skin. Her perky tits point right at me. The look in her eyes is both vulnerable and turned on.

She glances down at her chest. "Do you want my tits pressed against the window?" She asks it like it costs her something to say that. But like it frees her too. To have *book sex*.

"I fucking do," I tell her. "Go stand there. *Now*."

She practically sprints. Fine, it's only ten feet away, maybe less, but what a sight, that peach of an ass wiggling as she scurries.

Then, she presses her hands on the glass, tits pressed, ass up. I stalk over to her, taking off my glasses and setting them on the table, tugging off my shirt and tossing it to the floor.

From my wallet, I grab a condom, and once that's safely in hand, I undo my jeans, take out my eager cock, and smack her ass with it.

"Oh!" she yelps.

"Like that?"

I know she does. She's already moaning. But I'm pretty sure she likes to talk in bed. She likes the chance to say the things she's only ever written or read.

"Do it again," she urges.

Gripping the base, I slap my dick against her sweet ass. One cheek, then another, then I rub my hard-on between her thighs, where she's soaked. "Were you like this all day? Wet and needy for me?"

"I was a hot mess," she says, bowing her back, her body saying *take me now*.

What a wild admission. Hazel Valentine walked around Barcelona while hot and horny for me.

I press my palm between her shoulder blades, gently but firmly pushing her forward so those fantastic tits smush against the cold glass. "You were writing this scene all day, weren't you?"

"Yes. While you talked, I wrote sex in my head." She shudders as if reveling in whatever wicked feelings are whooshing through her body right now.

"You dirty woman." I praise her as I push against her, my cock sliding between her folds, gliding against her wetness.

I'm a live wire, sparking everywhere.

But I want tonight to be even better than last night—for *her*. It's a tall order, but I'm up to the task, especially when she trembles, then turns her face to me. "Need you."

Ah, hell. There she goes again with a direct plea that works on my heart and dick at the same damn time.

Quickly, I suit up, then I grab her hips, and I push against her entrance.

She gasps sharply, a high-pitched keen.

"Tits against the glass, baby," I tell her.

She complies.

"You want all of France to see the romance writer getting fucked on a train," I command as I ease in more.

"I do. I really do."

I sink in, filling her completely.

She feels incredible.

She's hungry, needy, and her sex drive matches mine.

I ease out, then back in, and soon, I'm finding just the right pace for the woman who's been aching for me all day.

It's such a privilege, a filthy, beautiful privilege, to be the man she craves. I don't take it lightly. I treat it seriously, fucking her with purpose, with intent. "Want it harder? Deeper?"

"Yes. Please. Both," she says.

I've learned a thing or two about Hazel over the years. She's never let a heroine come magically. No man in her stories possesses a magical cock. The hero always makes sure he's taking care of his woman right where she needs him.

I slide a hand to her clit, stroke her faster and faster still.

Like that, I give her the train fuck she's craved, harder, deeper, and designed to make her come.

There's nothing magical about my dick.

My ears and eyes deserve the credit. I've paid attention to her, and I've read both the lines and between them.

As she gasps and pants and I fuck and stroke, I take her over the cliff, with her tits pancaked against the reflection and her whole body trembling as the towns of France watch her come.

She cries out *yes, yes, oh god, yes,* and I'm right there with her, her sounds pulling me over the edge. I join her in bliss, wishing I could do it again tomorrow and the next day and the next.

But we can't. I don't need ground rules to know the game with Hazel has already changed. It changed in the bar car when we agreed to write together again.

There's even more at stake now. We can't disappoint our readers twice.

And if we fall into anything more than a brief train-trip fling, the two of us will blow up again. We just will.

After we clean up, and get into bed, I draw a deep breath, and begin another confession. "You know that photo of Max and that woman at the nightclub?"

The picture that broke them up.

She knows the pic. Knows I was in it, toasting with my writer bud, Vince Caine.

"Yeah?"

"I told Vince to take it. Then I told him to post it. I wanted you to see what Max had been doing, and I couldn't stand it anymore, the way he was cheating. I couldn't tell you face-to-face, so I engineered that picture."

She props her head in her hand, looking perplexed. "You did?"

"Yeah," I say, wincing. It felt noble at the time. Now it just sounds manipulative. But she deserves the truth. "I probably sound like a bigger prick now."

Shaking her head, she smiles softly, then presses a hand to my chest. "No. You don't. You sound like you were looking out for me. Like you were still my friend."

She's right. "I cared about you. I did, and I do, Hazel."

No sarcasm, no teasing. Just the truth I've always owed her. Night by night, I peel back a little more. But I still keep my fountain wish in a cage. That won't ever come free.

Hazel leans in and presses the most gentle kiss to my lips. It's too tender, it's too sweet.

It's too dangerous because it nearly unlocks me.

But I can't serve up the rest of my heart. She's told me time and time again that she missed me as a friend. As a writer. As a creative partner. She's made it crystal clear she likes my dick. But she's never once even hinted she suffers from terrible things like *feelings*. I'll just keep these wretched things to myself. Don't want to lose her again now that I've got her back.

We need to be friends for a long time. The corollary is we can't be lovers beyond this trip. It'll fuck up everything. Most of all, *me*. "So this is the get-it-out-of-our-system trope? The trip-only trope, right? Those are the ground rules?" Someone has to say it.

For a few seconds, she's quiet. Pensive. But a touch sad too. Then her expression shifts. She's resolute. Or, as she'd say, *resolute-ish*. "Yes. Don't you think?"

I think I want all of you. But I also know we could damage our careers now that we've publicly committed to finishing the final book in *Ten Park Avenue*. We have unfinished business at the computer, and that means we'll have to finish our business in bed after a few more nights.

"I do," I answer. Then I give her space to *not* cuddle.

Turns out she told another lie. Soon after she falls asleep, she wraps her lithe body around mine and stays like that, koalaing me all night long.

I don't care for cuddling, but I will miss this.

I will miss her.

* * *

I wake in the morning to a text from my agent.

> Mason: Normally, I'd give you a hard time for not telling me first, but when it's news this good, even I can't give hard times.

He links to the Book Besties' posts from last night. The comments go on forever. Wow. I park a hand behind my head as I read them. It's humbling. I still can't quite believe anyone wants to read my words—or in this case, *our* words—let alone all these people.

But there it is. In black and white on the Internet.

And for one of the first times in a long time, I don't have to picture anyone naked to navigate past this putting-myself-out-there feeling.

That's a welcome change.

28

TWO TICKETS

Hazel

You can't go wrong with a night in Paris.

Words I've lived by ever since I fell in love with this city when I first visited it with my mom. I've traveled here with friends a few times over the years, falling a little harder each time. That's why I set *The I Do Redo* here.

Naturally, I was excited when Aaron and Cady sent the trip agenda a few weeks ago and Paris was the one stop where we'd disembark from the train and spend a whole day and night.

But now that I'm here, taking a shuttle bus with the group from a late breakfast in Le Marais to our hotel in the Eighth Arrondissement, I don't feel excited. I feel a strange sort of dread.

As the van rumbles past the Louvre, my stomach lurches, and it's not from the quick stop at the light as pedestrians from all over the world cross, heading toward the famous museum.

It's the hotel arrangements. I wish I could hack into the hotel's computer system and rearrange the rooms.

But there's nothing I can do. I worry away at my cuticles as the destination looms closer. Soon, we pull over and clamber out of the shuttle bus. The maroon-uniformed man swings open the door with *Hotel Particulier Eighth* calligraphed across the gleaming glass. It's a new hotel that opened after the one in the tenth was sold out every night.

"Bonjour," I say to him, but I'm not feeling at all like Belle.

I'm jealous of her. I want that spring she has in her step as she carries bags of books through her quiet little town.

The spring in my step has gone missing, and I know why.

I just don't know what to do about it.

As the group fans into the lobby, that feeling of dread intensifies, climbing higher in me. With efficiency, Amy handles the reservations, telling us the hotel arranged to check us in earlier than usual. One by one, she hands out the keys, starting with Axel and me.

"For you," she says, setting a key card in Axel's palm, "And one for you," she says, placing one in mine, beaming with relief. "Finally. Sorry it took so long. We have everything sorted for the Copenhagen leg of the trip, so you'll have separate compartments at last as we travel to Denmark. Jay extended his apologies too and he's happy to comp you for another train tour another time, he's said."

That jolts me from my momentary funk, her first-name basis relationship with the billionaire. I steal a glance at Axel next to me, wanting to nudge him with my elbow, but all I have to do is lift a brow slightly. He lifts one in return.

"That's so kind of Mr. Bettencourt," I say when I snap my gaze back to Amy. I can't bring myself to call him Jay. Then I smile, gripping the card for emphasis. "And this is great."

"Much appreciated, Amy," Axel chimes in.

I'm careful not to smile too much or look at Axel too long. No one needs to whisper or wonder what happened behind closed doors.

But I wish I were sharing a room with him tonight. Mine already feels lonely, and I'm not even in it. I wish I could bump into him as I head to brush my teeth, then bicker over who takes up more of the bed.

I don't even know what our *trip-only ground rules* mean anymore. Did they apply to the first few nights only? Do they stop tonight? Why didn't we think about this hotel situation earlier today? Oh, maybe because we were making out as the sun rose and we had to scramble out of bed in a rush.

Again.

As the door to the elevator opens, I try to sort through my thoughts about last night, this morning, and then all the days to come in New York as we share a brain and a heart over the fate of our characters.

But I'm tongue-tied as the door closes and I hit the button for the sixth floor.

Axel stabs the button for the fifth. The share-a-room part of the trip is over, and I already miss it so much my chest hurts.

When Axel steps off on the fifth floor and says casually, "Have fun today," I can't untangle the words to say, *Wait! What are you doing? Sneak off with me. Let's play hooky in Paris before I see Rachel later.*

I only manage an awkward, "You too."

"Brooks will be on a boat tour," he says confidently. He's so sure of himself. He seems so sure of what's going on between us—what it is and what it isn't.

I'm momentarily confused by his comment, till it dawns on me. He'll be writing.

Something I should do too.

Maybe I can sort out my annoying emotions through words—they have always seen me through.

But an hour later, my room is too empty. The hotel is too quiet. I can't concentrate on the story in front of me on the screen.

What is Axel doing in his room?

Ugh. I can't obsess over him like this. I should talk to friends instead. Grabbing my phone, I click to my texts. I confirm with Rachel where I'm meeting her this afternoon, then click over to my thread with TJ. He's an early riser, so he might be up.

His gifs from our last exchange still cackle at me. Fitting. I tap out a reply.

> Hazel: I adulted so damn well that Axel and I are writing together again. Do I get cheese now?

> TJ: Whaaaaat???? Don't make me get out of bed to call you, girl.

> Hazel: Wild, right?

I SparkNotes him on the entire Axel situation, minus the sex. We can talk about the sex another time. Mostly, I don't want TJ to hear about Lacey rising from the dead from the whisper network. I want him to hear it from me, so I finish with one more text.

> Hazel: You were right. I missed him and I missed writing with him. When we wrote together, I wasn't in my head all the time, wondering if I was any good, if my story worked, if anyone would like it. I relished having someone to create with, someone to nurture a story with, then see it into the world. I liked having a partner in crime. (Well, you know what it's like from our book!)

TJ and I wrote a rom-com together last year. We had a blast, but that was a one-off, and we haven't made plans to write together again. I suppose for a mostly solitary, primarily feline-like creature, I crave companionship now and then.

Or more than now and then. Axel was my greatest companion, and we navigated the dark and dangerous waters of art and passion together. I can't wait to do it again with him.

> TJ: I do get it. I get it completely. Second chances are kind of my thing. Well, third chances, so I understand wanting to reconnect with someone you care about.

TJ and his husband met years ago in London, then met again, then finally, after one more time, got it right. I don't think Axel and I are headed down that path, but it's good to know TJ understands all my reasons. That's another thing I love about our friendship. There's an emotional shorthand we have, perhaps from mining so much emotion on our keyboards all day long.

Hazel: Thanks, friend.

TJ: Go have some fromage. I'm going back to sleep with my third chance.

Hazel: Show-off 😐

I say goodbye and set the phone down, returning to my screen, but all I manage are the words *She tastes like plums*, and I'm thinking of kisses again, and tastes again, and Axel again. Is he penning a daring escape on a boat tour? Or has Brooks met the woman of his dreams? Does he kiss her passionately on the deck, her hair blowing in the breeze before he has to cover her, saving her from a hitman's gunfire from across the riverbank?

I shiver, excited at the thought.

But thinking of his story isn't helping my fictional sommelier and his heroine. I shake off the thoughts of Axel's book, but five minutes later, I'm staring at white space.

"Fuck it," I mutter.

I'm in Paris. I have a free afternoon. I want to experience the world, not imagine it. I grab my phone and call him, hoping words come easily this time.

He answers on the first ring. But it's loud where he is, and he says above the din, "Hey there. Hold on one second." Then he says to someone else, "Oui. Un billet, s'il vous plait."

My heart speeds up. I know what he's doing. But I wait patiently for Axel to finish. When he returns to me, he says, "I don't normally pick up while I'm talking to someone, but what's going on?"

He sounds concerned about me, but also hopeful. I'm hopeful too, since he's not writing about a boat tour. He's buying a ticket—un billet—to take one.

"Can you get deux billets? If you're near the hotel, I can be there in twenty minutes."

29

HOLD THE TUNA

Hazel

I lean against the railing, the summer breeze fluttering my hair, the boat slowly curling along the Seine. "And to think I was going to spend the day in the vineyards," I say with a contented sigh as I drink in the view.

We're motoring toward Notre Dame, passing under a bridge, the cathedral in the distance.

He lifts a brow in a question, and I answer, "My current book. He owns several vineyards."

"Please tell me they fuck among the sweet raccoon wine grapes."

"The barrels, babe. He bends her over the barrels. You just can't hold on to vines with the way he fucks her."

Axel doffs an imaginary top hat. "You win."

"Oh, were we playing?" I rub my palms. "I don't

think you misused a word, but hey, I'll happily take another lunch."

And I would love it. Truly, I want another lunch with Axel. Maybe today. Maybe tomorrow too.

"I meant you win for the new game. We're playing... devise dirty scene scenarios on the fly," he says.

"And you let me win already?" I ask, offended, utterly offended, he'd give in so easily. So offended I slug his shoulder. *Maybe* to touch him a little more.

"Fine. You don't win. I take it back." Then boom, he says, all rat-a-tat-tat, "A rooftop garden. He bends her over the railing." Axel points to a pretty building on the Left Bank, wrought-iron balconies hugging the windows.

My turn. "In the Rodin Museum. Behind The Thinker. A fingerbang."

He gives an approving nod, then tips his forehead toward the Left Bank too. "The Tuileries. At night. Behind the flower bushes. She sucks him off."

"That would work in a public park, so points for realism," I say. He smiles devilishly, and I toss him another one. "At a brasserie in the Latin Quarter. Under the table."

Axel furrows his brow. "We already listed a fingerbang."

My lips curve up. "This time..." I pause, slide closer, then tiptoe my fingers down his shirt. "...she fingers herself while they wait for the *salade niçoise*, hold the tuna. She's quiet, concentrating fiercely, and he watches her every move with avid eyes." I say, painting a delicious scenario.

Axel's irises flicker with sudden heat, a burner turned to high.

"She lets him lick it off when she's finished," I continue.

He swallows, breathes out hard. He looks like he can barely speak. It's a good look. Then he rasps out, "What are you doing for lunch?"

"I think you're taking me out," I say.

"You definitely won."

"It was the *hold the tuna* bit, right?"

He laughs, then drops a quick, possessive kiss to my lips. "It was definitely for the *hold the tuna* bit."

At lunch, I'm feeling as risqué as expected. But also safe, as a red tablecloth hangs low enough to cover my lap, both the corner and the cloth giving us some privacy.

Only some.

But I don't need much.

In two minutes, I'm close, so close I'm pursing my lips, swallowing my moans. Axel's fingers roam up and down the back of my neck, and his soft, feathery touch is nearly as erotic as my fingers tripping the light fantastic.

"Don't say a word, baby," he commands, low and powerful.

I rein in a whimper as pleasure whips through me, fast and fierce.

"You dirty fucking woman," he praises me.

I tense as that familiar, electric pull pulses through me. I'm almost there.

"Bet you look maddeningly sexy when you come in public," he whispers, and that does it.

I'm there, cresting, crashing, coming.

And I can barely hold back.

Right when I think I'm going to embarrass myself in public with a loud cry of pleasure, his lips slam onto mine, and he swallows my sounds.

When he ends it, he utters one word: "Mine."

I shudder.

I don't know if he's claiming ownership of me or my climax, but right now, he can have both.

He reaches for my hand and licks my fingers, staring hotly at me with each deliberate suck. Then he lets go. "I won too."

What a game indeed.

The server swings by. "Your salad niçoise. Hold the tuna."

* * *

A little later, we walk along the Seine, this time admiring the river cruises from the banks.

"Admit it," I say. "Brooks is going to make out with some gorgeous beauty on a boat, and then he'll save her."

I tell him what I pictured a few hours ago in my room. His eyes blaze with amusement. "I have one question for you. Did you come up with that scenario so I'd kiss you on a boat?"

Busted and I love it. "Maybe I did," I say, feeling daring. Maybe the fingerbang gave me courage to say the things that have been welling up in my chest. "I wanted to see you on the boat."

I say it without guile. Without teasing. Only truth.

His smile grows bigger. He seems happier in ways I've never seen before. I'm happy too.

He glances around, gesturing to the water, then the land where we are. "But we're not on a boat now, Hazel," he says.

I exaggerate a sigh. "Such a shame."

He steps closer, getting in my space. "Ask for it," he says in a low but demanding tone. A hero's voice.

"Kiss me," I say, eager for more of him.

He inches closer, cups my cheek, then brushes his lips against mine. It's better than the kiss I imagined in my room. Maybe because there's no hitman hellbent on killing me. But mostly because I like kissing Axel so much.

I like talking to him.

I like spending time with him.

I want to sleep with him, and I want to fall asleep with him.

When he stops kissing me, I ask, "Want to sleep in my room tonight?"

His smile is both genuine and soft when he says yes.

30

ADULTING REWARD

Hazel

Rachel waits for me on the corner of a quiet street, a red silk scarf tied around her neck, gold-framed sunglasses covering her eyes. Her chestnut waves curl over her shoulders. She's the picture of sophistication, and it's been too long since I've seen her.

Picking up my pace, I walk toward her on the narrow sidewalks in Île Saint-Louis. The green shutters on the windows and iron lattice-work balconies give this Parisian neighborhood a quieter, back-in-time feel. It's an island in the middle of the Seine, and it's as if the city slows down in this place.

She whips off the shades, flashing me a bright smile. "Fancy meeting you here."

"You're one to talk about fancy," I say, pointing to the scarf. "You look très chic. I love it."

She flicks her hair off her neck, bobbing a confident shoulder. "Divorce. It's been good to me."

That's reassuring to hear, even though I know it hasn't been easy. I wrap an arm around her, squeezing her, glad she's doing better. "You mean it?"

I talk to her every week, text her often. But I haven't seen her since I was in California visiting my friend Ellie and helping my sister host a party for the businesses on Rachel's block in Venice Beach. Since then, she's moved to San Francisco and expanded her jewelry shop there.

She nods crisply. "Yes," she says, then gestures to the sidewalk, and we walk. "Mostly."

I laugh, but it's sympathetic. "Mostly is good." I pause, then add, "It's a lot." The end of her marriage blindsided her in ways no one could have expected. The secrets her ex-husband was keeping were book-worthy —no, saga-worthy. Her ex is the poster child for shocking behavior from ex-husbands.

"It is, but what can you do except..." She pauses to finger the end of her scarf and lifts her chin, defying the gods of divorce. "...be fabulous."

"Words to live by." We pass a Mediterranean café; the scents of hummus and falafel drift from the open-front restaurant. I'd love to go back there later, have a lingering meal, watch the people go by. But right now, I'm exactly where I want to be. "However, I think you've always been fabulous. Now, are you taking me to this jewelry extravaganza?"

She tosses her head back and laughs. "It's hardly an extravaganza. More like an artists' fair."

"Even better," I say as we walk past buildings that seem to tilt from age. I wonder about the love affairs these buildings have witnessed, the kisses they've seen under streetlamps and on rain-dappled corners. "So tell me how your new life is in San Francisco."

She shakes her head. "Nope. Don't distract me. You go first. I want to hear all about this trip with your... nemesis."

Oh, shit. That's right.

Everyone knows Axel and I are enemies.

Were.

But mere hours ago, we were under-the-table lovers. We aren't even enemies who fuck. We're not hate-banging. We're just...

What are we?

I don't know, but my stomach flips, and my brain gets loopy as I think about him. The clip of my heart speeds up, and I set a hand on my chest to settle it down.

"You said this time today would be your reward for adulting. Have you? Adulted?" Rachel adds, prompting me.

Right. I told her what TJ and I had decided the day I took off on this trip. That was five days ago.

Feels like a lifetime.

And I'm astonished by what I'm about to say. I haven't told anyone the whole truth. "We're not enemies anymore."

I whisper like I'm testing the idea.

She stops outside a boho boutique that peddles

purses and scarves, and tilts her head my way. "You're not? That's good. Right?"

"It is good."

A smile spreads on her face, a proud-friend smile. I feel lucky to be its recipient. "So you two worked through some of your issues? Put them behind you?" she asks.

Ha. Something like that.

For a few silent seconds, I feel trapped in a lie. Because I could shrug, smile, say something vague.

But I desperately want to tell a friend about this strange and weirdly wonderful thing that's happening to me. "We did, and we've also been spending our nights together."

I offer a *what can you do* smile. Rachel's expression shifts like the gears of a sports car, from shock, to *are you serious*, then to *tell me everything*. "You. Are?"

I feel a little incredulous myself. "We are. Who would have thought?"

"I need details. Time, place, position, etc. Also, number of orgasms, and possibly how high your fever is."

I crack up as we stroll leisurely past cafés and ice cream shops toward the fair. "Number of Os? Too high to count."

"I hate you," she mutters. "From your wine write-offs to your hot sex. Hey, can you write off sex now because you write romance?"

I grin, like I'm imbibing this whole damn beautiful blue-sky day. "I can write off sex toys, I can write off dates, I can write off anything and everything. Every single thing I do is research."

She shakes her head, annoyed, but not really. "This is not fair. You're getting laid *and* saving money." We turn down a street where a bustling fair full of tents and vendors awaits us. Rachel slows her pace again, setting a hand on my arm. "Wait. Is this more than sex?"

That's the question, isn't it? "I don't know. Sometimes it feels like it is. Which is hard to wrap my head around. But the thing is," I say, my heart an anchor now, weighing me down, "we decided to write together again. So I can't let any of these sex feelings distract me from our new partnership."

She hums thoughtfully. "That's a lot too," she adds, using my words.

"I guess we both have things going on." Something nags at me. "Hey, are we failing the Bechdel test?"

"The one that says women shouldn't talk only about men?"

"Yup."

"But we're not talking about men. We're talking about what we want in life. Our hopes and dreams."

I chew on that as we near the fair. Lilting French music drifts from a tent, and it's surely about love and longing.

"We are." Writing isn't just my daily reality. It's still my hope. It's still my dream.

Writing romance has helped me make sense of a messy world. It's my heart and soul. It's how I've found a way through the storm of emotions inside me, the leftover feelings from being raised by a controlling, angry man who wanted to put women in their place.

My feelings, too, about how my mother handled things then and how she handled them better later on.

I've poured those complicated feelings into all of my books.

My books I write alone.

The ones I write with Axel.

My stories have given me this life, this freedom, this chance to write off wine, to travel to Paris, and to live on my own terms.

Independently from anyone else.

From any controlling man.

As we wander through the fair, focusing on jewelry, studying pretty baubles and bling for Rachel, she asks me more about the tour. I tell her about the Book Besties—their big hearts, their goals, their careers, and their passions. "Most of all, they're so supportive, even though they hardly see each other."

"Like us," she says, with a happy but vulnerable look. One I return in kind—I'm grateful to have a friend like her.

"Just like us."

We talk more about Rachel's business, then it's time to go. I catch the Metro so I won't be late for our evening signing, and as the train rumbles along, my mind drifts to another friendship—the one I'm rekindling with Axel.

I replay earlier this afternoon with him, then I imagine later tonight.

I badly want to see him again, and I fear my feelings are only getting messier and a lot less friendly.

31

IRON DICK

Hazel

Show me a writer who's an extrovert and I'll show you a liar. I feel like I have jet lag again after the evening's signing at a bookstore in the Latin Quarter, followed by a tasting at a chocolate shop—one that was the inspiration for the chocolate shop in *The I Do Redo*.

By the time Axel, the VIP readers, and I return to the hotel near midnight, I'm crashing from the wonderful, but long day.

The Book Besties invite me for a drink in the lobby, but my yawn wards them off before I can even answer.

Jackie holds up a stop-sign hand as I close my mouth. "Nope. I take it back. No drinks for you," she says, going all mama hen.

"But can we have breakfast?" I ask. These ladies are so fun. Their friend energy is goals. I want to inhale it for a little longer.

"Of course," Jackie says, sounding thrilled. "There's a cute boulangerie around the corner."

"Let's do it," I say, then she shepherds me to the elevator. I don't bother to resist. I don't look back, either, to see if Axel is coming now or later. I have faith I'll see him.

"Night, Jackie," I say. "See you in the morning."

"Get some rest, hon. Tomorrow's another busy day."

"It is," I say, then I head up to the sixth floor.

When I shut the door to my room, breathing in the silence and enjoying it this time for much-needed replenishment, my phone buzzes.

I slide it open right away. Maybe it's Axel telling me he'll meet me here any minute. I guess that means I don't need a break from him at all. But I don't entirely want to contemplate what that means as I read his text.

> Axel: Try not to be shocked. Steven the Nikon Man has corralled me into a drink. He wants to talk shop some more.

> Hazel: Talk shop but don't get whiskey dick.

> Axel: As if I could get whiskey dick.

> Hazel: Anyone can get whiskey dick.

> Axel: Not this guy.

> Hazel: You're immune to it?

> Axel: Yes.

Hazel: I guess you'll have to prove it.

Axel: I will, Hazel Horny-All-The-Time Valentine.

Hazel: Did you just rhyme?

Axel: I believe I did. Do not hold it against me.

Hazel: I will absolutely hold it against you.

Axel: I'll hold you against me and my iron dick.

I laugh, then set the phone down on the table by the door, kick off my shoes, and head to the bathroom. After I wash my face, brush my teeth, and change into a tank top and undies, I slide into bed.

I finished that celebrity memoir on the train, so I download Saanvi's new romance about a cop and a firefighter fighting their burning feelings for each other. It's scorching and emotional from the get-go, but the day is catching up with me, and by the time jeans are being unzipped on my e-reader, my eyelids are fluttering.

A boat floats by. I see a woman laughing, a man smiling. A warm, hazy feeling wraps around me as I slip away.

* * *

A faint knock tugs on my blurry mind. Then, it grows louder. I bolt up. What time is it?

I squint at the clock. It's after one. Bleary-eyed, I hop out of bed and head to the door, where I peer into the peephole.

My chest squeezes when I see a guy in glasses, dragging one hand through his hair, holding a tumbler of amber liquid in the other.

I open the door, careful to stay out of sight just in case readers linger in the hall on the way to their rooms.

Axel marches in wearing a satisfied grin.

Making a show of it, he takes a swallow of the liquor, then sets down the glass with panache. He points to his pelvis. The outline of his erection is visible, and I crack up.

"Told you. That's a fucking iron dick, right there."

I squeeze it, assessing the goods. "I'd say granite."

He thrusts both arms in the air. "Granite, iron, steel. You name it, my dick can imitate it."

After he toes off his shoes, he glances down at his clothes. "Dammit. I didn't bring my jammies."

"Aww," I say, frowning. "Whatever will you do?"

"No idea." He whips off his shirt, shimmies off his jeans. Wearing only boxer briefs, he scoops me up and carries me the few feet to the bed.

He sets me down on it, then takes off his glasses and gets under the covers with me. I settle back on the mattress too, and the pillow feels awfully comfortable.

So does this duvet.

I sigh contentedly and then yawn contentedly too. It's nice being in bed like this, the faint sounds of the

Parisian streets floating through the half-open window, the moonlight streaking across the duvet, the fading notes of his forest scent tickling my nose.

It makes me want to…just kiss him.

But he'll probably want to have sex. Guys always do. They never want to just kiss. If you kiss them, they always think sex is coming.

Not that I'd object. I really like sex with him. But I also like kissing him. I'm also so tired.

And…oh…that feels nice too.

He's stroking my hair. Gently. Taking his time. Running his fingers over the strands. I snuggle a little closer to him. Maybe it's his tender touch or maybe it's this new trust we're building, but I'm curious about something, and I hope he'll answer. "Why don't the characters ever just make out in books? Is it because men don't like to make out?"

"They don't?" he asks, like that's a ridiculous question.

"Seems that way to me. And, sometimes I just want to kiss for a long, long time. Even if it doesn't lead to sex, but men…I don't know…" I say, trailing off.

He presses a kiss to my hair. "You really pick the wrong men."

It's not an accusation. It's just the truth from someone who knows my terrible track record. "I do," I say simply.

"But I've picked the wrong women too." He doesn't emphasize *picked*, but I hear the past tense in his statement.

I hear what's unsaid—maybe he's changing.

"What if we picked right?" I ask, musing like it's whether I want to order fries or salad when picking right is the essence of my work. "I don't even know what that would look like. It's hard to pick right."

He nods against me. "Daddy issues. We have them," he says into the dark.

A pang of longing knots in my chest. What am I longing for, though? For a new choice? Perhaps that. "I know. But we can make better choices for our characters."

It's easier to talk about imaginary people. We can test our theories on them, like the one I've been noodling on for the last two days.

I flip around so I can fully face my writing partner. There's something I want to tell him. Something that may surprise him. It surprised me. I feel incredibly vulnerable, like I'm cracking open a piece of my mind that no one has ever had access to. "I think Lacey should be with Noah."

Axel's eyebrows lift, but it doesn't take long for him to say, "Yeah?"

He sounds…delighted.

"I do."

"You think Jackie's right?" he asks, like he needs to double check my answer.

But I'm sure. I've been sure all day long.

"I think maybe the one for her has been in front of her all along," I say. This feels right for our heroine.

"We'll need to rewrite a lot of the story." It's not a warning. It's not a no. He sounds open to this new direction for our characters.

"We'll probably need to," I concur.

"Sounds hard, but it'll be worth it."

I feel bubbly. I'm so glad he agrees. "It'll be weird writing with you again."

He rolls his eyes. "You and your weird."

"Hey," I say playfully. "I did say sex with you was good weird."

"So this is good weird too?"

I set a hand on his chest, playing with his smattering of chest hair. "Writing with you is a good weird, Axel. I'm excited to work with you again."

He's quiet at first, then he sighs, almost resigned. Finally, he says, more upbeat, "Me too."

I want to ask why he sounded resigned, but I don't want to ruin us again. "I want this to work," I say, seriously.

"So do I," he says in the same tone, letting me know he's on the same page I am. Then, he strokes my cheek, studies me like he wants to say something important. "Can I show you something?"

My skin tingles even before I know what he'll say. "Yes."

He runs the backs of his fingers along my jaw, making me tremble. "I can't speak for other men, but this guy can just make out."

My heart catches, then thumps faster. "Show me."

And he does.

We kiss forever, and it's druggy and delicious. It doesn't lead to sex. It leads to a wonderful night in his arms.

32

VODKA AND TONIC TOGETHER AGAIN

Hazel

I crunch into a croque madame, hold the ham, the next morning. Cheese oozes over the edge of the toasted bread, but I dart out my tongue to catch it.

Jackie laughs from across the tiny orange table outside the boulangerie. "You go, Frog Hazel."

"I love cheese and I cannot lie," I say after I finish the bite.

"Who doesn't?" Alecia seconds. "When my wife felt well again, she was like *bring me all the cheese.*"

"Your wife is smart. Cheese might be the meaning of life," Maria adds, then takes a bite of her croissant, humming in appreciation. "Can I move to France some-day? Well, after I finish my degree and meet a hot billionaire."

Alecia nods knowingly. "May we all either meet them or become them. Speaking of, I think Amy and

JHB have a little something-something going on." She whips her gaze to me. "You should write about them."

I've already thought about that. But I don't want to let on any secrets about future story ideas. So I shift gears to the ladies. "Maybe I'll write about someone who becomes a billionaire making dog bandanas."

Jackie laughs, clearly tickled at that idea, but then she sighs. "I really hope the bandana business takes off. I have a chance to partner with a pet supply store, but I don't know what to say in my proposal. Well, I do know what to say. I just think I've said it badly." She frowns, looking embarrassed. "I haven't sent it in yet."

I put down my coffee cup and seize the opportunity. These ladies have done so much for me. This is one thing I can do for them. "Want me to look at it?"

Jackie's eyes pop. "You would?"

"I'm not too bad with words. I could help if you need it."

Alecia slugs Jackie's shoulder. "Take the help, Jackie. Let five *Calgon Take Me Aways* help you."

"That would be great," Jackie says, then she fishes out her tablet from her purse. I spend the next thirty minutes fine-tuning her pitch.

"Thank you," Jackie says sincerely before we go.

"It was my pleasure," I say, and truly, it was. I want her to have all the good things. Then I take them and the rest of the group on a tour of my Paris, and somehow it feels even more special to share this place I love with all of them. The readers who have become friends.

And that guy too. There at the back, listening

intently to every word I say about the curving cobbled street in Montmartre where the hero in *The I Do Redo* realizes exactly what he wants.

My stomach swoops annoyingly.

Or perhaps not too annoyingly.

* * *

The tour is over and I'm wandering with the Book Besties through a map shop in a covered passage when my phone trills with the theme from *Jaws*.

Normally, I don't answer or look at my phone when I'm out with others like this, especially when I'm the host. But that's Michelle calling with the special ring-tone I gave her since, well, she's a shark when she needs to be.

"That's my agent," I say apologetically to Jackie, Alecia, and Maria, who are checking out a cartoonish map of Europe. "I'll call her later."

Except when I hit ignore, Michelle just rings again a minute later. That's her shorthand for *pick up fucking now.*

I wince, unsure what to do.

Jackie, though, is certain. She waves at the phone, shooing me out. "Go! Agents must always be answered."

"Hi, Michelle," I say as I head to the door and press the phone to my ear.

"Hi, cutie-pie," she says in her Georgia accent. Everyone's *cutie-pie* to her. I suspect it makes her shark bite sharper. "Is Axel there? Get that peach too."

I catch Axel's attention. He's checking out globes

with the Nikon Man and his wife. I waggle the phone, and he follows me outside the shop, then around the corner, where he slides in next to me, shoulder to shoulder, as we lean against a pretty yellow column. He's close, so close I can smell him, a hint of soap, a bit of rain. My new favorite mix.

Must focus.

"We're both here," I tell Michelle, holding the phone between us.

"I am calling with delish news," she says. She's well trained. I hate being blindsided, even more so after last year, so Michelle knows to preface her calls with whether the news is good, bad, or ugly.

"I like good news," I say.

"Guess who got you two cuties a twenty percent raise?"

I blink. Axel's jaw drops. "Wow," we say in unison.

"Apparently that disappearing act made your next book even more valuable. Fans are clamoring, and Lancaster Abel wants to put the preorder up soon. So they're offering to pay you a bigger advance on the book. And they want you to deliver it in four months. What do you think? Can you pull it off? If you do, there will be a bonus on delivery, and the usual bonuses for bestseller lists, which you'll hit because everyone, and I mean the whole dang Internet, is talking about you two being back on. It's like vodka and tonic got back together after a terrible year apart."

I gulp.

Holy shit.

This is real.

We're truly doing this.

I knew that. Of course I knew that. But now everyone knows. And even if Michelle is exaggerating a tidge, this is a reality check.

As in, we'd better deliver, or our careers are toast.

I look to Axel first. My answer hasn't changed, but I want to hear him say yes again. I kind of can't get enough of it. "Thanks, Michelle. That's a lot, and it'll let me keep writing," he says, sounding honest and grateful.

He's still amazed he gets to do what he loves for a living. I am too. To tell stories is heady and humbling all at once.

I chime in with a cheery, "Send the contract anytime."

"Great," she says, and it sounds like she's about to hang up, but then she adds, "And by the way, *The I Do Redo* is a bona fide hit in France. The U.S. too, but your French publisher is très, très happy. They called, raving about how it's selling there. Just wanted to pass that along."

"Good to hear," I say, briefly flashing back to Veronica's advice when I FaceTimed her in Rome—*focus on work*. In a way, I did focus on work. On being fully present for every moment of the tour, on listening when the readers shared ideas, then on plotting new stories with Axel and revisiting old ones. Somehow, that all worked out, and here I am, lucky enough to *still* write for a living. Pinch me. Just pinch me.

It's almost all too good to be true. But somehow, it's real.

We finish up, and when I end the call, I'm still in a

state of shock and wonder over the Axel news. "We're really doing this," I say.

"We're really doing this," he repeats.

I've wanted this reunion badly. But now, I'm also starting to want something else. Something beyond the characters, beyond the coffee shop camaraderie, beyond the partnering in crime.

But my track record sucks. I guess you can't have everything.

A little later, we arrive at Gare du Nord for the final leg of the train trip. As I roll my luggage along the platform, Amy by my side, I glance at the clock on the station wall. It's early evening. This is our longest train journey —fourteen hours to Denmark.

Axel's behind us, chatting with others, while Amy rattles off details of the last night of the tour.

"And I checked and double checked. You'll be all set with lots of space," Amy says as we near the car. We'll have separate compartments on this journey north. That should make me happy, but it doesn't. I can't rely on a reservation snafu this time around to bring me closer to Axel. I'll have to take the step.

"Thanks, Amy," I say.

I shift the conversation to her, asking about her kids in Los Angeles, if she misses them, if she's excited to see them. I listen attentively, even though my shoulders feel heavy. Time feels too fast. It's running out for real.

This is our last night on a train. Then Axel and I will

spend tomorrow night in Copenhagen before we leave for the airport to return to New York.

Less than forty-eight hours, and this brief and lovely tryst on a train, in a hotel room, under the table in a brasserie, will end.

But it's been more than the best days of my so-called sex life. It's been boat rides and meanderings in foreign cities. It's been games we love playing and wishes in fountains.

When we return to New York, it'll be contracts and deadlines. It'll be keeping the promises we made to our readers. I won't break those again.

But we made promises to ourselves too—to finish the story. To see our characters all the way through. That's what we do. We write.

It's how I understand the world, and I don't want to break my understanding of myself either. I want to finish what we started.

There's only one thing to be done.

Once we step onto the train, Bettencourt is there waiting, sporting an expensive suit and an intensity in his gaze. "There you are, Amy," the billionaire says, and her name contains multitudes. He's eager to see her, he's hungry for her, he only has eyes for her.

I wave goodbye to the single mom who looks a little enchanted as she talks to the man waiting for her. I can't wait to tell Axel about the two of them and how they deserve a train romance.

When I reach my compartment, I flop down on the same bed we shared earlier in the trip, and I call him.

"How's your compartment?" I ask when he answers.

"You trying to trade, Valentine?"

I smile. "If yours is better, we should sneak into yours tonight."

I can hear him smile over my boldness, over the way I ask for what I want.

"Get over here now. Act casual, like we need to, I dunno—"

"—plot."

"Yes. *That*. Brilliant."

Seconds later, he's opening the door to his compartment, and I'm stepping inside so I can ask for something from the guy I couldn't stand when I shared a table with him in New York more than a month ago.

And it's not about Amy and the billionaire. It's about us. I'm eager to wring as much joy as I can from the waning days. "What if we make the most of these last two nights?"

"What do you mean?" he asks, sounding full of hope too.

"We finish the book tour tomorrow afternoon in Copenhagen. But we don't leave till the next day. Spend it with me. Just me. All day, all night." I take a beat, gearing up for the real ask. "Like a date."

His blue eyes twinkle. Then, he lifts a finger, swipes it across my eyelid gently and holds it up. "Eyelash. Make a wish."

I blow on it, wishing there were a way for Axel and me.

"What did you wish for?" he asks.

I already know it won't come true, but I still don't

reveal my wishes. "I can't tell you, but I can tell you what my fountain wish was."

"Yeah? Does that mean it came true? It was my iron dick, right?" He's trying to make me laugh, to keep the moment light, but I can tell he wants more from my wish.

I play with the neck of his shirt. "I wished to have a good trip, and I did. What about you? What was yours?"

He shakes his head. "It hasn't come true, but I'm close. So damn close."

"Tell me then?"

He just shrugs, noncommittal, and I hope to learn his wish someday. I hope, too, that it comes to pass.

Then he kisses me, and I taste both wistfulness and joy.

33

NO MORE WORDS

Hazel

Dinner is finished. Drinks are flowing. The train rumbles across the rolling hills of Germany as we travel deeper into the night on our way to Denmark. I finish the last of my chardonnay, but it's my only glass this evening.

I don't want to be tipsy or drunk on my final night on the train. I do want to be alone with Axel, but I also feel a little guilty for ditching our guests.

So we stay a little longer at the table in the dining car—now the liquor car.

The conversation with the group bends like the tracks, and eventually it turns once more to us.

"Have you thought about Noah and Lacey?" Jackie asks, bolder than she's been before, determined.

I put on my best polite, happy face—this is a secret we need to keep. "We'll see who catches Lacey's eye."

"When do you start writing?" Steven asks.

"After we return to New York," Axel answers, and that makes me happy and sad at the same time.

"Are you looking forward to working together again?" Jackie asks, but before we can answer, she tilts her face. "You know, I don't think I know this. How did you two even meet in the first place?"

It's been so long. Axel's been a part of my life since I became the person I always wanted to be.

Alecia jumps in with her own answer: "I bet you have a meet-cute like in a romance novel."

I glance at Axel with a smirk. "Too bad we didn't meet in an elevator," I joke.

"That got stuck," he adds.

"And then there would have been a power outage," I say.

"And I'd have had to single-handedly climb out the top of the elevator shaft to save the building."

Nice finish, I mouth, then I start a new made-up meet-cute. "Or at an ice-skating rink, where you bumped into me skating."

"Naturally, you were wearing a cute hat," he says in a too-charming tone.

"You caught me before I fell," I say the same way.

"But then you sliced my shin open with the blade," he says, his voice growing darker, matching the shift in our fable.

"You stifled a groan, but when you spotted a man with dead eyes in the back of the rink slinking off, you quickly scooped me up and got me out of harm's way."

He shakes his head, sighing all over-the-top. "Too

bad we didn't meet in an art gallery when you were trying to steal a painting that I was trying to retrieve."

My eyes brighten. My whole soul does too. "And then we spent the entire four hundred pages in a cat-and-mouse game, falling for each other but working toward opposing goals."

Wow, that hits close to reality.

Too close?

I don't even know anymore, but soon, it's like no one else is here as we write our mash-up meet-cutes, marrying our two genres and making up a whole new starting point for us.

After a final scenario involving a picnic then a chase on a motorcycle, Jackie claps, and Maria bows, and Steven lifts a glass.

"But what's the real story?" Uma the Redheaded College Girl asks pointedly.

The truth? It's simple and not exciting.

"We met in a coffee shop," I admit. "I was there with TJ, writing with him, but when he stepped out to take a call, I looked around and saw Axel a few tables over, tapping away on his laptop. His leather jacket was on the back of the seat, he ran a hand through his hair, and he concentrated so fiercely on the screen that I knew. I just knew. Still, I asked him if he was a writer and said I was one too."

"What did you think when she talked to you?" Alecia asks.

"I thought...*what a nosy writer*," he deadpans.

I slug his shoulder.

He straightens. "Fine, fine. I thought…" His mouth is soft, his eyes warm, as he finishes, "she was interesting."

Uma snorts. "Bullshit. You had a crush on her."

For a second, Axel goes still next to me. Uncomfortably still.

She can't be right? Axel didn't have a crush on me then, nor has he ever. He set me up with Max, for all intents and purposes. He was only ever attracted to me. That's not the same as a crush. Not the same. Not at all.

But the car remains silent. The only sound is the chug of the train, the rattle of the wheels.

"Of course he didn't," I say lightly. Someone has to break the heavy silence. "We became friends then."

"We did," Axel says quickly, but his voice is strained.

Does this conversation touch a sore spot? Maybe because of the attraction he felt then—an attraction he still feels.

One I feel, too, growing stronger and bigger every day. Every hour.

So much I don't want to stay in this car another minute.

* * *

We make it to the sleeper compartments thirty minutes later, next to each other.

"Don't take long," he rumbles, and it's an order.

No, it's a command, and it sends a shiver down my spine.

I turn the handle for my compartment—appearances and all, but as I unlock it, these appearances seem pointless. It's one more night. I'm not sure I care if someone sees us.

I turn around, catch his gaze, hold it for a long, heady beat. My stomach flips. What is happening to me?

From several feet away, doors open and shut, voices carry, but I ignore them as I close the distance between us and follow him to his sleeper car.

The second the door shuts, we kiss. It's chaotic and consuming, a hot, wet kiss that's somehow both poignant and sexy.

When he breaks it, he's breathing out hard, holding my face. "Uma was right." He swallows roughly, like it hurts to say that.

I smile, a little shocked, and curious too. "You had a...?" I can't quite finish the question—*had a crush on me* —it's too unexpectedly wonderful to say out loud.

"I did," he admits plainly.

"You never let on," I whisper. This moment feels fragile, like in it we could break whatever this is between us.

He gives a rueful shrug. So unlike the cocky, sarcastic smart-aleck man I've known. But I've been learning new things about Axel on this trip. He's been revealing his other side. His hurts, his heartaches, maybe even the things he doesn't like about himself, the parts he's trying to change.

We all have those parts. But it takes a real man, or woman, to see them, more so to admit them, then to change them.

He's that guy, flawed and so damn real it makes my

chest ache. I shake my head, a little amazed. "You're a good secret keeper," I say.

"It was easier," he says quietly, then he lowers his face, wincing. But he lifts it again quickly, his gaze resolute. "I wanted you to meet Max because I knew you'd like him. I knew he was your type. But it made it easier too. *For me.*"

I nearly reel from the admission. His crush was so consuming he engineered another romance for me. That's so huge I don't know what to say or to think.

"I thought it would help me get over my crush on you," he adds, apologetically. "I didn't want to ruin our partnership by telling you about this stupid fucking crush." He's so frustrated with himself, but then he sighs, a worried sound. "Now you hate me for real, don't you? But I had to tell you."

My heart squeezes even harder. It's beating so fast. "I don't hate you," I whisper, emotion already knotting my throat, and like that, I do know what to say. "I really, really don't hate you."

Then, before I tell him how I truly feel, how much I don't hate him at all, I cover his lips with mine.

I kiss him again.

It's messy and needy as we tug at clothes and jerk at zippers, then fall into bed together.

I ache, and I can't wait a second longer. When he takes off his glasses, I grab his face. "I need you," I say.

"Need" is only the start of how I feel. But I don't want to say more and ruin this fragile new us.

Axel grabs a condom, rolls it on, then pushes the back of my thigh, bending my knee toward my shoulder. He settles between my legs and sinks into me with one deep, delicious thrust that has me moaning.

In no time, I'm panting and gasping.

He's groaning and grunting.

Neither one of us talks. We don't demand dirty deeds, or ask for it harder, rougher, deeper.

I'm too afraid to talk.

Too worried I'll say the wrong words or say the right words at the wrong time.

Like *I'm falling for you.*

I have so much more than a crush on you.

Instead, for two incessant talkers we're remarkably, disturbingly quiet.

But we're loud in the only way we can be now. Speaking with our bodies, our sounds, our touches.

And with the way we come together in a desperate tangle this last night on a luxury train speeding across Europe toward its final destination.

34

THE FINESSER

Axel

This is dangerous. I'm too damn close to slipping. As she sleeps next to me, an arm flung across my chest, her red hair spilling onto my shoulder, I vow to do better tomorrow.

There's only one more day to survive, really. Once we leave Europe, the spell will be broken. We'll return to New York. I'll refill my salty supplies, slap on my armor, and do my goddamn job.

Come morning, all I have to do is make it through twenty-four more hours without telling her I fell in love with her once.

And, over the last few days, I've fallen in love with her again.

* * *

The sunrise brings a bright idea.

To survive the next day with her, I need to go back to the way we were. To arrows and barbs.

When Hazel's brushing her teeth, I don't come up behind her and dust a kiss onto her neck like I want to.

Instead, I pull back the bow, meeting her gaze in the mirror as she saws her toothbrush across her teeth. "Have you added one yet to your next rom-com?"

Her eyes become question marks.

"A quirky pet," I clarify. The conversation at our unexpected dinner seems longer than a little over a month ago.

She nods sagely, then speaks through a mouthful of mint. "Do snakes count?"

Damn.

She wastes no time.

I try again, grabbing another arrow from the quiver, tossing a glance at the bed beyond the door. The duvet is tangled on her side of the mattress. "I'm kind of amazed I survived the cover ambush the last few nights."

She spits then shoots me a curious look. "Want a T-shirt that says I Shared a Bed With Hazel Valentine And All I Got Was This T-Shirt Since She's a Cover Hog?"

Well, fuck. Someone is sharper than I am. She returns to brushing her teeth. Or rather, attacking them with a toothbrush.

"Careful now. That toothbrush might file a restraining order against you," I say.

I grab my toothbrush as she shoots me a narrow-eyed stare in the mirror, then spits in the sink. "I'll have you know I do some great thinking while I'm destroying toothbrushes," she says.

I can't keep up with her, so I go for the low blow. "Then by all means, attack it again...*sweetheart*."

She stops brushing on that word. Like it's dirty.

Because it is.

I probably shouldn't have said that.

I definitely shouldn't have said it. She knows it was a weapon.

But she doesn't call me on it. Instead, she lifts the brush again, then, meeting my gaze in the mirror like a cat refusing to look away, says coolly, "I will, Axel. Or should I call you my nemesis again?"

Ah, hell.

I should have known better. She's too sharp, too clever, too perfectly matched.

"That or...jerk," I say, apologetically.

With a roll of her eyes she mutters, "Sexy jerk."

And like that, I'm forgiven.

And like that, I fall a little more.

And all I want to do is tell her how I feel. Words well up inside me, threatening to burst free. *I'm in love with you and it sucks.*

I really need to keep my mouth busy today.

Maybe this toothbrush will save me. I jam it in my mouth and imitate her. Attacking my teeth as I brush so damn hard.

This is not us.

This is not real.

We don't brush our teeth together in the morning and bicker as foreplay.

That's it. I know how to stay the course and survive. But it'll require some finesse. Good thing I'm an expert finesser.

Once she leaves the tiny bathroom and roots around in her suitcase, which I relocated to my room last night, I come up behind her, sliding a hand up her back just the way she likes, slow and seductive.

She shivers, then murmurs.

Over the last few days, I've learned some of the things she likes. I wish I could learn more. I wish I could help her discover new things she likes too. And, conversely, I wish I could unlearn so many things about her as well—that she wishes on fountains, that she hogs the bed, that she wants to choose better, that she loves to explore and lift up others, and to tell stories all day and into the night. And that she supports me, encourages me, and sees through me.

I don't know what to do with this Hazel knowledge. All these facts and details are overflowing in my head, and there's hardly room for them, yet I want to fill my brain with more, more, more.

I bring my lips to her ear, flick my tongue against the lobe. "I was a jerk just then," I whisper. I need to apologize but it'll also help my shut-my-mouth cause.

"You were, but you don't scare me, Axel Huxley."

My heart spins faster. I am so fucked.

"I shouldn't have called you sweetheart," I continue, and this time the nickname comes out tender, full of all the feelings for her.

She leans back against me, warm and eager. "Or say it like that instead," she urges.

I need to escalate. Right fucking now. I shift gears, full speed ahead with dirty talk. "I don't want to make out. I want to fuck you again." I take a beat, then add, low and smoky, "With my tongue."

There's a sharp intake of breath, then she drops the blouse she just picked up. She leans back against me. "And you think I want that?"

She's so fucking good at our games too, whether it's bickering or banter, whether it's one-upmanship or word play. She's the perfect partner in crime, in games, in…everything.

"You do. So sit on my face, Hazel."

A minute later, I'm lying on the bed, and she's not hovering; she's sitting, pressing, pushing. I love that she grinds against me shamelessly. My mouth is thoroughly occupied as I make her come hard.

Too bad it defeats my purpose.

Because when she flops next to me, running her fingers down my chest, I want to get closer. I want to tell her that she can come over every night in New York. Or I'll go to her place. I don't care where we are. I just want to be with her.

And on that never-going-to-happen thought, I need to get some coffee and eggs really fucking soon to shut me up for the next day.

* * *

At breakfast, the last-day-of-vacation mood blankets the group. Everyone moves with a little melancholy, a little wistfulness as we grab plates and pour coffees.

I don't sit with Hazel, but when Bettencourt strides through the car, beelining for Amy, who looks his way with a *trying to wipe the sex glow* smile off her face, I can't resist a glance at the fiery redhead I adore. Hazel gives me an *I know what they did last night* look. And I return it.

That gives me one more idea for how to make it through the next thirty minutes till we arrive in Copenhagen.

After we return from breakfast, we zip up bags, gather phones and books. We're twenty minutes from Copenhagen, and I know how to make my wish come true.

We'll talk about work the entire rest of the trip.

Just work. That is all.

Once she closes her suitcase and brushes one hand against the other like she's saying *that's done,* I beckon her with my finger.

I'm sitting on the tiny love seat by the window. It's hard as stone, but I don't care. The view is unbeatable as we roll toward the Danish capital. The view will keep me rooted in my cause.

"But the couch," she says, a little whiny.

"Come here anyway."

I figure she'll sit next to me, but she surprises me and sits on my lap.

And that fries my brain. I catch the scent of her wildflower shampoo, and I'm done. I don't want distance. I want to savor every last second with her.

I wrap my arms around her, nuzzle her neck, like a lovestruck fool taking his last hits. Then I let go, look out the window, and try to resist the too-fast, too-painful speed of my heart. I try so damn hard to talk about work, only work. "I had this fantasy the other night," I begin.

She lifts a brow seductively. "You and your iron dick are insatiable."

I laugh softly, but then kill the laughter. "Shockingly, it's not about sex. Ninety-five percent of my thoughts are, but not this one."

"I like your anti-sex thoughts too. Tell me."

"I am never anti-sex," I say. I can't have her thinking that.

She rolls her eyes. "I know, Axel. I know you."

My heart clutches. I fight like hell to ignore the tight squeeze in my chest. And I try, dear god, I fucking try to focus. "I pictured a man and a woman who meet on a train," I begin. "At first, I thought she was feisty, and he had a chip on his shoulder. But then, what if she's the single mom PR woman, and he's the reclusive billionaire who's captivated by her?"

There. Amy and Bettencourt will get me through.

She gasps. "Oh my god."

"I mean, it's sort of obvious, I know," I say. "But maybe we could write it someday."

What in the holy fuck am I doing? I'm trying to be tough, but I'm talking about the thing that makes me most vulnerable.

My passion.

My love of stories.

My burning need to tell them.

She holds my face. "I've always wanted to write a train romance too."

"Yeah?" I ask, my dumb heart flipping. I can't catch a break with her.

She lowers her voice like she's sharing a deep, precious secret. "Confession: when my publishers first told me about the trip, I imagined an elegant train romance. Velvet gowns, a dapper man, and long, lingering glances as the train sped across the coast."

Like it has for the last few nights.

"We should write one," I say. Because when I try to resist her, I do the opposite.

"We should. A broody billionaire with secrets. And a single mom with a wounded heart," she says.

"He's determined to win her over," I add, and that's not me, that's not us. Though, perhaps it is.

"She tries to resist," she says, and yeah, maybe it is us after all. Maybe we've been writing ourselves this whole damn time.

"But she's helpless to his charms," I say, then run my fingers up her arm, into her hair.

"She wanted to resist," Hazel says, locking those green eyes with mine.

"But he wore her down," I counter, my voice low, my heart thudding painfully. I'm aware I'm speaking in the past tense now. I'm definitely no longer brainstorming Amy's romance.

I'm retelling this one.

Wanting to give it a new ending.

"He did," she says, and her voice is soft and sad at the same time.

I'm such a fool. I pull her close, kiss her lips, and then...fuck it.

I can't keep swallowing my feelings anymore. When I break the kiss, I say, rough and full of emotion, "Hazel."

Her breath hitches. "Yes?"

I gear up to speak my heart to her, right here, right now. I part my lips, the words forming to say *I'm so in love with you*—when there's a rap on the door.

I blink, suddenly unsure what to do. I clear my throat, ready to speak my truth anyway, but the other person is faster.

"Hello! We'd love to do a group photo as we pull into our final stop."

It's Amy, bright and cheery.

Breaking the moment.

"Of course," I call out, my voice rusty. It hardly sounds like my own. "Be right out."

Then Hazel turns to me with expectant eyes, a soft mouth.

And I search through my mind for a beautiful lie. "I just wanted to say...we should write that book."

Her expression is blank, confused. But then there's a smile. It's slow and a little uncomfortable as she says, "We should."

A few minutes later, we assemble for the photo, then step off the train for good.

35

DATE NIGHT

Hazel

As Axel and I lead the readers on the final activity of the final day of the tour—an hour-long bike tour around the city—I'm thinking about our date tonight when the tour ends.

We're going to the Tivoli Gardens, the amusement park in the center of town. I can't wait to ride The Demon and its three ridiculous vertical loops.

Bring on the adrenaline.

I'll use it as fuel to say, *What did you really want to tell me on the train?*

I don't think he was talking about books. I think—*I hope*—he was hinting at something more, something better.

Like, maybe we can try dating when we finish writing Lacey's book at the end of the year. As I pump the pedals, riding past a fountain by the harbor, I picture that scenario down the road.

We could go back to New York. Meet up for our writing sessions. Finish the story we promised, and the second we write *The End* we can explore bougie coffee shops in Brooklyn and mock their ridiculous pour-overs, go to art galleries and figure out how to sneak into them late at night to steal things back (for research of course), then take a tango lesson together because we could both incorporate tango into our stories—him for subterfuge, me for sexual tension.

And all of that, every second, would be foreplay.

The bickering, the bantering.

We could crash into each other at night.

I glance at my phone in the phone holder on the handlebars. Ten more minutes and the tour will be over. We'll arrive at the hotel in the center of town.

We'll say our goodbyes to Jackie, Alecia, Maria, Uma, Steven, and all the others. Amy and Jay too.

Then we'll run off for our date. It'll be one last night, but maybe a promise of what's to come.

As I pedal, I practice the words. *Want to date me in a few months?*

Tonight, under the twinkling lights of the adorably Scandinavian amusement park, will be the perfect time for me to take a chance.

But something nags at me as we cover the final blocks.

What if I'm asking for too much? What if this was just a vacation fling after all? What if I scare him away for good?

When we reach the hotel and lock up our bikes, I can't shake this doubt. But I shove those thoughts aside since it's time for goodbyes.

Axel works his way around the group, shaking hands, giving hugs. I do the same until I reach Jackie. "I'll miss you most of all, Scarecrow," I tell her softly.

Her eyes shine. "Thank you for everything."

My throat tightens, but I clear away my own emotions then tell her, "You better email me and tell me how the deal went for the dog bandanas."

She crosses her fingers. "I hope it goes well."

"I know it will," I tell her, then I hug her once more as my breath hitches. This was a special week in so many ways. It rejuvenated me. It reminded me that I might be the woman who works through her issues with words, but at least those words are reaching people, touching people.

Including myself.

The Book Besties head into a different hotel—I'm glad we have separate ones—and then I walk to Axel, more nervous than I'd thought I'd be. There are no more buffers. It's just us for one more night.

Will I be brave?

I watch him, still talking intensely to Steven, still giving the guy all his attention, and I decide it's time for me to change.

To choose better.

Axel's the best choice I have ever made. I just know it.

There. That's settled. My pulse evens like a boat lolling on peaceful waves.

But as I wait for him to finish, my phone trills. I grab it. Oh, I know this number. It's the one that brings a cocktail of nerves and excitement.

My publisher.

Did something happen with the contract? What if they don't want the book anymore? What if they want ten more books with Axel and me for one million dollars?

"Hello," I say as I answer, and my voice is rusty.

"Hazel!" It's Aaron, the publicist.

"Hazel Valentine," Cady chimes.

"That's me," I say, stepping away from the hotel entrance and stopping at the quaint street corner.

"We have news," Cady practically sings.

"Such good news. You know how well *The I Do Redo* is selling?"

"Like, everywhere," Cady tag teams. "The U.S. and the world, and France and just everywhere."

Everywhere is indeed everywhere. "I've heard. Michelle said the same. I'm so glad."

"Oh, good. So you'll go?"

Did I miss something? "Go where?"

Aaron tuts. "Cady, you didn't even tell her."

"Ack! My bad," Cady says. "I got ahead of myself. Hazel, An Open Book wants you to do a special signing tomorrow."

"In New York? When I return?"

I can hear Aaron roll his eyes. "I got this, Cady," he says to her, then to me. "No, sweetie. In Paris. The store wants you to do a solo event tomorrow, a reader Q and A, and to sign both the French and English editions. Since you're already there, we thought, easy-peasy. We'll tack it onto the end. If you can just grab a flight to Paris tonight, you can do it tomorrow and leave from Charles de Gaulle. We'll handle everything."

That's...incredible and awful. I turn toward Axel, unsuspecting as he chats with Steven. Axel glances at me, a dirty look in his eyes, like he can't wait to get me alone.

I have to look away and confirm I heard right. "You want me to leave tonight?"

"Well, sort of. More like in the next two hours. I've got my Google Flights open and we can get you on the next flight out of Copenhagen to go to Paris for the event tomorrow. Lancaster Abel would be so happy if you could do this."

My heart hurts. I want so badly to stay here, to have one wild and free night with Axel. To talk.

But I don't want to disappoint my publisher or my readers. "Of course," I say, sounding hollow. *Feeling* hollow.

They rattle off details, including that a car is coming for me in fifteen minutes.

When I hang up, Steven has taken off. It's just Axel and me outside the hotel on the Danish street.

I must be frowning because his expression shifts as he walks to my side. His sly smile burns off, replaced by question marks. When he reaches me, he looks... guarded. "What's going on?"

My throat is too tight to speak. I feel sick. This is so dumb. I should not feel this emotional. "I have to leave.

I'm going to Paris in…" I croak the next words. "Fifteen minutes."

He blinks, startled. His eyes flicker with surprise, maybe even hurt. "You do?"

I quickly explain, finishing with, "I'm sorry."

But that sounds so weak. Except I don't know what else to say. *I was going to ask to maybe date you in a few months, but hey, gotta go.*

I can't say that before I take off. I can't ask him what I haven't truly figured out myself.

Especially when a black town car pulls up to the curb ahead of schedule. A driver hops out, holds up a sign.

Valentine.

No Huxley.

Just me.

There isn't even time for goodbye. I need to grab my bag from the bell desk. I rush inside, snagging my stuff, then return to the sidewalk, right outside the entrance. Axel's still here, but he no longer looks shell-shocked.

He seems cool. In control. He's sporting his *nothing bothers me* face as he leans against the hotel facade.

"Sorry about tonight," I say, but that barely covers it.

He waves a dismissive hand. "No big deal."

But it's a huge deal, I want to scream. Only he seems like the Axel of before, and I don't know what to make of it.

I manage a confused, "I'll see you in New York."

Then, like a confident, aloof hero in a romance novel, he cups my jaw and presses a quick, final kiss to my lips.

Final. It feels final.

"This was fun. And we'll get back to work in New York," he says, and that's that. "Like we planned."

The only-for-the-trip trope is over. And so are we.

I slide into the car, feeling rattled and thrown. The vehicle pulls onto the road to head to the airport.

I turn my face to the window, looking back, but Axel is already walking away.

36

ROMANCE FUCK-UP

Hazel

I need to revise my prior statement.

*You can never go wrong with a night in Paris...*unless you're sitting stupidly on your hotel bed, staring blankly out the window at the Seine.

Feeling empty. Sad. And utterly confused.

What the hell is going on?

I've played those last two minutes in front of the hotel in Copenhagen over and over. I replayed them on the short flight to Paris. I replayed them in the car on the way to the hotel. I replayed them when I ate dinner with the bookstore manager from An Open Book and she prepped me for tomorrow.

But alone again, as moonlight streams across the city, I still don't get it.

Axel was so...Axel 1.0.

With a heavy sigh, I pick up my phone, checking the

screen in case he's called or texted or sent, I don't know, a gift certificate for a lifetime supply of coffee. Or maybe a note that says he'll always hold the tuna for me. Instead, my messages are empty except for a note from my mom.

> Mama Valentine: You must really be having a wonderful time on your trip if I haven't gotten a single note.

I'm a bad daughter. I didn't reach out to her while I was traveling. But she ends her note with a smiley face, so I know she's not really mad at me.

Maybe she knows I need her. Mother's intuition. It's late in Paris, creeping toward midnight. But it's early evening in Connecticut, and she's probably just starting to close up at the garden shop she owns in Wistful.

The ache in my chest is too intense to weather alone, so I call her.

She answers right away. "Hey, are you having an amazing time?"

My heart sobs. But I swallow the tears and choke out, "Mom, do you think I have a terrible track record in romance?"

A door squeaks. She must be shutting the door to her office. "Sweetheart. Of course not."

What? How can she say that? "Have you seen the string of failed relationships behind me?"

She laughs softly, sympathetically. "We all have that."

True, true. But doesn't she get that mine is embarrassingly bad, especially given what I do for a living? I pick at unseen lint on the duvet. "But I choose cocky, unavailable men. I choose men who cheat on me. I choose men who care only about themselves."

"And from each one, you learn something about what you want and what you don't want. I certainly have from my string of mistakes."

She makes a good point, but I'm not sure I'm ready to listen. "I'm just such a shitty little liar." I flop dramatically onto the bed, staring at the painting on the ornate ceiling in the hotel room. Women in flouncy dresses swing languidly in gardens. So French. "I peddle happy endings, and look at me." I feel sad and foolish. "How can I write these books with these fantastic romances when I'm flailing around at dating and love? I thought I was getting better, but I'm clueless."

Today was a classic example. I was sure Axel was going to say something so swoony I'd melt, and then the moment shattered, and I couldn't figure out what to do at the hotel in Copenhagen.

Did I read everything wrong?

Probably.

I got it all wrong with Max.

But really, it's for the best. We made a promise on a train not to ruin our resurrected partnership. Does it even matter why I'm bad at love? We agreed we could go only so far, and we reached the last stop.

"Oh honey. You're so hard on yourself," Mom says,

gentle and caring. Her voice feels like a hand stroking my hair when I was younger.

I squeeze my eyes shut. Tears well up in them. Her words hit straight in my bruised heart.

Someone else was hard on me. Someone else was hard on me my whole freaking life. The man who hurt my mother. The man who put her down. Who controlled her. I squeeze my eyes a little harder as I think of my mean, absent father.

I'm just like him. But...*with me.*

I can't even speak, but Mom keeps going. "But maybe you shouldn't be," she continues, and the tears start to leak.

"But I don't know how not to be," I say, my voice breaking. Judging myself is all I know.

"I think you do. You're just letting yourself believe that you have to be as hard on yourself as..." she stops, takes a beat, "As you saw others be."

She's careful not to blame him now. Maybe this is part of *her* healing. Her moving on. "But you don't have to be perfect in romance or life," she adds.

"I'm not even remotely close to perfect," I point out.

"Hazel, you want to win everyone over. You want to make everyone happy—your readers, your friends, the people you date. But especially yourself. It's the reason you write. Every time you sit down to write a new romance, you recreate the world. You remake it, ultimately, into something wonderful. But you're not broken. You have to stop telling yourself that you're broken. That you choose badly. You just choose, and then you learn, and then you move forward."

More tears fill me up then spill out, slip-sliding down my cheeks. "Why do you have to be so freaking right?"

She laughs gently. "Because I did the same thing. It took me a while to undo it. But I did. Stop telling yourself that you're no good at this romance thing. Besides, there's no requirement that a romance writer has to be in love. Don't put that on yourself. It has to be a heavy weight to carry."

My shoulders do feel leaden. My heart feels like concrete. Maybe she is right. I've spent so much time judging myself. Feeling like a fraud. Wanting to please the world.

But that's only part of it. There's another reason I don't want to be hard on myself anymore. "I don't want to be a romance fuck-up because..." My throat hitches. "Because there's this guy, and I fell in love with him. And I don't know what to do."

Before I can give her any details, she asks, "Is he a good man?"

I'm surprised she doesn't ask if he's in love with me. She doesn't even ask what's happened.

Perhaps the *only* point is how I feel about the choice of him.

Deep in my heart, I know that Axel is good for me. I know, too, we're great together.

And right now, I know something else. I've been hard on myself about *Ten Park Avenue.* About the rigid way I expect us to write it—*without* acting on these feelings for each other when I *want* to act on them, and I'm pretty sure he does too.

If I don't have to judge every choice I make, maybe I don't have to judge the act of falling in love with my writing partner. And maybe I don't have to erect boundaries around that romance either.

What if we can have it all, try it all, do it all?

For the first time in ages, I see possibilities rather than roadblocks. Wide open paths rather than rigid rules.

My mother is right. Every chance is a new one. Every mistake is an opportunity to learn. Every day we can change.

And every story is a new beginning. Axel and I can start over in every way. We can rewrite the way we work. We can recreate our own world. We don't have to ruin our partnership. We can forge a new one. We aren't the first co-creators to fall in love. We won't be the last.

That is, if he's in love with me.

I hope he is.

Because I'm so in love with him.

At last, I answer my mother with a simple, "Yes, he's a good man."

We talk a little more, then I let her get back to closing up the store, and I stare out the window, feeling lonelier than I have in a week.

But I also feel like I understand myself a little bit more than I did when I walked into this room.

And like maybe, just maybe, I can see my future.

37

THAT LUCKY GUY

Axel

This is fun.

Not.

The last thing I wanted to do tonight was to wander the streets of Copenhagen all alone. But you don't always get what you want and c'est la fucking vie.

I pass a sidewalk café full of tall men and women drinking beers, enjoying each other's company.

I jerk my gaze away.

Maybe I'll stay out all night long. I couldn't get an earlier flight out of this godforsaken city, so I'll just turn it into a work night. I'll spend the next several hours wandering Copenhagen till dawn.

What else am I going to do? Not like I can ruin my fountain wish now by spewing up love professions to Hazel. She's *au revoired*.

As I stalk through the city, I record the surroundings, taking pictures with my phone, writing notes on an app. I'll return to all of this later when Brooks will have to escape from a villain in this city.

Maybe he'll even do it over there. Yup. Across the street by the harbor.

I wait at the red light at the corner, then bound toward the canals that wrap around the city. I stop at the edge of a bridge, staring at the boats docked for the night—the ones that are used for boat tours past palaces and opera houses and all the sights I want to see with Hazel.

Why the fuck did I have to stop here?

That's it. I'm nixing boat tours from my next book. Especially boat tours where the hero kisses the woman he's been in love with for so long it messes with his whole head, his heart, his sense of the universe.

Instead, Brooks will come here, and he'll have no other way to evade the villain than to jump off the bridge and land in a motorboat right below, then take off.

Sort of like I did this afternoon, jumping away from Hazel before she could leave me.

Introspective much?

I shake my head, annoyed at the intrusive thoughts brought on by doubt. I do my damnedest to ignore any and every emotion as I write more notes under a starlit sky when a smooth, deep voice interrupts my thoughts.

"Let me guess. You're pondering."

I jerk around. It's Bettencourt. What is up with him? The dude really does appear out of thin air. Billionaire superpowers.

"What are you doing here?" I ask, like it's a cross-examination.

"I just finished dinner nearby." Oh. Okay, so he doesn't really materialize. It's just a coincidence. He waves toward the starlit river. "And I saw you staring at the water, contemplating the meaning of life, love, and a woman you can't stop thinking of."

Get out of my fucking head. "Why would I be doing that?"

"Occupational hazard of being an utter romantic," he says. It's not even a question. It's just a statement.

I snort. "I'm not a romantic."

He smiles, like *okay, have it your way.* "Then perhaps it just seemed familiar. I've been there. I've done that. Did it in Paris last night. Sorted out some things."

The character bio I wrote for him was all wrong too. Billionaires aren't supposed to figure shit out in one night. "You did?"

"Yes. Like what I want most out of life." His gaze strays to the restaurant as if he's hunting for someone, hope in his eyes.

"I'm just researching tonight. That's all," I say, firm and decisive since I don't want to admit more. I don't want to crack open my heart to somebody who is hitting way too close to home.

"Research is good too. Nothing wrong with that," he says, generously.

Giving me an out.

Right now, I hate him on principle. Because I see myself in him. Or maybe I see who I wish I could be when, seconds later, Amy's striding over to his side. He turns away from me, eyes only for her. When she joins him, he kisses her. Quick. Declarative. She's his. Then he turns back to me, keeping an arm wrapped tightly around her. "Good luck with your research, Axel. I hope it leads you to an answer. And thank you."

"For what?" Is he talking about the exchange we just had?

"For the books you write. For what they led to. They led to this tour. It led to your publisher hiring this amazing woman for the tour. It led to her entering my life. It led to me pondering but not for long."

Amy laughs then squeezes his hand. "Thank god you didn't ponder for long, Jay."

"If you and Hazel weren't on this tour, I might not ever have met my Amy," he says.

Then he says goodnight and walks off with a woman he's fallen in love with after only a few days on a train.

That lucky guy.

He makes it look so easy.

38

STUBBORN FOOL

Hazel

My mother's words stay with me the next morning as I brush my teeth.

Or attack them.

I am hard on myself.

I do beat myself up, judging and berating all the time.

So today, I choose differently. I don't have to be as hard on my heart as I am on my teeth. I ease up on the brushing, and perhaps I can learn to relent too, on the way I beat myself up over my past.

I finish, then get dressed to head out for the afternoon. I convinced Rachel to meet me for lunch. Once my blouse is buttoned and my hair dried, I quickly Google nearby brasseries.

When I find one named after the French word for

eat, I burst into laughter. That name is so similar stylistically to the restaurant where I ran into Axel again in New York the other month—Menu. I want to tell him that I found another minimalist-named restaurant. Just like I wanted to tell him about the sweet raccoon wine. And how I want to tell him about how miserable last night in bed was without him, wrapped around a duvet with no one to steal it from and no one to talk about beets or pistachios or chief foragers with in the morning.

What I remember most about the night at Menu is how I felt when he left. I hated to see him go. I've always hated to see him go.

I couldn't stand it yesterday either.

But soon, I plan to do something about it. To choose differently. I can have a whole new track record with Axel Huxley. A new one that I make with him.

As I trek to Le Marais to meet my friend who's starting over too, the Parisian summer sun warming my shoulders, I feel like I do when I begin a new story.

There's a blank page waiting for me to write on it.

I call my sister as I walk the bustling streets of the trendy neighborhood, past boutiques and cool cafés. The second she answers, I say with so much enthusiasm and excitement, "You were right about Axel."

It's such a relief and a joy to say those words.

Veronica gasps. "How you wanted to bang him?"

"That and pretty much everything else," I say, laughing.

I can't see her, but I know her jaw is dropping. "You

and Axel Huxley? That is kind of wild that you fell for him." She sounds astonished, but also delighted.

There's no judgment from her either. She doesn't ask how I made peace with the fact that I used to hate him. She just trusts my decision. Just like I need to trust my own heart.

"I did," I say.

"So what are you going to do?"

"That's the question," I say, but I'm starting to find the answer.

* * *

Over olives and cheese, I tell Rachel my revelation. "I think it's time to leave the past behind," I say, a little nervous but excited too.

She shudders. "Sounds terrifying."

"I know."

"Especially when it's your own past. Your own issues. Your own hurt."

I nod. "Exactly. Because I realized I've moved past our split. I moved past it days ago. That's not what I have to let go of. I have to let go of all these old beliefs about myself. But I'm ready, finally. And I think when I see him in New York, I'm going to tell him in the only way I know how."

"Which way is that?"

I take a breath, meet her friendly gaze. "I'm going to write him a story. And the next time I see him, I'm going to show it to him."

She smiles, the warm supportive smile of a friend. "Look at you."

Look at me indeed. One trip through Europe and I'm ready to move past...well, myself.

39

OF COURSE A FOUNTAIN

Axel

Eight more hours and I can leave.

"You'd think it'd be easier to get out of town and change your flight," I grumble to Carter on the phone as I nurse a coffee, heading toward the fountain that we passed on the bike tour yesterday.

"You'd think it'd be easy because you want to run away," Carter says, all nonchalant as he works out, the sound of pump-me-up music in the background of our call.

"Fuck you," I say, because damn, my brother figures me out too easily.

"Fuck you too. Also, I know that your *fuck you* loosely translates to *my little brother is right.*"

I snort, all defiant. But also damn curious. I take the bait. "How do you figure I want to run away?"

"You like to jump ship when you've had enough," he

says in a simple, damning assessment. I slow my pace at the street corner, the fountain one block away.

I want to deny it, but dammit. I can't. "You dick."

He laughs. "So, are you running away from Hazel?"

"No," I bite out quickly then sigh, giving in. "Yes."

"Why?"

Why is the question of the hour, of the week, of the whole year. It's the question of my life. "Because we work together, because I made a promise to myself, because I made a wish on a fountain." But that barely scratches the surface. "Because I don't want to disappoint our readers. Because I don't want to have tricked everyone." There it is. The core of the painful truth.

I don't want to fool others, but I also don't want to fool myself.

I don't want to be a mark or to make others a mark.

Which means...I'm trapped.

"And?" Carter asks.

I've told him the whole damn story of the trip. Of Hazel and me. What else is there to say? "And what? I just gave you the answer."

"Good. That's an excellent step. But take another one."

I knit my brow as I reach the huge Gefion Fountain, where stone oxen pull a plow, driven by a Norse goddess. There's a metaphor in there somewhere for my life. "There is no next step," I say.

Or maybe there's no metaphor. Maybe I should just stop pulling a pointless plow.

He scoffs, huffing as he climbs endless stairs at the gym. "You came this close and you're going to stop?" He sounds shocked—disappointed too. "Do you just stop writing before the climax?"

"No. Obviously."

"So finish the job, Axel. Tell her. Stop running away. Just stop stopping," he says, and I bristle.

"This isn't law school," I counter, but with each assessment he levels at me, another layer of my defenses slips away.

"I didn't say it was," he says, and he's firm. He's not bending. "All I'm saying is you've been crazy for her for a long time, and you're this close and you just shut down."

"How do you know I shut down?"

"Because I know you. Because you've conned your-self most of all—into thinking you need to shut her out to protect yourself."

I swallow, feeling naked and embarrassed. Unable to counter him. I have no move to make because he's right, once again. Maybe the long con of my wish on a foun-tain is that I'm my own mark. I grumble, then mutter, "It's so irritating when you know exactly what I've done."

He laughs, deep and satisfied. "Tell her how you feel. Just finish the story."

I drag a hand through my hair, as if I can undo everything I've messed up. But I don't have to undo it. Hazel's already forgiven me. We've already moved on. We've already started over. But then I did what I've done before—*I stopped.*

She might be the one who left yesterday, but with

my cold, dismissive goodbye, I'm the one who walked away.

I have to stop leaving. And I have to start walking toward her, no matter the risk. I can't keep this wish secret any longer. "I'll tell her I love her when I return to New York," I say, and Carter slow-claps from across the ocean.

A throat clears behind me. I spin around.

Jackie is here. The blonde booklover smiles like she has a secret. "You could tell her sooner."

Alecia and Maria are with her too. I end the call quickly, then ask, a little amazed, "How did you find me?"

Alecia rolls her eyes and points to the water dancing across the stone, then all the coins sparkling under it. "We thought you might be here. You've got a thing for fountains." Then she smiles and says, "And for Hazel."

Does everyone see through me? Maybe I haven't conned anyone at all. Good. That's good. That's damn good.

"I do," I admit. I'm over fighting my feelings. "I'm in love with her."

Jackie squeals. "That's soooo great."

"You don't care about what it might do to—"

Jackie shakes her head and pats the stone edge of the fountain. "Sit, and let's come up with a plan."

And that's that. They're not worried about a book. And honestly, I'm not either.

So I sit on the edge of a fountain, and I let them help me come up with a plan. It's nice that I don't have to plot alone.

40

THE HERO

Hazel

"There is no way we are ever going to share a thing in this flat. Not a meal, not a bed, not even a single moment together. Mark my words," I say, reading from the opening chapter of *The I Do Redo*.

I don't even have to look down at the page. I know these lines by heart.

But still, I shut the paperback dramatically and smile at the crowd from the front of the event room in the store. An Open Book is packed. It's standing room only at the bookstore in the heart of Paris.

"I guess we'll see if they share anything," I say with a coy smile, then stage whisper, "Like a kiss."

A few attendees laugh, then the bookstore manager opens the event to the audience. "Just go ahead and line up. My assistant manager will bring a mic and take your questions."

Even though I wanted to stay in Copenhagen, I'm so glad I'm here. I'm grateful for all these people who showed up for a last-minute event. Sure, I might not have been able to spend another night with Axel, but life has a way of giving you second chances. You just have to spot them and take them. I plan to take mine. Maybe even tomorrow night when I land in New York. I'll stop by his place and read what I wrote for him this afternoon.

For now, I shake the thoughts of a possible *us* away, and I answer questions about the book I'll be signing tonight, about what I'm working on, about my favorite moment from *The I Do Redo*, and then a question that doesn't surprise me at all.

"Are you excited to start working on Lacey's book with Axel Huxley?" a French reader asks.

No matter what he says when I show him my new idea, I'm outrageously excited to work with him. And I know, too, that we'll find a way to honor our contract, and, I hope, our hearts. "I can't wait," I say. In fact, I wrote a scene today for his eyes only. A brand-new one with a heroine who steals the covers, and likes to play word games, but then is terribly vulnerable when she asks the hero if he'll give her another chance, and also to hold the tuna. It needs polishing, but I can do that on the flight home tomorrow. "We have lots of ideas for where to take the characters."

"Next question." The bookstore manager points to someone in the back of the event area.

I can't see who it is, at first, but then a familiar

blonde sidles into the aisle, wearing a Book Besties shirt.

"Hi there! Just wondering what you'd think of a romance where the hero has been in love with the heroine for a long time?" A smirk tilts Jackie's lips.

That's a random question, but I answer honestly. "Sure. It's always nice when he falls first."

Then Alecia appears, grabbing the mic from Jackie. "And maybe they've known each other for a while. And even worked together?"

We're getting more specific, but I don't know where we're going. "I'm open to that," I say cautiously, curiously.

Maria's there too, and she grabs the mic. "And then he finally gets the cojones to tell her his feelings in front of everyone."

This feels...scripted.

My heart speeds up to one hundred miles per hour. I'm not sure if I should connect all the dots, but I want to.

"And then he tells her."

That's...*him.* He's somewhere in the crowd. That raspy, sexy voice is an arrow straight to my heart.

"What is he going to tell her?" I ask, barely able to breathe as I hunt for him.

Axel steps forward and Maria thrusts the mic to him.

Is he really here? In Paris? At a bookstore? Striding toward me in front of all these people?

Yes, yes, yes, yes.

"He's going to tell you his wish," Axel says, his deep blue eyes locked on mine.

My heart beats in my throat. Emotions spill over inside me. I'm one giant nerve of hope. "Tell me yours and I'll tell you mine. Because it came true," I say.

"Here goes," he says as he reaches me at the table, never taking his gaze off me. "I made a wish to make it through this trip without telling you how I felt about you, and I did make it. Well, mostly. But I'm going to break it right now. I love you. I fell in love with you years ago, and then I fell in love with you all over again this week. And maybe I'm breaking all the rules of wishes, and maybe this means mine won't come true—"

I pop up, stretch across the table, and grab his face. "I'm in love with you too."

His smile spreads like wildfire. "You are?"

"I'm so in love with you I wrote you a story."

"I'm so in love with you I told a whole bookstore," he says, the fucking show-off.

"I'm so in love with you I planned to tell you in New York tomorrow."

"I'm so in love with you I caught a last-minute plane to Paris to tell you today."

And I don't need to play competitive-monster games anymore. I'm too happy. "You win."

But when I scurry around the table and kiss his fantastic lips, I'm pretty sure we both win. Everyone claps and cheers as we kiss in a bookstore in front of a crowd.

When he breaks the kiss, he brings his lips to my ear and whispers, "Can I stay in your room tonight?"

I'm so ludicrously happy that I kiss him again. "As if I'd let you stay anyplace else, you sexy jerk."

He smiles stupidly and runs the back of his fingers across my cheek. "What was your wish, sweetheart?"

Axel says it in a whole new way this time, full of love and tenderness. I want to hear that affectionate nickname over and over. "To have a good trip with you. And I did."

"I guess some wishes come true," he says.

"They sure do."

Then I finish the event, and I leave with the hero of my love story.

41

VEX ME

Hazel

We race to the hotel. I want to be alone with him so badly.

Well, big gestures make a gal frisky. Obviously. But it's hard to walk fast when I just want to kiss him.

I give in to the impulse because I can. As we near a streetlamp across from the river, I tug his hand, stopping his pace under the glow. "This is what it's like. That moment in a story. I feel all…floaty," I say, in awe that this is my life.

He shakes his head appreciatively. "Who knew the romance writer was a total sap?"

I slap his chest. "Shut up. You better feel this way too."

He covers my mouth with his, kissing me slow and deep in the Paris night, as if he's making sure I know he feels the same. When he breaks the kiss, he murmurs, "I do, Hazel. I really do."

"Good. Now stop distracting me with your kisses and get me naked."

He plucks at my blouse. "So, it's the Tuileries for ten points? You want to bang in a park?"

My eyes widen. "We get points in our game?"

He scoffs, then runs a finger over the curve of my right breast. "Yes. We get points, you competitive monster. I'm making up the rules as we go. And if you want it in a park, you'll get it in a park. You'll get it on a boat. You'll get it in the bathroom of"—he stops, surveys the scene, then tips his forehead to a busy bar down the block—"*that bar*. Hard and up against the wall."

I shiver, loving that he's still the same. He's everything I fell for. He never stops challenging me, and that's what I want.

I wrap a hand around the back of his neck, playing with the ends of his hair. He needs a haircut, and I like that too. It's so him. A little messy and rough around the edges. "Can we play that game when we return to New York? That seems like something they'd do in a book."

He presses his forehead to mine. "You and your incessant need for book sex."

"Your fault. You introduced me to it," I taunt, then I flash him a sexy smile. "So, can we?"

"We can play that game every day. But there's something we need to do in the room tonight," he says, his voice rumbly, dominant.

I tremble. I'm already excited and he hasn't even told me what we're doing. "Name it."

"How about I show you?"

I grab his hand and I run.

Yes, I fucking run.

* * *

"Show me now," I tell him the second the door closes.

He grabs my face, hauls me in for a greedy kiss. It's passionate and possessive, and also...romantic.

His hands cup my cheeks tenderly as his lips devour me hungrily. It's so very Axel—he's rough and demanding, but passionate and sensitive too.

When he breaks the kiss, his lips quirk into a vulnerable grin. "I want you to show me something, actually."

"Yes?" I say, already breathless.

"How you look riding my cock." His words are filthy, but his tone is thick with longing. "I've been fantasizing about this for so long. I need you on top of me. Need to watch you climb on me, straddle me, and take me fucking deep."

I go up in flames.

A few minutes later, I'm close, so damn close. I'm riding Axel, and he's gripping my hips, and not taking his eyes off me.

"Beautiful," he praises, and that word strikes me as... almost odd.

"You've never called me beautiful before," I say as I rise up, then down, a burst of pleasure radiating through me.

He grabs me harder, fucks me deeper. "I know," he grunts.

It's purposeful. His word choice. Everything he says is intentional. It means something. But then pleasure spins higher in me, and I can't think anymore.

I can only feel these intense sparks.

"Play with your tits for me," he demands.

As I ride him I comply, fondling my breasts while he stares at me savagely, his gaze pinned to my hands on my tits.

He's breathing so hard, almost feral. And there's something wild in his eyes. Something I haven't seen the other times we've slept together.

"You look so fucking sexy. You feel so fucking good," he says in a mad rush, then it's like he can't stop. "I've wanted you for so long. Craved this so many times. Fucking needed you."

His words ignite a storm of bliss inside me. Then he reaches between my thighs, strokes my clit, and sends me soaring.

My world blurs. I'm groaning, panting, crying out as I crest.

Then, when the orgasm starts to ebb, he flips me over in one rough move, pushing me down on the bed, hiking my legs onto his shoulders. He slides back into me, and he's unleashed. Unlocked. He's fucking me ferociously. "I swear, Hazel," he mutters. "Need you so much. Want you so much."

And on that naked admission, he shudders, then stills.

I grip his ass hard, holding him tight to me, feeling all his…pent-up emotions as he comes.

That's what was in his eyes.

Love and passion. Lust and years of longing.

It's so surreal, and so wonderful at the same time.

After we separate and clean up, we return to bed.

"That was...different," I say.

"A Hazel weird different?" His eyebrow arches in question.

"Weird good," I say, setting my palm on his chest, savoring the slick warmth of his skin.

He meets my gaze, unapologetically. "I was a little... overwhelmed."

"I noticed."

"Yeah?"

"I liked it," I add.

"Did you now?"

"You were very intense. It was like a whole new level of sex. Were you holding back before?"

With a sigh, he nods. "I was. I had to. I didn't want to let on. I didn't want to blurt out *I fucking love you* during sex."

I furrow my brow, unsure if I want to hear that during sex. But if he wants to say it, I think I'd be okay with it. "Will you say it now?"

He scoffs. "No. It's cheesy. I'm not cheesy. Also, it was a metaphor, Hazel."

I roll my eyes, slug his arm. "I know that. I was able to identify the metaphor from the context clues. But then I wasn't sure if you were hiding the truth inside a metaphor."

He laughs, then runs his fingers through my hair. "It's the truth of how I feel. And I just...had to hold back." His laughter ceases. His eyes turn intensely serious. "I don't want to hold back now."

My heart pounds harder for him. "Don't hold back anymore."

"I won't," he says, then he exhales hard, a long sigh of relief, like he's been waiting to sigh forever. It's humbling to be the one he feels all those things for. I want to deserve all these emotions. I want to keep earning this...adoration.

"I won't hold back either," I say, then I snuggle against him. But I'm not ready to crash. Something else tugs at my mind. "You called me beautiful for the first time. I don't think you've ever called me pretty or beautiful."

It's not an accusation. It's a question.

"Because that's not why I fell in love with you," he says simply. "I fell in love with you for who you are, not what you look like."

My heart clutches. It's all soft and squishy. "You're making this really hard," I mutter.

"Making what hard?"

"To keep up the bickering," I mumble.

He laughs. "Sweetheart, I intend to vex you for a very long time."

"Is that a threat?" I taunt.

"It's a promise. Prepare to be vexed, flummoxed, irritated, and driven mad. Also to be fucked very well and thoroughly."

I thread my fingers through his hair. "You know how I said I won't hold back?"

A line digs into his forehead. "Yeah?"

He sounds so concerned, but I can make that worry go away. I run a finger down that line. "I don't hate cuddling," I say in a confession.

And Axel Huxley cracks up. He laughs so hard the Left Bank can hear. "That is so very you."

I flip around so my back is to his chest. "Cuddle me."

"If I have to," he says, then wraps his arms around me, and holds me tight.

* * *

In the morning we're sitting at a sidewalk café, downing coffees. I'm watching the city roll by as Parisians march to work, or to fun, or to school.

Axel's head is down, bent over his phone. He's reading the scene I wrote.

I'm not nervous. I'm just grateful he's here. Happy I can show it to him. It's not long—just a thousand words or so.

He's done quickly, and when he looks up, he's a little dumbfounded.

Oh, shit. Was I too sappy? "You didn't like it?"

He parts his lips to speak, but nothing comes.

Oh, god. Axel is never speechless. What's wrong with my words? Maybe it needs a little editing, but when the feisty, bossy, chatty heroine says to the grumpy, talky, sarcastic hero that the guy for her has been in front of her all along, and she wants to try, doesn't he get it? Oh, no. "It's too cheesy and you hate cheese?" I ask, wincing. "Is it the *hold the tuna* bit?"

He dips his head, smiling, maybe embarrassed. Then

he raises his face. "I just love it so much I don't even know what to say."

I'm swept up with so much happiness that I stand, close the distance between us, and sit on his lap. I wrap my arms around him, and I kiss his stubbly jaw. "I love you."

He sighs happily as he pulls me close.

42

TEN POINTS

Axel

*A **week** later*

I down the last of my coffee then set the mug in the sink amidst an embarrassingly large pile of empty mugs.

But, whatever.

Who's going to see them? I leave the kitchen, grab my messenger bag, and head for the door.

You dumbass. Hazel will see them.

Don't want her thinking I live like a pig. Setting down my bag, I double back to the scene of the messy crime and wash the mugs, putting them in the dish rack to dry.

Then I head to the door again, surveying my pad one more time before I take off. Yup. It's officially acceptable for a lady to see tonight.

Lady?

Fuck that.

She's not simply a lady. She's my woman. My girlfriend. My big love.

On that thought, I smile.

The goddamn grin doesn't leave my face as I head down the hall of my building and step into the elevator. My buddy Bridger's in the lift, sporting a ruby-red shirt, checking out his phone. He looks up when he must hear me. Then he arches one brow. "What's wrong with your face?"

"What *is* wrong with my face?" I ask, lifting a hand, hunting for…coffee residue?

He points at me, his eyes narrowed. "Your mouth is doing something funny. I think…" He peers quizzically. "Is that a smile?"

Asshole. "Yes. They are common in the species of men when they fall ass-over-elbow in love." Then I grin wider. "Like yours, dickhead."

He laughs, but now he's smiling too. He was the first of the two of us to fall, and he and his girlfriend, Harlow, are disgustingly happy together. "Fine, you got me there," he says, then shoots me a wide-eyed look. "So, who did you hoodwink?"

The elevator slows at the lobby, and as we leave the building together I tell him. "The one and only Hazel Valentine."

"No kidding? Harlow loves her books."

"Harlow has good taste."

"I love her books too. I've been trying to acquire

them for my company," he says. Bridger runs a TV production shop.

"Want me to put in a good word? I imagine you'll need it. Everyone wants Hazel's stories," I say, feeling all the pride in the world.

"Sure, but the four of us should have dinner soon too. As friends. Go to a show."

"I like musicals," I say as we hit the street.

"You do?"

"I am a man of many mysteries," I say.

"You are, Huxley. You are," he says, then claps me on the shoulder. "You wear happiness well."

"Thanks, man," I say, then we head in opposite directions, and I make my way to Chelsea to a familiar haunt.

A coffee shop where I once paid rent. Hazel and I spent so much time at Big Cup that we left rent tips. A few twenties a week in the tip jar. Wi-Fi, caffeine, and a place to park your ass is all a writer needs, and I'm eager to pay it again, since I'll be working with her.

When I near the familiar shop, my pulse kicks up. I walk a little faster, and once I spot that mane of red hair, I feel both longing and peace. That's a welcome change—the peace part—from when I'd walk into the shop, twisted and torn over the unrequited feelings that had squatter's rights in my chest.

Back then, the pain of wanting someone I couldn't have, of loving someone in secret, ate me alive. Pushed to the emotional brink, I made terrible decisions I regretted.

I'd probably have let that regret eat me alive some more too if she hadn't come back into my life on that trip and insisted—absolutely, relentlessly insisted—on uncovering what went wrong.

God, I fucking love her for never giving up on us, and on me.

I grab the handle of the door and head inside, marching straight over to my fiery redhead. She's biting the corner of her lip, tapping away like a madwoman. She's lost in words, and it's a beautiful sight.

This is how I started to fall in love with her. Fierce and focused, she's the breathing manifestation of creativity.

My heart rockets as I close the distance between us, grab the chair, and sit across from her.

Seconds later, she looks up, then blinks. "Oh, I was—"

"Writing a scene where the hero answers the door wearing only a towel."

She shoots me a *don't you wish you were right* look. "As a matter of fact, no."

"I don't believe you."

"Don't make me prove you wrong."

"Prove it," I counter.

She spins her laptop around, and slides it toward me. I peer at the screen, reading the first line.

"Oh, no you don't. Read that shit out loud," she says, flapping her hand at the silver machine.

I stifle a laugh, then I clear my throat and read. "After an ungodly long shower, where I stood under the scalding-hot stream for a few days—it feels that way at least—I step out and wrap a fluffy white towel around my breasts. As I cinch it closed, the doorbell rings. Seriously? Like I'm going to open the door now anyway. But maybe it's my friend Penelope, since she just returned to town. It'd be rude to leave her hanging.

"I pad quietly to the door as a droplet of water slides from my hair down my shoulder. I peer in the peephole, and my breath catches. It's Noah, and he's dragging a hand through his thick, dark hair. He heaves a sigh, one of obvious frustration, perhaps from our fight outside the hospital last night. Admittedly, it had been a long night. But I said things, and he said things.

"I don't move, still unsure if I'm going to answer it when he mutters something under his breath, and it sounds like my name. Like a *c'mon Lacey*. And it's chased by a *please.* That last word undoes me, and I swing open the door, curious but still annoyed. Before I can even ask why he's here, his eyes roam up and down my frame and he mutters, '*Wow.*'"

I look up, then blow out a long stream of air. "You made the heroine answer the door in only a towel?"

She shrugs a playful shoulder. "I'm an equal opportunity towel-after-the-shower-scene writer."

I lean closer, park my chin in my hand. "Please tell me they're going to have hot hate sex next."

She leans across the table, her lush mouth inches from mine. "You tell me. You're up, Huxley."

I crack my knuckles and get to work.

It feels good to be back here with her.

It feels even better to leave with her.

And it feels great when she spends the night. Well, first we play a game. I fuck her in the stairwell.

Then call out ten points.

But she called out my name.

So we both won.

I can't believe my brother roped me into this. "Of all the escape rooms in New York, why did he have to pick a museum-themed one?" I ask Hazel as we leave the Christopher Street station, the chilly air slapping my face.

It's a few months later and we're nearly done with our book. But right now, it's time for friends and family.

"You're going to do great," she says, grabbing my hand with her mittened paw.

"This is like, half my books. This is what Brooks does every day. He's an expert," I say, dreading it a little more with every step.

"Then you'll do great. Since you write these escapes all the time."

I shoot her a withering look. "I'd do great if I had all day to plan and research it. Then to draft it, then beat myself up over how awful the first draft is, then throw the draft in the trash, drink ten coffees, chase them with whiskey, and finally find the answer in the shower the next morning," I say as we turn onto the next block, heading toward Conundrum on Jane Street, home of the place where my brain is about to be put to a horribly public test.

"I solve plot problems in the shower too," she says, all cheery and completely oblivious to my struggles. "Like this morning when the vineyard owner decided to buy a brand-new vineyard as a big gesture for his heroine. I came up with that under the hot water."

"Show-off," I mutter. "Also, is that your way of telling me to buy you a vineyard and name it Sweet Raccoon Vines? Because I do well, but I don't do that well, sweetheart."

She stops in front of a red-brick building, shaking her head, laughing. "No, and also, did you just see me *not* placating you about the escape room?"

"I saw it and felt it deep in my bones," I say with a scowl.

"Remember what I told you in Barcelona? Just have fun," she says, then presses a kiss to my lips. "And if you have fun, I'll reward you."

That lifts me from my escape room funk. "You mean if we're the last to solve it, I can go down on you in the escape room? Twenty points. I'm so there," I say, then I grab her hand and walk faster.

43

I'M IMAGINING

Hazel

He doesn't do bad things to me in an escape room. Please. Cameras and all. But we do win. What can I say? I'm a competitive monster too. We located the stolen work of art before Carter and Rachel, my sister and her fiancé, and my friend Ellie and her guy Gabe did. They're all in town for the holidays.

Now, with the escape room behind us, we're all hanging out at Gin Joint, a speakeasy in Chelsea. The fireplace roars and torch songs play overhead.

"I demand a rematch," Carter says, lounging on a blue velvet couch as he lifts his beer. "Who's in? Tomorrow. We'll find another one. And this time, Gabe and I will win."

Ellie's fiancé, Gabe, cracks up, then shakes his head. "Dude, do not volunteer me for another one of those. You're lucky you got me to go to one at all," says the football player. Carter and Gabe are both receivers—Carter plays for the San Francisco Renegades, and Gabe just retired from the Los Angeles Mercenaries. They're good friends too.

Carter rolls his eyes. "Big, tough football player hates escape rooms."

"I do not hate escape rooms," Gabe corrects. "I simply prefer poker, blackjack, and betting games."

My sister's fiancé, Milo, jerks his gaze toward the guys. "Poker? Did someone say poker? Let's play tonight."

"I'm in," Axel says, lifting his tumbler of whiskey in a yes. "And I will destroy all of you."

I roll my eyes, then ruffle his hair. "You're extra competitive when you think you can win."

"Damn right," my guy says, and I love that he's changed some things about him—like opening his heart —but he's remained the same in other ways. Like hating escape rooms and jumping at the chance to play a fierce game of cards. He leans in and plants a kiss on my cheek. "Just like you are."

From her cozy chair, Rachel sips her martini, watching the guys peacock. There's a sly look in her eyes. When she sets down the glass, she says, "Or we could all go to a new wine and beer tasting tomorrow. Hazel and I got tickets to a cool spot in Brooklyn. Want to come?"

If there's one way to capture a table's interest, that did it.

Carter jumps first. "I'm in," he says, then after yeses

abound, he switches seats with Milo and slides in next to Rachel.

"So, I had to come all the way to New York to see you. What's the deal with that?" he asks her playfully.

"I saw you last week in San Francisco," she points out with a smile.

"Yeah, yeah, yeah. I'm just saying...you're avoiding me."

She rolls her eyes. "I am not avoiding you. Ever."

"You better not be. Don't tell any of these guys, but you're definitely my favorite friend."

Rachel's cheeks flush pink, then she says softly, but not too soft for me to hear, "I'll keep your secret." Then she adds, "And you're mine."

As they chat more, I slowly turn my gaze to Axel, asking with my eyes if he heard that.

His irises say *yes.*

"My friend and your brother?" I ask quietly, just to confirm the obvious.

"They've been friends for a long time," he remarks.

I dip my face closer to his ear. "I'm imagining a friends-to-lovers romance."

He arches a doubtful brow. "You think so?"

"I sure do," I say, then lift my wine and clink my glass to his. "We have a little bit of that too."

He just smiles, speechless once again.

When we leave a little later, I'm not thinking of anyone else's romance. Just mine with this man who's my partner, my guy, and truly, my very best friend.

I go home with him, and it's where I belong.

EPILOGUE

SOMETIMES IT RAINS

Axel

Done.

Well, *almost.*

It's December, I'm in Big Cup with Hazel, and I just finished writing the best words in our way overdue *Ten Park Avenue* installment.

I smile slyly at the clever partner in crime across from me, who's waiting. Just waiting.

She knows what's next. She wants it. She's practically going to pounce on the laptop screen.

So I drag it out a little more, like a dick, taking my sweet time studying the screen. Just to taunt her.

Finally, she relents. "Axel! Just do it. Write the two best words, and then show it to me. *Now.*"

Ha. I knew she'd break first. Acting all blasé, I say, "Fine."

Then I type *The End*, and I share the final scene with her.

She dives right in, and if that isn't the sexiest she's ever looked, I don't know what is. Smiling, cackling, rapt. It's gorgeous, watching her read.

When she reaches the final words, she draws a deep breath, and gasps. Then reaches across the table and kisses me. "We did it," she says when she breaks the kiss.

We sure did.

It wasn't easy. We butted heads a few times, disagreed on some moments, and fought ruthlessly over whether Lacey would bang *her* head on the headboard during a particularly athletic sex scene—I shocked Hazel by saying no, she shocked me by saying yes—but in the end we found our way through. We wrote and rewrote and compromised, and we made each other better together.

Poor Lacey though. She wound up with a goose egg the next day. But hey, that was the price she paid for three orgasms.

After we polish the final scene—translation: Hazel adds a line here or there but finds zero, count 'em, zero grammatical errors—we take off into the chilly New York day.

"So, should we celebrate finishing our book by going to a billionaire's party tonight?" she asks. Then bumps her elbow with mine. "Confession: I'm going to be taking notes all night long on what his Fifth Avenue penthouse looks like. I've only ever written them. I've never seen one."

"Me too. And it better be grander than my imagination. Though I can imagine a lot," I say.

"I'm still kind of surprised we were invited."

"Baby, he likes us. We're the reason he's having this engagement party."

She smiles. "Maybe we are." Then she waggles an eyebrow. "And I get to see you in a suit tonight."

I roll my eyes. "You do love a man in a suit."

"Correction—I love *you* in a suit."

"How do you know? You've never seen me in a suit."

It's her turn to roll her eyes. "Some things you just know."

J. Hudson Bettencourt

I wasn't supposed to be on the train the day I met Amy Chandler six months ago. But that's how it goes with so many of life's moments.

They were never supposed to be on the schedule. Your flight is canceled, your car won't start, the snow keeps you in a cabin.

At the time, these beats certainly don't seem like moments. They seem like inconveniences. Annoying flat tires that threaten to ruin your day.

That was how I felt that evening in Nice. I'd been in the French city, meeting with a new green energy company I'd invested in, and I was slated to catch a flight to London. I had a meeting the next day with the JHB executive board, based in London, where I'd lived for the last few years as my holdings expanded in Europe.

But as I checked out of the hotel in Nice, my flight alert flashed on my phone. There was rain in London.

Well, what else was new? That city was always home to a gray storm.

This time, though, there was so much goddamn rain, so much infernal thunder and lightning, that the airport shut down.

All flights were canceled.

But man can't rely on one mode of transportation, one source of fuel. That's the foundation my business was built on. I'd simply go to London another way.

I headed to the train station in Nice instead, planning to catch the midnight train to Paris, then transfer to a London railway. But when I walked into the station and stood under the departure board checking the times, my attention strayed to a woman with chestnut hair.

She walked past me, chatting amiably with a group of tourists, perhaps. Three other women wearing T-shirts that said *Book Besties*. My gaze stayed on the brunette. She was tall, with lush hair cinched back in a ponytail, and the most inviting smile I'd ever seen.

Her smile was warm, real, and also…intriguing.

When the three women excused themselves for the restroom, the brunette headed toward the departure board and craned her neck to check the times.

"I've only double-checked the departure twenty times, but I can't seem to stop," she said, then shrugged. "You never know when they might switch times."

"A train line that switches departures capriciously? I might have something to say about that," I said, and I had a lot to say about it in fact. Efficiency was the cornerstone of my clean energy business.

She turned to me, her brown eyes curious and friendly. "I trust you don't like capricious train lines?"

"In fact, I forbid them," I said, and that was the truth, though of course she probably had no idea.

She laughed. "Well, glad you have your priorities straight."

Then she walked away.

That was that.

She was gone. I had no idea what train she was taking. Would she be on one of my trains to London? To Barcelona? Or one of the many others departing in the next hour, fanning out all over Europe?

What did it matter, though? She was simply a woman I had exchanged a few lines with in front of the departure board.

Except as I waited in the station for my train to leave, I replayed that brief exchange too many goddamn times for my own good. We'd barely talked and yet I couldn't get her out of my head.

There was something about her. Something about that moment.

She could be married.

Uninterested.

Unavailable in a million ways.

Shoving her out of my mind as best I could, I answered a few emails from the board and took a call from my vice chairman.

Then it was time to go—I had a meeting to attend. A job to do. I was headed for the platform to catch the train when someone with a *Book Besties* shirt scurried past me then darted onto the train on the other side of the tracks.

My pulse raced unexpectedly.

My woman could be on *that* train. She'd been traveling with the Book Besties.

I gazed at the long line of blue and cream-colored cars.

My skin warmed. Possibilities flickered through my mind.

This was annoying, this reaction to a woman. This reaction to anything that wasn't business.

But there it was, insistent, under my skin.

This was a moment. Because that was my train. My line. My choice.

And goddamn it, I was making it.

Purposefully, I crossed the platform and boarded the train to Barcelona.

Was I a stalker?

No, I wasn't a fucking stalker. I was a man who'd spotted an opportunity. And while I could be patient, I also didn't let a tantalizing chance pass me by. I said hello to the JHB Travel Manager, followed the blonde in the T-shirt, then scanned the car for the brunette I'd exchanged words with in the station.

If she was there, I could ask her a simple question.

That was all I wanted to do. *Ask.*

I headed down the first car, then the second. She was nowhere to be seen. This felt like a fool's errand. Then I caught sight of chestnut hair and warm brown eyes. She was turning toward her compartment.

I kept going, closing the distance between us, and she stopped with her hand on the doorknob, pausing like she recognized me.

Remembered me.

Letting go of the knob, she stepped into the aisle, tilted her head, studied me.

I was caught up and determined all at once.

When I reached her, I didn't waste time. I had a question to ask. "I'm J. Hudson Bettencourt. And it would probably be terribly capricious of me to ask you to dinner tonight, here in the dining car, but if you're single and available, I'd love to take you out."

Her smile was my answer. "Are you capricious?"

I arched a brow. "Right now, I am."

She studied me a beat longer, her pretty pink lips parted in curiosity. "I'm single. And what do you know? I very much enjoy dinner."

I grinned. "I, too, like dinner."

It was simple. Unexpected. And the start of the best thing that ever happened to me.

I canceled my meeting in London. I had a new mission—get to know Amy. That evening over dinner, I learned more about her. She was clever, lovely, and a little wounded. Impetuously, I asked her if I could travel with her, and she said yes.

But truthfully, the request didn't feel impetuous. It felt right.

The next night in her compartment, she told me about the end of her marriage, when her husband came out. "We're still friends," she explained with a small smile of acceptance. "We still support each other, and I want the best for him, but there was clearly no spark."

"And how are your kids doing with that? The divorce, that is?" I asked, as we sat on the couch in her compartment. Though, I made a note that we needed new couches. This one felt like a stone.

"They're young, so they're doing well. I think. And Sebastian and I really want to make it work for them. I've got a very supportive family. I'm close with my brother and my parents, and they help with the kids."

That warmed my heart. My family was gone, and I was glad she had hers. "That's good. That you're close with them, and that the kids are doing well."

"What about you?"

I laughed. "I don't have kids."

"I meant family," she said, gently correcting me.

I shook my head. "My parents are gone. It's just me," I said, and even though I was one man against the world I'd rarely felt lonely. I had too much to do. Too many places to go. Too many things occupying my days.

But I felt lonely at that moment. Because briefly, in my evening with her, I didn't want to focus solely on the things that occupied my days. The meetings, the deals, the travel.

I just wanted more of this—this connection.

"I'm sorry they're gone, Jay," she said.

It was rare people called me by my first name. I was used to Mr. Bettencourt, or just Bettencourt.

"I like the way you say my name." I was eager to move on from the loneliness. I wanted to feel unlonely.

I wanted to focus on her lips, her hair, and her eyes. How her body might feel against mine.

"Do you now?" She licked the corner of her lips. Then whispered, "Jay."

All seductive and inviting.

I growled, low in my throat.

Her eyes flickered with heat.

Then I reached for her hand, threaded my fingers through hers. A bolt of heat raced through me. I rose, pulled her up, then tossed a careless glance at the couch. "I'm not going to kiss you for the first time on that miserable couch," I said, then lifted a hand to stroke her cheek, her jawline, then the corner of those lips.

She tilted her chin up, then said, "The first time?"

Anticipation thrummed through me. "This won't be the last time I kiss you, Amy," I said. Then I captured her lips with mine, and I kissed the stranger who'd caught my eye on the platform.

The stranger who'd driven me to change my plans.

The stranger who was no longer one at all.

I kissed her for a good, long time. Until it was no longer a kiss. It was hands on buttons, then fingers on zippers, then her and me crashing onto the bed.

She climbed onto my lap, wound her hands in my hair, then shuddered. "It's been…a while."

Those words were a gift, like she was. And I wanted to treat her with care and also make her feel incredible.

"I'll take care of you," I said. "I'll give you anything you need."

I took my time, kissed her everywhere, adored her.

Made her moan, sigh, and cry out my name.

And in the morning, I canceled the rest of my plans so I could finish the trip with her. When I told her, she said, "I was hoping you'd want to."

"I very much want to travel with you," I said.

In Paris, I took her out when she had a break from her tour group, and over a glass of wine at a sidewalk café by the Seine, she said she'd miss me when she returned to Los Angeles.

Right then, right there, I knew I had to make another change in my life. I wanted more than travel.

After I walked her back to the hotel, I told her I needed a moment alone. I left her and walked solo around the city, pondering.

Could I do this? Could I make this change for her?

I'd lived in London for the last few years. But one night by the river in the City of Light, with the glow of the street lamps and my unrelenting thoughts of Amy my only companions, and I had my answer.

The next night in Copenhagen, I told her I'd move to the U.S. to be with her, splitting my time between Los Angeles and New York, where I managed my U.S. operations.

"If you'll have me," I said, feeling wildly vulnerable as I asked her the question of my heart over dinner.

She reached across the table, took my hand. "I think I'll have you, Jay. I think I'll have you very much."

I laughed at the way she teased me. "Oh honey, I'll be having *you*."

She wiggled a brow. "Tonight?"

"Every night we're together," I said.

Then I reached for her face, cupped her cheek, and

kissed that gorgeous, flirty mouth. When I broke the kiss, I said, "Have I mentioned how glad I am that you led this group of writers and readers on this train trip?"

"Have I mentioned how glad I am that it rained in London?"

"You have, but you can say it again."

"I love when it rains in London."

Now, six months later, she's my fiancée, and tonight she'll be more. I adjust my black tie, smooth a hand over the lapels of my jacket, then look at the woman behind me in the bedroom of our home in Manhattan.

Ours.

She spends time with me here when she doesn't have the kids, and sometimes when she has them too. Mostly, I go to Los Angeles to be with her and to work from there.

She's worth it.

All these changes are worth it.

I'm not lonely anymore.

"You look very marry-able, Mr. Bettencourt."

I smile. "So do you, Ms. Chandler."

Hazel

This place is gorgeous. The view is stunning. I feel like I can see all of Manhattan. But I don't gawk at the city for long.

Because *Pachelbel's Canon* is playing, and Amy Chandler is walking toward Jay Bettencourt.

This is not just an engagement party. It's a surprise wedding.

And after they say I do, and he kisses the bride, he offers a toast that ends with an ode to us. "And I suppose I have Axel and Hazel to thank. If you hadn't written those books, I might not ever have met the love of my life."

Then he turns all his attention to his bride, and I turn mine to the guy by my side. "I guess we really do need to write that billionaire train romance," I say to Axel.

"I'm in." Then he kisses me and says, "With you, I'm always in."

FINAL EPILOGUE
ALL ABOARD

Hazel

A year later...

Lacey's story is releasing in one week, so Axel and I are slipping away for a vacation before we go on a tour around the United States together to promote the book.

His Brooks Dean romantic thriller released a few months ago to rave reviews. I'm so proud of him, and I read some of the best ones to him. Then his agent sent him a bottle of scotch. My vineyard owner story came out too, and I can't complain about how it did, especially since Axel's friend Bridger's production company bought the TV rights to it.

It's been a busy year and a damn good one. A whirlwind of creativity and sex and love and friendships. But I'm eager for some downtime with my guy, just him and me, taking a train trip. JHB expanded its operations, with a luxury train route that runs along the Italian coast and stops in several seaside towns. Bring on the pasta, the sunshine, the wine, and the long, lazy mornings in bed with my favorite person.

But first, we fly into Rome, where I'm a little jet lagged. It's nothing a day traipsing around the city won't cure.

After a cup of coffee, we head to the Fontana dei Libri, since Axel claims we need a picture.

I shoot him a look. "You're not a picture person."

"Give a guy a chance to change, Hazel. C'mon."

When we reach the small fountain where we first reconnected more than a year ago, I dip my hand into my jeans pocket, rooting around for some coins. I know what to wish for so I toss a nickel in right away, then turn to Axel to hand him one.

But he's no longer right next to me.

He's on one knee.

My heart catches.

"Don't marry a bed," he begins. "Marry me, Hazel Valentine. I love you more than coffee, more than wine, more than being right, more than books, more than stories. I love you more than I ever imagined, more than I thought you'd let me love you. And I want to spend the rest of my life bickering, bantering, loving, and being with you. Just you."

It's too late to stop the waterworks and I don't even try. I sink to my knees where the man I spend my days and nights with slides a gorgeous emerald onto my finger.

Then, I hold his face. "My wish just came true. To be with you always."

"Sweetheart," he says, full of swagger and love, "you're stuck with me."

"And hold the tuna," I say, then we kiss in front of the fountain of books.

Fitting for the next chapter in the story of my so-called love life.

* * *

Binge the entire HOW TO DATE spicy rom com series FREE in KU!

Grab Rachel's and Carter's friends-to-lovers, fake dating, sports romance and meet one of my favorite heroes of mine! Plays Well With Others is FREE in KU!

You'll fall hard for the fake engagement turned into marriage of convenience romance with the sexy single dad in The Almost Romantic, FREE in KU!

The small town, grumpy/sunshine, brother's best romance The Accidental Dating Experiment is here and FREE in KU!

Get your Hazel and Axel extended epilogue by clicking here or using this QR code!

You'll also love Veronica's boss/employee romance THE VIRGIN NEXT DOOR! The steamy and hilarious standalone is currently available and also **FREE in KU**! Turn the page!

EXCERPT - THE VIRGIN NEXT DOOR

Veronica

I Shall Call Him Mister Sexy Pants

I know a thing or two about fetishes thanks to my super-secret dating-in-the-city column, but I didn't know about my own fetish until it began a few months ago. I'd just landed the column gig, so I took myself out to celebrate, as one does, with cake.

The guy who served me the slice at Peace of Cake was sexy and clever, and we flirted over frosting for a few minutes, talking about nerdy things like fractions and synonyms. But then, a pack of teenagers swarmed the shop. I had to go, and I never got his name. He called me Miss Polka Dot. I called him Mister Dessert.

I returned a few days later, but he wasn't there.

Turned out he'd just been helping out a friend. I had no idea where to find him.

C'est la vie.

But a month after that, I was sitting on my third-floor balcony of my apartment in the Village, watching New York go by in the spring, when I spotted him walking down the street. And what a view. This specimen of bearded, inked modern man wasn't picking his clothes from the conventional dude-drobe of baggy pants, loose jeans, or Boring-with-a-capital-B khakis. He was clearly dressing for my delight in those trim, checked pants that hugged his legs.

Thank you, Mister Sexy Pants.

I, Veronica Valentine, had discovered a brand-new kink. I had a thing for men wearing trendy, tight trousers, as I went on to detail the following week in my anonymous column, *The Virgin Club.*

But then, a little while after that, life happened, things happened, trouble happened, and my crush crashed into the middle of my life, where I'd have to see him every single stinking day.

The plan? Make sure he never, ever knows he's the one and only Mister Sexy Pants.

Keep reading: THE VIRGIN NEXT DOOR!

BE A LOVELY

Want to be the first to know of sales, new releases, special deals and giveaways? Sign up for my newsletter today!

Want to be part of a fun, feel-good place to talk about books and romance, and get sneak peeks of covers and advance copies of my books? Be a Lovely!

PS: If you're looking for Veronica's story, you can find it **FREE IN KU** in THE VIRGIN NEXT DOOR!

DEAR READER

Dear Reader,

I had so much fun writing Hazel's romance! Since she's a sexy romantic comedy writer, I imagine some readers will wonder if she's based on me. Well, yes and no.

Sure, we have a lot in common. For starters, Hazel's a vegetarian, like me. But a lot of my heroines are. She can be stubborn. *Raises hand*. She also writes romances with quirky pets.

Gasp! Who else does that! And she has fabulous friends. (I'm looking at you Laurelin Paige, CD Reiss, Lili Valente, K. Loraine and Sarina Bowen, among many others!

She also sometimes dictates scenes in her books. Yup, I've done that. And, I can't believe I'm admitting this, but…she too hates cream cheese.

Okay, that wasn't hard to say, but this actually is. I maybe, possibly, also have a whiteboard like she does.

So, with that out of the way, let me just say — Hazel is her own woman. She has her own emotional wounds, her own hurt, her own heartache. And her own love story to tell!

I hope you love her like I do!

Xoxo

Lauren

MORE BOOKS BY LAUREN

I've written more than 100 books! **All of these titles below are FREE in Kindle Unlimited**!

Double Pucked

A sexy, outrageous MFM hockey romantic comedy!

Puck Yes

A fake marriage, spicy MFM hockey rom com!

Thoroughly Pucked!

A brother's best friends +runaway bride, spicy MFM hockey rom com!

Well and Truly Pucked

A friends-to-lovers forced proximity why-choose hockey rom com!

The Virgin Society Series

Meet the Virgin Society – great friends who'd do anything for each other. Indulge in these forbidden, emotionally-charged, and wildly sexy age-gap romances!

The RSVP

The Tryst

The Tease

The Dating Games Series

A fun, sexy romantic comedy series about friends in the city and their dating mishaps!

The Virgin Next Door

Two A Day

The Good Guy Challenge

How To Date Series (New and ongoing)

Friends who are like family. Chances to learn how to date again. Standalone romantic comedies full of love, sex and meet-cute shenanigans.

My So-Called Love Life

Plays Well With Others

The Almost Romantic

The Accidental Dating Experiment

My Favorite Holidate

A romantic comedy adventure standalone

A Real Good Bad Thing

Boyfriend Material

Four fabulous heroines. Four outrageous proposals. Four chances at love in this sexy rom-com series!

Asking For a Friend

Sex and Other Shiny Objects

One Night Stand-In

Overnight Service

Big Rock Series

My #1 New York Times Bestselling sexy as sin, irreverent, male-POV romantic comedy!

Big Rock

Mister O

Well Hung

Full Package

Joy Ride

Hard Wood

Happy Endings Series

Romance starts with a bang in this series of standalones
following a group of friends seeking and avoiding love!

Come Again

Shut Up and Kiss Me

Kismet

My Single-Versary

Ballers And Babes

Sexy sports romance standalones guaranteed to make you hot!

Most Valuable Playboy

Most Likely to Score

A Wild Card Kiss

Rules of Love Series

Athlete, virgins and weddings!

The Virgin Rule Book

The Virgin Game Plan

The Virgin Replay

The Virgin Scorecard

The Extravagant Series

Bodyguards, billionaires and hoteliers in this sexy, high-stakes
series of standalones!

One Night Only

One Exquisite Touch

My One-Week Husband

The Guys Who Got Away Series

Friends in New York City and California fall in love in this fun and hot rom-com series!

Birthday Suit

Dear Sexy Ex-Boyfriend

The What If Guy

Thanks for Last Night

The Dream Guy Next Door

Always Satisfied Series

A group of friends in New York City find love and laughter in this series of sexy standalones!

Satisfaction Guaranteed

Never Have I Ever

Instant Gratification

PS It's Always Been You

The Gift Series

An after dark series of standalones! Explore your fantasies!

The Engagement Gift

The Virgin Gift

The Decadent Gift

The Heartbreakers Series

Three brothers. Three rockers. Three standalone sexy romantic comedies.

Once Upon a Real Good Time

Once Upon a Sure Thing

Once Upon a Wild Fling

Sinful Men

A high-stakes, high-octane, sexy-as-sin romantic suspense series!

My Sinful Nights

My Sinful Desire

My Sinful Longing

My Sinful Love

My Sinful Temptation

From Paris With Love

Swoony, sweeping romances set in Paris!

Wanderlust

Part-Time Lover

One Love Series

A group of friends in New York falls in love one by one in this sexy rom-com series!

The Sexy One

The Hot One

The Knocked Up Plan

Come As You Are

Lucky In Love Series

A small town romance full of heat and blue collar heroes and sexy heroines!

Best Laid Plans

The Feel Good Factor

Nobody Does It Better

Unzipped

No Regrets

An angsty, sexy, emotional, new adult trilogy about one young couple fighting to break free of their pasts!

The Start of Us

The Thrill of It

Every Second With You

The Caught Up in Love Series

A group of friends finds love!

The Pretending Plot

The Dating Proposal

The Second Chance Plan

The Private Rehearsal

Seductive Nights Series

A high heat series full of danger and spice!

Night After Night

After This Night

One More Night

A Wildly Seductive Night

Joy Delivered Duet

A high-heat, wickedly sexy series of standalones that will set your sheets on fire!

Nights With Him

Forbidden Nights

Unbreak My Heart

A standalone second chance emotional roller coaster of a romance

The Muse

A magical realism romance set in Paris

Good Love Series of sexy rom-coms co-written with Lili Valente!

I also write MM romance under the name L. Blakely!

Hopelessly Bromantic Duet (MM)

Roomies to lovers to enemies to fake boyfriends

Hopelessly Bromantic

Here Comes My Man

Men of Summer Series (MM)

Two baseball players on the same team fall in love in a forbidden romance spanning five epic years

Scoring With Him

Winning With Him

All In With Him

MM Standalone Novels

A Guy Walks Into My Bar

The Bromance Zone

One Time Only

The Best Men (Co-written with Sarina Bowen)

Winner Takes All Series (MM)

A series of emotionally-charged and irresistibly sexy standalone MM sports romances!

The Boyfriend Comeback

Turn Me On

A Very Filthy Game

Limited Edition Husband

Manhandled

If you want a personalized recommendation, email me at laurenblakelybooks@gmail.com!

CONTACT

I love hearing from readers! You can find me on TikTok at LaurenBlakelyBooks, Instagram at LaurenBlakely-Books, Facebook at LaurenBlakelyBooks, or online at LaurenBlakely.com. You can also email me at lauren blakelybooks@gmail.com

Made in United States
Troutdale, OR
01/17/2025

28057695R00209